DEVILS DEN

A JUSTIN MCKNIGHT ADVENTURE

LEONARD D. HILLEY II

CHAPTER 1

Justin McKnight sat in the backseat of his father's Lexus while his parents, Jack and Rita, stared straight ahead at the interstate. They rehearsed their sales pitch for a scheduled insurance meeting when they returned to Lexington that evening. Their conversation drew no interest from Justin. He stared out the window at the passing hills and houses, and released a long, quiet sigh.

School was out for the summer, and he would spend the next two months with his grandparents in Cider Knoll—a small rural community outside of Somerset, Kentucky.

His family had made this trip many times, but today a boding evil loomed and threatened to sever the security he had known for so long. Contrary to the bright morning sun, a dark, ominous sensation shrouded the car that he didn't understand and couldn't comprehend. Inner turmoil and dread encapsulated him. He had no reason for his uneasiness, but the strange darkness lingered. He couldn't shake the feeling that something bad was about to happen.

Because his parents were too preoccupied with their careers they had failed to form the strong emotional bond he desired. A chasm needed to be bridged for him to reach the nurturing lifeline he needed from loving parents. He felt closer to his grandparents because they held uncompromising patience and love. The summers at his grandparents' farm were his fondest memories.

Justin was a veracious kid with a waggish smile, mischievous at times, like any thirteen year old can be, but he never caused trouble. He devoted himself to his schoolwork, did his chores in a timely manner, and never argued with his parents when it was time to go to bed. He was, for the most part, the ideal child.

To occupy his loneliness and the deep void provided by workaholic parents, Justin spent his time enraptured in fantasy novels, superhero comics, and drawing.

His biology classes introduced him to the world of insects. Over the past few summers, he had collected a vast number of butterflies, moths, and beetles. His interest in entomology was another reason he enjoyed his summers at his grandparents. The forests, fields, and meadows offered a larger number of species to collect than he could ever hope to find in the big city.

Bored, Justin tuned out his parents' sales pitch and searched through his backpack until he found his spiral-bound sketchpad and a charcoal pencil. He flipped through the pages and stopped at the first blank sheet. He lightly stroked the pencil back and forth, up and down, hoping inspiration came.

Suddenly, through the vague charcoal lines, an image surfaced. Justin moved his pencil more conservatively and concisely. Stronger characterizations broadened in the center of the paper. Within minutes, he had drawn a gnarled, leafless tree with jagged, forked branches that cut into a dark, sunless sky. Twisted roots vanished into the black waters surrounding it.

The scarred tree stood on mossy ground in the center of a marshland. Black, bubbling water pooled around the tree knotty roots. Small islands of sphagnum moss splotched the bog's surface.

The sudden inspiration pushed him to draw more. Hanging from the tree's largest bough was a frayed, leather noose. Justin understood the noose represented death. The dark tree seemed an evil entity poisoning the water around it.

In spite of the warm summer day outside, goose bumps crept up his arms. The eeriness and familiarity of the dark images iced through his veins and unnerved him. He tried to recall where he had seen such a place, but he didn't remember.

He rested the flat end of the pencil to his lips, contemplating his next strokes to further enliven the picture. His attention turned to something in the swampy water he hadn't noticed before. An apparition. The skeletal shape of a man's face peered through the water at him. He shuddered, closed the pad, and looked out the window.

Hidden within every shadowed crevice of the trees along the interstate's edge were entities he felt but feared seeing. The hairs on the back of his neck stiffened as chills ran through his body. He'd never experienced such seizing terror.

Justin had *not* drawn the face. It had *appeared*. In the few seconds he had studied it, he had no doubt the image somehow existed and watched him. Somewhere, this ghostly figure waited to cross his path.

The dark sensation overshadowing him was connected to what lay in the brackish water on the page. This wasn't one of his ordinary drawings. It was a warning of an impending threat. He feared this drawing was somehow a portal. The image within wanted to pass through to him and take him. He took a sharp breath and tried to swallow the growing lump in his throat.

His parents continued rehearsing their sales pitch, oblivious of him.

"So, Mr. McKnight," Rita said, deepening her voice. "What can your insurance company offer that our present company doesn't already cover?"

Staring intently at the road, Jack replied, "We can provide you the same benefits you already have but at ten percent less than your employees currently pay."

Rita laughed, brushing her auburn hair from her eyes. "You've got me sold," she said. "But, of course, I'm married to you."

Jack nodded and looked into her hazel eyes that sparkled when she laughed. "I certainly hope we can convince them as easily as you make it sound."

She closed the leather journal on her lap. "Honey, it won't be a problem. You've studied the competing market and know where we stand. You've won over other major executive firms before, so this won't be any different."

He sighed. "I know. It's just something doesn't feel right. I generally go into these meetings with a cloud of confidence. When I feel like I'm going to gain new business clients, I have a tugging sensation, almost like a sixth sense, that lets me know I have the account."

"You don't feel that now?"

"Not as strongly as I usually do. Something's off."

"Like what?"

"I'm not sure. I can't explain it. I have a bad feeling but I'm not certain why or what it's about."

Rita frowned. "You ever feel this way before?"

Jack was quiet for a moment as he thought. He ran one hand through his graying brown hair and then adjusted his glasses. "Yes, when I was a boy."

Justin wished they'd break away from the sales talk, but once they began, they seldom stepped outside their circle of business. Had his mother glanced back at him that very moment, she'd have sensed the terror that paralyzed him.

As he held his sketchpad he thought about the facial image in the swampy water. Surely what he had seen was magnified by his wild imagination. He opened the sketchpad.

Instead of the faint detail greeting him, the image was more pronounced, darker, and strangely, closer. The face no longer held a ghostly form but had fleshed out. The eyes were deeper, angrier. The human face was more appalling than earlier. The picture seemed to be coming to life.

Hollow eyes resided deep inside sunken sockets—dead, but also, *undead*. Justin didn't know what to make of the growing image. This wasn't his imagination, but he truly wished it were.

He put away his charcoal pencil and studied the picture with extreme curiosity. Far behind the evil tree was an old, crumbling tombstone. One at first, then another and another, until six gravestones shadowed an inset in the picture where his pencil had never touched.

The face tilted. Rows of teeth tightened into a grim smile.

An ominous voice whispered, "I'm coming."

Justin closed the pad and held it shut, fearing that whatever was in the picture would slink from the drawing, grab him, and pull him into the mire.

"I'm coming for you," it said.

Justin's heart raced. His growing fear made breathing difficult. Catching a glimpse of his pasty reflection in the window, he almost didn't recognize his own face. His lips quivered, and his eyes were consumed with horror.

He scanned the fields and gentle sloping ridges along the highway and hoped to forget about the strange drawing. But the threatening voice whispered again.

"I'm coming for you."

The roadside sign indicated that Burnside was three miles ahead. There, his father would turn from the main road onto a side road that crossed a small swollen pocket of Cumberland Lake. Soon after, they'd reach the quiescent Cider Knoll. He hoped his grandfather could make sense of the drawing, although he wasn't certain he should show his grandfather the picture at all. He certainly knew not to tell him about hearing the voice. His grandfather called such foolishness, "Hogwash!"

Justin no longer looked forward to spending the summer away from his parents. The voice wasn't a figment of his imagination. The threat came from a darker region, an unknown origin, perhaps even a hellish recess from deep inside the bowels of the earth.

Evil was coming.

For him.

Fear paralyzed him. His stomach turned with nausea and an unsettling anxiety intensified at the thought of never seeing his parents again.

Ten minutes of eerie quietness passed. If his parents had continued discussing their proposal, he hadn't heard them. He seemed to have passed into a void where outer sounds didn't resonate.

Opening the sketchpad, Justin noticed that the dark water now eclipsed the man's eyes but the rest of the face remained visible. His uneasiness didn't fade. The situation would be a lot different if *he* had drawn the face.

He gently rubbed his finger across the face, feeling for an abnormality in the paper's texture that might explain how the image had appeared. He wanted a reason to prove his imagination played against him. Perhaps the paper was thicker or convex in this area and the brushing of the charcoal pencil had stenciled out the bold facial expression. But the paper was as smooth beneath the face as were the surrounding edges. There wasn't any defect that he could find. He flipped the page over and examined the underside.

Smooth, too.

Out of the hundreds of pictures Justin had drawn, he didn't recall one drawing where an image self-evolved. In fact, this piece of art was darker than any he'd ever created.

"I'm coming."

He closed the pad.

Justin wondered what had drawn the face and the gravestones. Somehow the face detected his presence. Maybe it could actually see him. Whatever it was, it was coming for him. He didn't doubt the threat for a second.

His father turned the car onto a dirt road. Grandpa's farm was only a few miles away. Some comfort washed over Justin, but not enough to grant the security he craved. Grandpa was getting old, not feeble, but not young enough to provide a hundred percent protection.

In the horror movies Justin had watched, guns rarely destroyed undead creatures. Magic, specialized tools or just plain luck wrought victory against demons and undead ghouls. Of the three, luck was the only thing he could hope graced him, but that was seldom the case.

His father's cell phone rang. A rattling sensation shivered through every bone in Justin's body.

"Hey, Bob," Jack said. "You have great news?"

Bob Raymond worked as Jack's business partner and financial advisor. The two had been friends since elementary school.

"Rita's here with me. Let me put you on the speaker phone. She'll want every detail too."

Jack placed the cellular into the console phone cradle and pressed a button. Bob's voice resounded with a hollow ringing, which made him sound like he was trapped inside a metal drum.

"Just off the phone with Quinton McAbee," Bob said.

"From St. Louis Mutual Insurance?"

"Yes. You remember him?"

"Of course, he offered to buy our firm earlier this year. He's loaded and not ashamed to let you know, either."

"His offer still stands," Bob said with strong enthusiasm. "He wants to meet you today, if you're interested."

Jack chuckled. "I'm not interested."

"Come on, Jack. At least meet him for lunch. He flew to Lexington this morning just to talk to you. You know I'm ready to sell my shares if you agree to the offer. But, if you choose not to sell, I won't abandon you."

Jack sighed. "He's got determination to come all this way without phoning ahead."

Bob stammered, "Well, he did call."

"When?"

"Last week."

"Why didn't you say something?"

"I didn't have the heart."

"So just spring it on me, huh?"

"Jack, he's offering a very lucrative deal. Seven figures. A large seven figures. He's interested primarily because our business is one of the strongest non-national companies with the fewest complaints."

Jack bit his lower lip and shook his head. "All right. I'll meet with him. What time? We're dropping Justin off at his grandparents now."

"Eleven o'clock. At Red Lobster."

Jack glanced at his watch. "I'd be pushing it, but tell him we'll meet for lunch."

"Good. I'll call and let him know. If you can't make the eleven o'clock lunch, call me, and I'll drive him to our office."

"Okay."

Jack disconnected the call.

Rita took Jack's hand and squeezed. "You're really considering selling the company?" Her smile and the pitch of her voice revealed her excitement.

Justin leaned forward in his seat. He hoped his father sold the company. At least then they could be tighter-knit family. He wouldn't be a latchkey kid anymore.

Jack shook his head. "I don't know. I'm keeping our options open. I'd hate to sell a business that's so strong in its second generation. Dad worked too hard to make this insurance company successful. I feel I should offer the same sweat and blood he did."

The smile faded from Rita's face. She turned toward her window and looked at the lush countryside. "I miss it here," she said.

"I do, too. Do you want me to sell?"

"The final decision is yours, dear. I do and I don't. There are pluses and minuses either way."

"I just don't want to let my father down."

"Honey, he's told you for several years they want us to move closer."

"I know."

The car disappeared from the harsh sunlight, buried by the cool shade of the thick forest trees that shrouded the road. At the bottom of a steep hill, a shallow creek crossed the dirt road. His father grumbled his disdain for having to drive the new Lexus through the water and muddying the tires.

As the car passed through the creek, water hissed off the rolling tires, followed by the sound of wet sand and pebbles plinking off the under-carriage.

His father murmured.

Rounding the next curve in the darkening forest, the right side of the car dropped and sank.

"Damn," Jack said.

Rita glared at him. "What?"

"Sorry," he said with a red face. "Flat tire."

Jack parked the car, removed his safety belt, and opened the door.

Justin looked out the window. For early morning, the forest was darker than normal.

His father smiled. "Come on, Justin. You can help me change the tire."

Justin unbuckled his seatbelt and stepped cautiously onto the dirt road. He was disheartened that this was the first thing his father had said to him during the trip. He imagined other fathers and sons probably talked about upcoming football games, but his father was always too preoccupied with work to enjoy sports or outdoor activities.

No cars could be heard in either direction. The tranquil isolation soothed Justin. A gentle breeze whipped off the cool running creek and flowed around them. Birds chirped in the dark, sheltered branches. Insects buzzed, hovered, and chummed.

The forest didn't seem intimidating, but Justin still couldn't get the facial image out of his mind. He wondered if what had threatened to come might emerge from the shadowy trees and take him. He stood close to his father, not that his father was the heroic type to step between him and a ravenous beast. But perhaps his father could bore an attacking beast to death with the details of his superior insurance coverage. At any rate, Justin felt positive that a clause existed that provided the top of the line coverage for teenage boys eaten by monsters.

Jack popped open the trunk, tugged out the heavy spare tire, a wind-out jack, and a four-ended tire iron. He handed the jack to Justin. "You remember where to position it?"

Justin nodded.

"I'd do it except I have my suit on. After I drop you off, your mother and I have to hurry back to Lexington."

"It's okay," Justin replied.

Jack squatted beside the tire and quickly loosened the lugs. Justin cranked the jack.

Deep in the forest a strange noise bellowed.

Jack's head turned in the direction of the sound. With wide eyes, he asked, "What the hell was that?"

Justin swallowed hard. "I don't know." He was thankful he wasn't the only one that had heard it. Whatever it was had frightened his father, too.

Justin cranked the jack until the car was high enough to pull off the tire. Wrestling off the muddy tire, he rolled it aside. He picked up the spare and struggled to lift it onto the wheel studs. After two tries, he set the tire into place. His father hurried to hand-twist the lugs while looking toward the forest. He quickly stood and finished tightening them with the tire iron.

As Justin lowered the car, the bellowing cry echoed again.

Closer.

Whatever it was, it seemed to be following the creek bed toward the road. In minutes, it could be within attacking distance.

His father shut the trunk and said, "Hurry up, Justin. We need to get out of here."

Justin didn't reply.

His father glanced at him and said, "Son, what's wrong?"

Justin realized his inner fears had overtaken his facial muscles, revealing his terror.

Jack placed a gentle hand on Justin's shoulder. "You look like you've seen a ghost. What's bothering you?"

Justin's lips quivered. At thirteen, he never thought he'd experience the humility of crying in front of his father again. But he couldn't stop the tears and sobs that convulsed him. His father pulled him close and hugged him.

"What's wrong?"

Wiping tears from his eyes, Justin said, "Something bad is going to happen. I feel like I'll never see you or Mom again."

A stunned expression hung on his father's face. "Nothing's going to happen to us. We have a lot of meetings to attend this summer. You love spending the summers with your grandparents, don't you?"

"Yes."

"We'll be okay. So will you. I promise."

Justin nodded and climbed into the backseat. But the knot in his stomach didn't lessen, nor did his apprehension. A few minutes later, they arrived at his grandparents' farm.

His grandmother hung towels on a clothesline when Jack pulled into the drive. His grandfather rose from the side of his tractor and headed toward the Lexus. Charlie, the old redbone hound, sat on the porch. His ears perked when he heard Justin's voice.

Jack stayed long enough for Justin to get out with his suitcase. Grandpa managed a brief conversation with Jack and Rita before they backed out the drive and headed down the dirt road.

Grandpa ruffled Justin's hair. "How're doing, tiger?" he asked. "Ah, don't worry about them none. They'll be okay. As for us, we're going to have the time of our lives this summer."

Justin carried his suitcase to the farmhouse. The serenity of the farm he had known seemed so distant and so far away. He suspected he was in a different place altogether. He hoped after a big dinner and a good night's sleep, he'd feel better.

But if what appeared in the drawing had been a warning, this might be the last time he saw his parents alive. If it was coming for him at his grandparents' house, it wouldn't just take him. It would take them as well.

CHAPTER 2

$\mathcal{A}$wakening for the first time in twenty years, Elias Jackson was surrounded by complete darkness. Weak, emaciated, and slightly disoriented, he slid his hands along his body, checking for deterioration. Other than suffering from severe dehydration, his body seemed intact. His cold skin was shriveled, clammy. The rope scar around his neck had not disappeared, but neither had his hatred and desire for revenge. Between his thumb and index finger, he rubbed the bone necklace pendant and mumbled an incantation.

His faint, slow heartbeat steadily strengthened. His lungs ached and burned as he inhaled his first breaths of stale, musty air.

Elias pressed his aged hands against the cold marble slate that entombed him. Pushing with what little strength he had, the lid moved several inches. To his surprise, water rushed through the opening, flooding him while pushing out valuable oxygen. Large bubbles rose to the swamp water's surface.

Twenty years prior, when his master had performed Elias' ritualistic burial, the sepulcher was set beneath dry ground, not water. Elias had no idea how water saturated his grave.

Elias fought to push the lid off the sepulcher, but the water pressure increased the resistance. His long fingernails ripped as he clawed and pushed. Gnashing his teeth, he growled and shoved harder. The lid moved. He pushed until the gap widened enough to squeeze his thin body through.

After escaping the tomb, he faced another obstacle. Strands of sphagnum moss entangled him like slender ropes. He choked as water filled his mouth. He spit the water out and held his breath. His weak lungs ached for air. The water burned his eyes like acid. The faint glimmering light above revealed that he was only a few feet from the water's surface.

Opening the sepulcher had fatigued him, leaving him little strength to swim to the surface. As he pulled handfuls of sphagnum strands downward and kicked his feet, a small cushion of moss formed beneath him. The moss sustained his weight and buoyed him upward.

Elias' face broke through the water. He gasped violently for air. Thick sphagnum moss congealed around his weak body like a life preserver and kept him afloat. He pulled himself to the edge of the swampy pool. Exhausted, he lowered his head over his crossed arms. He took several deep breaths before crawling out of the water.

Beads of water dripped from his glistening, ebony skin. Gazing around, he tried to get his bearings. The landscape had drastically changed during his absence, and for a moment he wondered if he had been transported to another realm.

A thin layer of fog covered the marshy edge of the forest. A spider's fortress, weighted with silver dewdrops, swayed lazily in the breeze. In the neighboring field between tall fescue blades, smaller webs rippled like curtains ruffled in the wind.

Once the morning fog dissipated, direct sunlight would take its toll on Elias' body. His best shelter to deter rotting deterioration of his aged body was to hide in the cool, damp shadows of the forest.

Hunger gnawed his stomach.

Elias crawled into a grove of small hemlock trees. Each painful movement forward crunched dry, brittle needles. The sharp needles stuck to the underside of his wet body. He panted and closed his eyes, too exhausted to move further. The thick lower branches prevented sunlight from reaching him.

As he lay in the cool shade, his stomach rumbled. His hunger intensified. He needed nourishment immediately to reverse the decay before the elements of nature claimed him. This was his seventh awakening and should he die, he lost any hope to gain immortality. He didn't want to fail.

All his spells, sacrifices, and evil deeds over the past one hundred twenty years had been in vain if he died now.

Elias had to keep his bargain with his dark master so his body would return to normal. Failure meant eternal suffering rather than reigning on

Earth with the living where he could continue his evil activities, preying on the pure. His end of the agreement required sacrificing one innocent soul every twenty years for seven terms. He had succeeded this undertaking six times. This resurrection signified the seventh and final sacrifice. Becoming immortal was within his reach.

The pact with his dark master had seemed easy at first, but only because he didn't realize the odds against achieving success were greater than actually completing the task. His master had withheld the details of Elias' bodily decay and offered no spells to totally counteract degradation. Nothing stood to preserve his body during the twenty-year dormancy periods. The ramifications were more than Elias imagined. His eagerness for reward blinded him to reality. His dark master never hinted or whispered the toll and expense to Elias before he signed his name in blood. The Voodoo hibernation spell Elias cast upon himself, as a Bokor, was the only reason he awakened every twenty years. But his body grew weaker, leaving him less time or strength to search for a pure, unblemished sacrifice.

Freeing himself from the sepulcher had drained valuable energy. His muscles cramped with tight spasms. Too weak to lift his head, he closed his eyes, believing he was doomed to fail. Sleep coaxed him without revealing its selfish betrayal to reclaim him.

As Elias prepared to surrender defeat, the smell of fresh blood aroused him. His eyes opened quickly. A freshly killed rabbit lay inches from his face.

A sleek ferret with burning red eyes chattered and pushed the rabbit closer with its nose.

Elias hungrily accepted the gift, lapping the blood seeping from the rabbit's slit throat. After swallowing the warm liquid, he gnawed small chunks of rabbit flesh. He chewed the tiny bits of meat slowly. Swallowing solid food challenged his throat muscles to work after two decades of dormancy. As his esophagus muscles contracted to push food into his stomach, he almost choked. Breathing hurt.

Keeping food down wasn't easy. Once his gag reflex slowly subsided and his stomach was full, he became drowsy and sleep took him. He needed rest before he could complete the ritual.

Strange dreams crept through Elias' mind. Vivid images of a teenage boy presented themselves to him. He saw the boy but from an odd view. A premonition. This was the boy he must sacrifice. Purity gleamed in the young man's eyes with radiance too bright to ignore. Somehow the boy saw him, too. For a brief moment, Elias felt their connection through this unusual channel. Perhaps his magic as a Bokor had manifested over the years and granted him this new power.

Staring at the boy, Elias said, "I'm coming."

Fear creased the young boy's face.

Elias smiled. He preyed on fear and weakness. The boy's fear gave Elias more power, strength, and an upper hand.

"I'm coming," he repeated.

For several minutes the connection was broken. Cold and darkness separated them. When the channel reconnected, Elias taunted, "I'm coming for you."

The young man disappeared from view again, but Elias didn't worry. He had seen the boy, and oddly, he knew the boy's name: Justin McKnight.

When he awakened from his brief sleep, the ferret had returned with a companion—a black cat with golden eyes. The ferret dropped two voles before Elias and the cat clutched a fat quail in its teeth.

Somewhat stronger, Elias sat against the trunk of a hemlock. He ate the dead animals, savoring the taste of blood. His mind returned to the teenage boy and how to find him. He had little time. The full moon was near.

During the heat of the day, Elias would stay in the coolness of the thick trees and eat whatever his familiars brought. Come dusk, he'd be stronger. He entertained the thought of finding others to sacrifice until he found the boy. Performing such homage not only strengthened his favor with his dark master, it bestowed added stamina should his offerings be pure. Their ages didn't matter. But the master would insist having the child as the final sacrifice in order for Elias to gain immortality. No other sacrifice he had offered possessed such purity.

Crushing the quail's head in his mouth, Elias envisioned Justin and how to make the sacrifice. He could smell the burning flesh, the coppery scent of spilled blood, and hear the anguish the child suffered and screamed during the offering. The more pain, the greater satisfaction the master enjoyed.

NIGHTFALL CAME.

Thick clouds overcast the sky.

Elias wandered through the woods. His strength had increased and some of his deterioration had mended, but without another sacrifice his healing was short-lived.

He came to a small, whitewashed church near a bluff overlooking

Cumberland Lake. The final night of the Hope Chapel's weeklong revival was coming to an end. The quaint church thrived with the boisterous harmony of bad singers. The off-key cacophony of music and voices was enough to keep Elias at a distance.

Peering through the darkened trees, he studied at the white church building. A single yellow bulb glowed above the front door. Less than twenty cars were in the gravel parking lot. A few more were parked in the short-cropped grass near the forest, out of the light's glow.

A small pavilion stood to the side of the church where parishioners picnicked on warm Sunday afternoons. Two rhododendrons walled the closest end of the pavilion.

Elias crept through the parking lot and slinked behind the rhododendrons. The music inside the church faded and the singing stopped. A man prayed aloud. Elias spoke a prayer of his own.

Not a minute after the man finished praying, the old church door creaked open and people dispersed.

Elias waited.

His seasoned patience was phenomenal. He understood he couldn't just kill anyone for a sacrifice. Purity of heart was essential. He needed an offering to replenish his vigor. Food and sustenance weren't enough to repair his weakened condition. Without added energy, he doubted he'd live long enough to sacrifice Justin at the full moon. A blood offering appeased his master and granted essential vitality to his ragged body.

The young pastor stood at the door shaking hands with each member of his congregation as they left. No one seemed interested in staying longer than necessary as they shook his hand and headed for their vehicles. The amber glow of the single porch light cast weak courage against the contrasting darkness of the forest. As they rushed to their cars, the congregation held little faith that the light was protective against their fear of what hid within the shadows of the night. In previous decades people trusted the sanctuary of their churches and tabernacles, but no more. Homage seemed replaced by the lust to be seen and present, not in deed or to deity. Detecting the pure from the evil wasn't difficult, but finding someone who actually possessed purity was rare.

CAR ENGINES REVVED AND SLOWLY, one by one, they headed down the narrow dirt road.

Pastor Ledbetter pulled the door shut and locked it.

A strong breeze swayed the trees and shrubs. A storm was coming. The warm air stirred through the forest and brought with it the sweet aroma of honeysuckle and cocoa butter. The heavenly fragrance dissipated, followed by an intolerable, rotten stench. The smell was stifling, like the reeking odor of a sun-ripened carcass.

He pulled out his handkerchief and covered his nose and mouth to keep from gagging. Something large and dead lay nearby.

Alone, Ledbetter peered across the gravel lot. His small Micra hatchback was parked near the pavilion. Something rustled in the bushes. Deer, perhaps?

He shuffled through his pocket for his keys. Once he found them, he quickly walked to his car.

Opening the door, he froze. From the overhanging tree branch something hissed and spat.

A black cat with piercing, narrowed eyes landed on the car roof and slashed his face. The burning pain was instant.

Ledbetter wiped the fiery wound and pulled back his hand. Blood covered his fingers. The cat arched its back and growled.

He jumped in the car and slammed the door. Turning the key in the ignition, he noticed a tall figure hobble from the rhododendrons. Stealthily, the black figure shambled toward the car. At first he wondered if one of the parishioners hadn't left yet. But the man's steps staggered, unsteady, like a drunken man.

The beam of the headlights brightened the man's hideous, deteriorated face, which had more bone exposed than flesh. Without thinking, Ledbetter's foot slammed down the accelerator. The car spun in the loose gravel from right to left.

Ledbetter cut the wheel sharp and gunned the small engine. It whined as it pulled away. Fear breathed in him.

Looking into the rearview mirror, he could see the man start to run.

A living corpse, he thought, shaking his head. Nothing in that condition should breathe life. Such a nightmarish being couldn't exist, but for reasons he couldn't fathom, he accepted it as real and chose to get the hell out of there.

Topping the hill at the end of the church lot, eyes gleamed in the glow of the headlights. Deer. Ledbetter slammed the brakes and the car pivoted to the left, spraying gravel and dirt into the air. The alarmed deer trotted into the woods.

Ledbetter's heart hammered so hard that his throat hurt. Breathing was difficult. He mashed the gas again. Before the car straightened out, the hatchback's rear window shattered into a million shards of raining glass.

He glanced over his shoulder. Large hands reached for him. He couldn't believe that what he had seen near the pavilion moved this fast. Growling like a raving animal, it stretched its arms toward him.

The undead man was crawling into the car.

Ledbetter gunned the engine, hoping the sudden burst of speed jarred the man out of the back of the car. It didn't.

He picked up the Bible resting on the passenger seat and held it behind him at the creature. The action was crazily desperate, like using a silver cross to ward off a vampire or shooting silver bullets at a werewolf, but he hoped the feeble act worked.

With a blunt thud and loud crash, the Bible was knocked from his hand through the side rear window.

Ledbetter wanted to scream, but his dry, hoarse throat was strained from his thunderous sermon. His vocal cords refused to hasten his command, and he doubted screaming would deter his attacker. No one was within shouting distance to rescue him, either.

By his best estimate the dirt road intersected the paved highway less than half a mile away. If he pushed the engine to its maximum throttle, he might be able to make a sharp enough turn onto the blacktop to dislodge the man from the car. As it was, that maneuver was his best and only chance for survival and escape.

The car topped the next hill with enough momentum to lift the tires off the road. His stomach fluttered. Upon landing, the shocks failed to absorb the impact and sent the car into another skid. As the car slid sideways, Ledbetter jerked the wheel sharp to the right. The car straightened for ten yards before careening the opposite direction.

The tail end of his car struck a large oak and violently pivoted back the other direction. The collision sent a heavy object from beneath his seat that struck his foot.

His gun.

Weeks had passed since Ledbetter had last fired practice rounds at the target range, but he kept the Ruger 9mm loaded and tucked under the seat. The bumpy road had knocked the gun loose and if he was able to retrieve the weapon, he still might have a chance to escape.

With his left hand he held the steering wheel while blindly reaching down with his right to find the gun.

Heavy breathing rasped from the rear of the car. The collision hadn't knocked the man out of the vehicle, but the labored sound of his breath indicated he might be injured.

Cold metal met Ledbetter's hand. He grabbed the gun and dropped it in his lap. The car skidded again, and he fought to keep it on the road. The last thing he needed was for the car to plummet over the embankment and get lodged against a tree. If his car stopped, he had no hope of losing the undead man in the backseat.

Clammy hands with sharp fingernails wrapped around his neck from behind. The smell of decay permeated from the man's slick flesh. His hands tightened and choked Ledbetter's throat.

He slammed his foot hard on the gas. The engine whined from an overdose of RPMs. The sudden acceleration was enough to pry the weak hands from his throat.

Ledbetter gasped for air, clicked off the gun safety, and fired three shots behind him without glancing back. The man shifted in the seat, but no obvious sounds of pain echoed from his adversary.

In such a small car, he didn't understand how he could have possibly missed. He fired again. The fourth round struck bone. A painful wail howled in the backseat.

For just a moment, he hoped that he had killed the man, but that flicker faded fast. The undead man grabbed Ledbetter's right wrist and yanked his arm behind the seat. The hyperextension did excessive damage.

Ledbetter screamed as the tendons and ligaments in his right shoulder tore and snapped. The gun dropped to the floor as the man released his grip. Ledbetter's useless arm hung limp at his side. The burning pain made his head spin and nausea churned his stomach. He fought to remain conscious.

The car smelled of gunpowder and rotten flesh.

Ledbetter leaned against the steering wheel. The road dipped and turned sharp to the right. He slammed the brakes, a bit too hard, and the car spiraled out of control.

A cloud of dirt puffed and drifted with the scent of brake fluid and burnt rubber. Involuntary tears leaked from his eyes as he attempted to bring the vehicle under control, but with only the use of his left hand, he overcompensated the turn. The rear tire spun on sandy soil at the edge of the road. The tire failed to gain traction and forced the car to dip front-first down the ravine.

The car bounced and shook. The undercarriage ground against a large rock. Something popped beneath the car.

Ledbetter mashed the brakes, but the pedal dropped to the floor, useless. The brake line was busted.

Small deciduous saplings covering the sloped ravine snapped and lashed at the car. A thick tree branch smashed through the windshield as the vehicle's speed increased. The end of a large log shattered the right headlight. A few seconds later, the left headlight burst. Darkness prevented him from knowing what he approached.

The undead man snarled and reached for him.

Ledbetter shut his eyes and fell to his side. The abusive bounces and the lashing tree limbs made it too dangerous to sit upright. He hoped to hit a large enough tree to stop the vehicle before it hit the water.

The slashing saplings whipped the air as the speeding car plowed through them. The front of the car suddenly tipped up when it struck a large rock. The gas tank ruptured and the front wheels turned to the left and suddenly straightened back out. The surface beneath the car changed from rocky to smooth, which let Ledbetter know the vehicle was descending down a concrete culvert.

At the bottom of the ravine was a deep inlet of water from Cumberland Lake. With his throbbing, useless arm, he was in no condition to pull himself out of the car before it sank in the water, and he certainly couldn't swim.

He was destined to plunge into the chilly water. Nothing he did could stop it.

Ledbetter smelled gasoline.

Grinding metal beneath the car produced sparks and ignited the leaking gas. Flames licked the sides of the car, and seconds later, engulfed the vehicle in a ball of fire. The unbearable heat intensified. Death by fire wasn't the way he hoped to leave this world and a rather ironic way for a minister to die.

Ledbetter closed his eyes and sought to pray, but he doubted a prayer reached God before death claimed him.

The glowing flames danced around him. His skin felt like it would melt. He expected the fire to spread to the car's interior, but instead, the car hit the water. Fire hissed as the water quenched its fury.

Some comfort came as the water sucked the car down. He'd rather die drowning than engulfed in flames.

Arms wrapped around him and tugged him upward. The undead man pulled him ashore and stood over him. Ledbetter coughed, sputtered, and shivered. The dark man's hollow eyes stared down at him. A strange smile spread across the undead man's face.

Ledbetter lost consciousness.

CHAPTER 3

*J*ustin had finished his morning chores, which included feeding
the chickens, cows, and pigs. Then he shucked a few bushels of
Kandy Korn and weeded his grandmother's flowerbeds. By
concentrating on each task he hoped he'd forget about the drawing from
the day before, but even the tranquil, sloping hills surrounding his grandparents' farm didn't erase the sinister face in the picture or its verbal threat.

He flipped open the pad and studied the drawing. The black tree held its
ominous evil presence, but for some strange reason, the hideous face in the
water had vanished.

Justin shook his head. The face had been there. He had seen it. His imagination had not placed it on the page. The threat had been real, too.

After the heat of the afternoon sun subsided, clouds drifted overhead
and a gentle breeze flowed through the orchard. He grabbed a freshly fallen
apple from the grass and took a big bite. Juice trickled down the sides of his
mouth.

Deep in thought, he inspected his drawing and waited for the voice to
whisper again, but it didn't. The face was gone, and now he wondered if
what was in the water had escaped the picture and was hunting him.

Justin closed the pad, stood, and nervously studied the apple orchard.
The unsettling sensation he was being watched brought chill bumps down
his arms. Holding the sketchpad, he thought about similar frightening
ordeals in the area.

Since it was Saturday he had biked to the old country store near Mill Springs Mill after he finished his chores. Old Man Harper owned and operated Harper's Grocery and stocked new comics each week. Justin liked the old store because a lot of older men sat on wooden crates and told hunting and fishing stories. They dipped snuff or chewed tobacco while they weaved their rambling stories with occasional arguments. And sometimes, just for fun, they told the creepy legends to frighten kids and teenagers. Devils Den, the haunted cave, was one such story they told with conviction and certainty that no one ever questioned that something horrible had happened there. But none of the men ever divulged the specifics, adding more mystery and suspense to the legend.

Old dusty spider webs hung from the wooden rafters. A pile of peanut hulls had been swept beside a large barrel filled with roasted peanuts. Floorboards creaked whenever people walked through the store. At other times, when no one moved or spoke, the sound of footsteps rasped across the weathered hardwood floor, which was another invitation for the old men to tell eerie paranormal stories.

Harper sold bait and tackle, and his store housed a small post office. On occasion, Harper bought some vegetables from Justin's grandfather or let Lib hold quilt raffles.

Justin stared at his sketchpad. For a moment he considered showing the picture to some of the old men at Harper's store, but he was too tired to bike back. Even though he had bought a stack of comics, he wasn't in any mood to read them. Perhaps later in the evening they'd be of more interest.

The face and the whispered threat lingered in his mind. His arms pimpled with goose bumps. A gentle breeze brushed the back of his neck like heavy breathing. His apprehension returned.

As he walked through the apple orchard, Charlie jumped to his feet and barked. Justin turned to see what upset the dog. One apple tree's branch swayed and shook in a manner that looked like someone was climbing the tree.

Justin's stomach tightened. He couldn't see a visible threat, but the dark eeriness he had felt the day before had returned.

The wind wasn't forceful enough to move the branches.

He tucked the sketchpad under his arm and watched the tree. The branch sagged. Although he didn't see anything, he felt eyes watching him. He wanted to turn and run.

Laughter rang in his ears. An angry voice whispered, "I see you."

Charlie rushed between Justin and the tree and snarled. He dug his front paws into the clover-covered ground and kicked dirt into the air. Spittle and foam sprayed the air as the dog gnashed its teeth. The dog's ears flattened and his bark lowered to a fierce growl. His upper lip curled, revealing sharp teeth. The dog sensed something was there, too.

The branch suddenly sprang upward and swayed. The dog darted through the trees, chasing and growling with ferocity after something Justin didn't see.

Justin ran to the farmhouse.

His grandmother sat on the porch swing and sewed her latest quilt.

Justin walked between her flowerbeds. Swarms of honeybees and bumblebees buzzed from blossom to blossom. Fluttering spicebush and tiger swallowtails hunted for nectar as well. Not quite past his uneasiness, his heart jumped with excitement when he stopped at the zinnias. A Giant Swallowtail tapped its long tongue into one flower. Its large wings expanded.

Without a second thought, he ran to the house, stormed across the porch and flung open the screen door.

"What's your hurry, young man?" his grandmother asked with a broad smile as she looked up from sewing.

"I need my butterfly net!"

"There are plenty of butterflies out there."

Justin rushed back to the porch with his net in hand. "I know, but not like this one. A Giant Swallowtail. It's the only swallowtail I don't have."

He ran off the porch and back to the flowerbed where the butterfly perched on a large coneflower. The swallowtail sipped nectar. As he stepped cautiously toward the butterfly, a lump rose in his tightening throat. He had never been so nervous in his pursuit of a butterfly, but if he captured this one, it would be the prize of his collection.

Justin wiped his sweaty palm on his shirt and then held the net tight. As he brought the net back over his head, the butterfly sensed his alacrity and took to flight. In a few seconds it drifted over a barbed wire fence and across the pasture.

"No!"

He flung his net over the fence and squeezed between two strands of wire. Without hesitation he grabbed the net and rushed down the sloped pasture. The butterfly darted and erratically swooped up and down, side to side, and avoided each desperate sweep he swung.

A winding creek divided the lush pasture. In the middle of the pasture a small grove of trees offered the butterfly an excellent refuge. Justin had to catch the swallowtail before it darted into the trees, or he might never see another one like it for years.

The butterfly flew over the creek. The wind caught the butterfly's delicate wings and lifted the creature upward, out of his reach. Still following the creek, the swallowtail headed for the trees.

Before Justin realized it, he was wading knee-deep in the creek and swinging his net wildly at the butterfly. He swung the net well over his head, hoping he didn't lose balance and fall face first into the water. His desperate behavior was already an embarrassment to Lepidopterists everywhere.

The breeze changed direction as he made one last desperate sweep. To his disbelief and pleasure, the butterfly fluttered inside his net.

"Gotcha!" he said with a broad smile.

Justin closed the end of the net so the butterfly couldn't fly out. Then he pinched its thorax and stunned his captive to prevent it from tattering its wings. He wanted the specimen to remain perfect.

After he stunned the butterfly, he looked around. He stood inside the tree grove, knee-deep in water. His feet sloshed water as he moved to the sandy bank and sat under a large maple tree. Sweat and water soaked him. All he could do was stare at his prize butterfly. His heart raced and slowly, his breathing calmed.

Justin took a large glassine envelope from his shirt pocket and carefully slid the butterfly inside. The envelope's glossy texture ensured the wings didn't get smudged or damaged. When he glanced toward the farmhouse, he hadn't realized he had run over a half mile while pursuing the butterfly.

He shook his head and looked at his muddied pants and shoes. With his adrenaline surge waning and his excitement gone, he was tired, exhausted, and he dreaded the long walk back.

A tree branch snapped in the trees. Justin turned in the direction of the sound. About twenty yards away stood a man. His face was exactly like the one in the drawing. Justin was on his feet in an instant.

The man's repulsive, rotting face sickened him. The thin undead man propped himself against the trunk of a thick tree. His bulging yellow eyes peered more menacing than those in his picture. A sleek ferret with cold, red eyes stood to the right of the man. A black cat stared from its crouched position on a low tree branch. Their eyes were as evil as the man's.

Justin ran.

He didn't look back to see if the man pursued. He just ran. Judging the deteriorating condition of the man, he didn't believe the man could catch him, but he knew without question that the picture had been a forewarning.

By the time Justin reached the fence, he was panting hard. His lungs hurt and pain dug in his side from running.

Coldness chilled him.

The threat was now present in flesh, not in a drawing. The hollow eyes, the withered face, were real.

Justin crossed the fence and dared to look back. The grove of trees shrouded themselves with new darkness. Evil lurked within. He didn't fear the being leaving the protectiveness of the trees. Not in the heat of the blazing sun. After sunset and midnight came, that's when he believed the man would act on his threat. Darkness was the proper environment for evil.

He wanted to tell his grandparents, but it didn't matter how he tried to explain what had happened, they wouldn't believe his story. If he hadn't seen the undead man, he'd have soon forgotten the drawing and filed it away as weird imagination.

Justin stood on rubbery legs. His wet clothes hung heavy as he trudged through the yard toward the front porch. Seeing the undead man dwarfed the elation of capturing a prize butterfly. The threat wasn't to be ignored, but he wasn't certain how he'd defend himself.

His grandmother had set aside her quilting and sat shelling peas. When she glanced up and noticed him, her eyes widened. "What'd you do? Take it swimming?"

"No, Gramma. It flew over the creek. I waded after it."

She laughed, and then she took a more serious tone. "You should be more careful around water in this heat. The copperheads stay near water when it's hot. I bet you didn't even consider that, did you?"

"No, I didn't."

"Be more careful. Lots of dangerous things in the woods and creeks. Your life is worth more than a butterfly."

"I know."

She smiled. "You'd best go change out of those wet clothes before your grandfather gets home. You know how he is. He'll tan your hide if he knows you've been in the creek."

The familiar roar of his grandfather's pickup approached down the dirt road. Billowing clouds of dust churned as it raced toward the drive.

Justin left his muddy socks and shoes in the downstairs washroom. He ran upstairs to his room and yanked out dry clothes from the dresser drawers. He quickly dressed and took the butterfly to the porch for his grandfather to see.

The brakes squealed as his grandfather stopped the truck and got out.

Justin sat on the porch step with a broad smile, holding the glassine envelope in his hand.

"What you got there, boy?" he asked.

Justin stood and slid the butterfly out into his palm. "Look!"

His grandfather took a handkerchief and wiped sweat from the side of his face while he studied the swallowtail. He shook his head, "I've not seen one of those in years."

"My butterfly field guide says they're tropical."

Grandpa nodded. "Yep. I've never seen them around here. When your grandmother and I lived in Florida for a few months, they were everywhere. Some citrus farmers consider them pests because their caterpillars eat orange leaves."

Justin smiled. "I'd never consider something this spectacular a pest."

Grandpa laughed and ruffled Justin's hair. "If your livelihood depended on your harvest, you'd think differently."

He frowned. "I don't know."

"You gonna to put it in your collection?"

"You know it!"

"Well, get to it. I've got something to talk to you about when you're done mounting it."

"Okay."

JUSTIN'S GRANDFATHER, John, took a stack of empty baskets from the truck bed and carried them to the barn. His day at the farmers' market had been successful. He sold ten bushels of purple hull peas, ten bushels of blue lake green beans, twenty bushels of Kandy Korn, and thirty bushels of tomatoes. The abnormally early warm spring had allowed him to plant crops a few weeks ahead of schedule and if weather permitted, he might have a successful second planting by July. Last year, he had barely broke even, but this year he expected to turn a large profit.

After he retired and handed over his insurance agency to Jack, John's gardening hobby had become a gardening obsession. His wife, Lib, teased him endlessly that he didn't have a green thumb. He had two green hands.

John planted far too many plants for the garden space. What produce he didn't sell, he gave away or they canned for winter. What had once been a hundred foot garden patch was now a three-acre mini-farm. He invested in a John Deere tractor and a Troy-bilt tiller.

He never expected to ever sell so much produce on a Saturday afternoon, but he was pleased to see his retirement hobby was becoming lucrative.

It was a shame he wouldn't be around much longer to enjoy it.

CHAPTER 4

*E*lias was greatly disappointed in sacrificing Ledbetter. He had hoped the pastor was a man filled with purity, dignity, and sanctity, but all those attributes were absent.

Being a man of faith, Ledbetter hadn't exactly lived what he preached. His soul was tarnished by darkness and evil. He seemed to believe his sins of womanizing and bars would eventually be exposed. His premature day of reckoning had expired along with his life at the hands of Elias.

When the pastor had awakened after crashing into the ravine, he mistakenly believed Elias was a dark angel sent to destroy him and rid the world of his many injustices. Confessions and pleas for forgiveness spilled from his mouth, which angered Elias.

Elias wasn't a holy priest and he hated being considered sanctified because he opposed all that was righteous.

By the time he finished impaling Ledbetter, he had learned all of the pastor's perversions. The babbling revelations tested Elias' patience. After several minutes of rapid repentance, Elias finally silenced Ledbetter.

The details of his sins pained Elias. Neither he nor his dark master benefited from the sacrifice. If anything, the master was probably more agitated about the sacrifice. Elias had inadvertently tipped the scales in favor of good by killing a man festered with pure evil.

He was too appalled to drink the man's blood. Tainted souls held no value or vigor for him.

Elias thought of the boy.

Justin McKnight.

Purity radiated from him. He sensed it when they made eye contact in the grove of trees. Had he been stronger and the day nearer dusk, he'd have pursued the boy across the pasture. But he didn't have long to wait. Sunset was only a few hours away. With the darkness he preyed.

Immortality was within his grasp.

CHAPTER 5

*J*ustin turned on his desk lamp. He grabbed an empty pinning board and placed the butterfly's pinned thorax into the center groove. He meticulously positioned the forewings and tightened thin bands of wax paper across them to hold them in place. Then he set the hind wings.

When he was content the wings were positioned properly, he stared at his growing collection with pride. This swallowtail was indeed his greatest prize, but the cecropia, Luna, and polyphemus moths held glories of their own.

The Harvest Festival at the county fairgrounds was a few weeks away. Justin believed his collection would finally beat Tommy Johnson's from Carver Creek Road. Although they were best friends, they had a strict sense of heated competition burning between them. Each tried to outdo the other in every contest. Often their competitions ended in a draw.

Their friendship was loyal and unquestionable. Neither allowed jealousy or anger to divide them if the other won. They congratulated each other no matter how coveted the prize they sought was.

Justin turned off his lamp and walked barefoot to the barn to find his grandfather.

Grandpa stood beside the barbed wire fence at the right side of the enormous, aged barn. The loft held so many hay bales that it appeared the hay supported the rusted tin roof. Hay strands poked through the slatted black boards.

The painted chewing tobacco advertisement on the roof was slowly being eaten by rust and the passage of time.

As Justin approached the barn, his grandfather puffed his cherry wood pipe. He reached into a brown paper bag and tossed cracked corn on the ground. White leghorns flocked and scrambled across the barnyard, pecking and scratching at the corn.

"I fed them this morning, Grandpa," Justin said. He stepped up on the wooden fence slat to be near his grandfather's height.

"I know, son. I like to watch them eat. It comforts me. These animals depend solely on us. They trust us to take care of them. Because of that trust, they're our responsibility. After all, we got them from a hatchery, so in a sense, we're their parents. We fostered them until they were old enough to get about on their own. In some ways, you depend on Lib and myself to take care of you during the summers. We foster you because your parents don't have the time."

"I know."

Deep creases of sadness formed around his grandfather's eyes.

"What did you want to tell me?"

His grandfather swallowed hard. "Well, son. Some things in life are difficult for us to accept or understand. Sometimes . . . sometimes things don't happen the way you plan them, you know?"

Justin shrugged. "I suppose."

"Well," Grandpa said. His voice grew solemn in spite of its shakiness. "I received some bad news a week ago. Something that I hoped would never happen, but it has. I should probably wait until your mother and father get you in August to tell you, but there's no reason why it should wait that long. Maybe you can deal with it better now than right before school starts. I've debated the matter over and over the past few days on how to tell you, what words to say, and what your reaction would be once I tell you."

"What is it?"

"I'm dying, Justin," he said bluntly. "Cancer. The doctors tell me I have chronic lung cancer. I probably won't be around next summer to look after you. I regret it. Smoking all these years and destroying my lungs. I regret it most because of you."

Tears welled in Justin's eyes.

"I love you, boy. I love you so terribly much. It pains me that your parents aren't doing their rightful job raising you. They need to spend more time with you and not with that damned insurance business." He cleared his throat and wiped his eyes. "Of course, I can't say that I didn't do the same thing. I wasted your Dad's childhood building up that insurance business to house and feed us. Your father's doing the same thing I did. Maybe those traits are hereditary, too."

Justin couldn't speak. A lump rose in his throat. It was painful to swallow. Tears streaked his red cheeks. He wiped them away with his sleeve.

His grandfather continued feeding the chickens. Not once did he turn to face Justin. Justin understood why. If his grandfather, the man known for his rock hard stature, if he turned toward Justin, he'd break down and lose his composure. Although Grandpa was a tender, compassionate man, he did have his pride. He was still a strong man, thin but muscular. His hair was sprinkled with silver, but he looked ten years younger than his actual age. He forced himself to remain strong by not showing signs of fear and hopelessness.

Grandpa fought tears and held a stern chin. "I feel like I'm deserting you. You're not old enough to handle life on your own, which is partly what you'll have to do once I'm gone. Perhaps your Mom and Dad will be more attentive after I've passed on. But I still feel like I'm failing you."

Bravely, Justin forced the inevitable question though his cracking voice. "How long?"

"What?"

Wiping fresh tears away, Justin said, "How long did the doctors say you have to live?"

"Six months."

Justin felt his heart shatter as undreamed dreams died. He reached over and wrapped his arms tight around his grandfather.

"Don't die, Grandpa. I love you. You can't die."

Grandpa rubbed the back of Justin's head with his calloused hands.

"Easy boy. It's not over yet," he said, still not breaking down or losing his composure. "Not by a long shot, I assure you. I've not given up, so don't you give up on me, either. I'm a fighter, you know? With your help, we'll fight this thing together. You and me. There are treatments, chemotherapy, but there's no guarantee any of them will fix it. But one thing I *can* guarantee you."

"What?"

"Each new day is another opportunity for me to enjoy more thoroughly than the last. By God, we've got a whole summer to fill with adventures. Don't forget that. There's no time for grieving. Not yet."

Justin forced a smile.

Grandpa ruffled Justin's hair.

Justin didn't see anything other than the dismal outcome. Cancer. It killed by slowing eating a person's body. He'd watched documentaries about it in biology class. He couldn't bear to see his grandfather suffer something so terrible.

They stood silent for more than a half-hour and watched the sunset. As dusk settled, the chickens flew to their roosts for the night.

His grandmother stepped to the edge of the porch and yelled, "Supper!"

"Come on, boy," Grandpa said. "Let's go eat. Maybe we can figure out what we want to do tomorrow."

Justin went to the washroom and closed the door. He scrubbed his hands with warm water and soap, grabbed a towel, and sat on the edge of the bathtub. He wiped tears from his eyes.

Several minutes passed before he finally had the courage to look in the mirror. His eyes and cheeks were red. He ran cold water and doused his face.

Justin walked into the kitchen and took his seat. The kitchen normally gleamed in pure white—white linoleum, white sink and cabinets, and white table and chairs. But this evening, everything seemed tarnished, cold, and empty.

His grandmother smiled as she set an iron skillet of cornbread at the center of the table beside a large kettle of pinto beans and a plate of fried potatoes.

Grandpa handed the plate of potatoes to Justin. "After we eat, why don't we sit on the porch and see if any large moths come to the porch light?"

Justin nodded. "Okay."

Lib smiled. "How'd things go at the farmers market?"

"Great. I sold everything."

"Wonderful, dear," she said.

Grandpa nodded with pride. "Yep. I bought a few eggplants to plant tomorrow."

"Like you need any more plants to tend to, John."

"Oh, now don't go harping about my gardening," he replied with a grin. "You know it relieves my stress. That's why you pour so much time into your flowerbeds and quilts, isn't it?"

"I know. I'm teasing. I love my flowers because they bring so many different butterflies for Justin to collect."

Justin picked at his food, occasionally taking a bite, but he wondered how they could be playful with one another after what his grandfather had just told him. Didn't they worry about how little time Grandpa had to live? Or were they being strong for him, trying to make the ordeal *less* than what it really was? Although they might be able to ignore it, he couldn't.

He pushed his plate forward and said, "May I be excused?"

Grandpa nodded. "If you must, but this is the best supper your grandmother has made in some time. Sop up some of these beans and cornbread."

"Maybe later," he replied. "I'm not very hungry right now."

"Did you buy some snacks at Harper's Grocery today?"

Justin grinned. "A few."

"Just like your father. Jack did that every weekend when he was a boy. Never able to save a dime. Did those Butler brothers chase you again?"

"They tried. I lost them though. Their ten-speeds can't catch my dirt bike when I jump ditches."

"The porch light's on. Go see if anything's flying around."

"Okay."

AFTER THE SCREEN door creaked shut, Lib gave John a sharp glance. "You told him, didn't you?"

John nodded, swallowed a bite of food, and washed it down with buttermilk. "Had to, Lib. He needs to deal with this pain before school starts. At least he'll have accepted it by then. This way the trauma won't affect his schoolwork."

"You're probably right, but he's taking it hard."

"Of course he is. He's losing family stability. Jack and Rita aren't spending enough time with him. They send him to the Y or let him play video games all evening. We're the only real balance he has right now."

"Just like when Jack was little, right? That's what is really bugging you, isn't it? You're feeling guilty for neglecting his childhood because you were building your business. Jack is doing the same. You feel like you're getting paid back for your absence."

The words cut John deeply.

"Yes, Lib. That's exactly how I feel. I said just about the same thing to Justin earlier. I told him that I placed my job over his father, too, and it was wrong. I realize it now. I just wish I had seen it years ago. At least Jack had you. Rita's as obsessed as Jack is as I was about my career."

"I know." Lib formed a bridge with her fingers and rested her chin on them.

"It digs at you," John said, shaking his head. "It really does. In the back of your mind, you believe if you work a bit harder, you'll earn enough extra money to take your kid to an amusement park, fishing, or camping. But, before you know it, you've turned around and your kid's graduating from high school, heading off to college, and soon, he has a family of his own to support. All you're left with is giving him a handshake and a clap on the back. Then you have to live with the regrets for all the lost time."

Lib reached across the table and placed her hand on his.

"You've mulled this over for a long time, haven't you?" she asked.

John massaged his temples and sighed. "It's haunted me for years. Now that I'm facing death, I'm afraid Justin will be deprived like Jack was, or maybe worse. That's why I obsess over gardening. It's the best way to work out my frustration. But no matter how hard I work in the garden, I can't keep the weeds from growing. The burdens keep coming, just like weeds, but you can't yank out a burden like you can a weed."

"No, dear. You can't."

"So I apply my constant energy and devotion to the plants. They're bountiful because of me. And plants don't argue with mule-headed opinions, either. I've yet to have one ask for the car keys."

Lib laughed and eased back in her chair. "I'm glad you still have your sense of humor."

John smiled.

"But," she said. "We've got a more important task right now. That young man on the porch thinks the world of you. He's as low as a boy can get. He knows he may be losing you. That part of him is scared."

John wiped a tear as he stared at the front door.

"I remember when you father passed away," Lib said. "You were young, and his death paralyzed part of you. I don't think you ever got past losing him."

"Death has a way of doing that, no matter how old you are. I believe death troubles us because we never have a chance to talk to that person again. There are always things you wished you had said, but never did. The secrets you'd like to have told them, but once they're dead, you don't get the chance to tell them. It's too late."

Lib stood and started clearing the dishes.

John stood, stretched, and yawned. The phone rang, and he jumped.

~

"Hello?"

"John?"

"Yes."

"This is Tommy's dad."

"Hey, Mack. How are you?"

"Fine as frog hair. Tommy wanted me to call to see if Justin is staying the summer with you."

"Yes, he is. He's on the porch if Tommy wants to speak to him."

"No, that's fine. He's outside catching moths."

"So is Justin."

"Tommy wanted me to tell you about the frog-jumping contest next weekend at the voluntary fire department raffle. Tommy's caught one granddaddy whopper of a frog and can't wait to see if Justin can find one to challenge it."

"Okay, I'll tell him."

John hung up the phone and walked out the screen door. Justin sat on the steps in the darkness and rubbed Charlie's long, droopy ears.

Small moths circled around the porch light.

Justin watched the moon creep above the ridge. Two brown bats swooped acrobatically around the barn security light. Charlie nuzzled Justin's hand while he patted the dog. Charlie's tail wagged.

John sat beside Justin. "How you holding up?"

"Okay, I guess."

"You're not going catch any moths sitting way over here."

Justin forced a smile. "I'll check them out in a few minutes."

"Son, I know what's going through your head, but lots of folks get cancer nowadays and with proper treatment, they come out okay."

"It's not fair. Why did you have to get cancer?"

"Fair?" John chuckled. "Nothing in this world is fair, my boy. Nothing. This isn't anything compared to what I've seen in the newspapers and magazines about Nam. You had a great uncle who served nearly his whole life in the military. He fought in Nam. The tragic stories he told were far worse than anything I ever imagined. How he survived the memories is beyond me."

Charlie chuffed. Justin scratched the redbone's ears.

"But," John continued. "You need to understand that the McKnights' are fighters. When problems arise, we don't run from them. We stand our ground and do our damnedest to win. You have my word that I'm going to fight this cancer tooth and nail."

"But what if the cancer's really bad?"

"I'm a fighter. I'll fight this. I have to."

"You still smoke."

"Not nearly as much. I'm not entirely certain cigarettes caused it. It could have been from using pesticides and herbicides over the years. There are a great number of factors that may be responsible for my cancer. But, as a major precaution, I'm doing my best to quit smoking."

"I love you, Grandpa. I believe in you, and if you want to quit, you'll find the strength."

John smiled. "I appreciate that, and I love you, too."

The moon grew brighter on the horizon, and for some odd reason, it seemed larger than normal with a haunting aura.

"Oh," John said. "I almost forgot. Tommy has caught the biggest bullfrog in the world! His father called and said it's a sure win at next Saturday's frog-jumping contest. And, get this, he *dares* you to find a frog that can jump anywhere near the distance his can."

"Really?"

"Yep. So I have a favor to ask."

"What?"

"Tomorrow, I want you to go down to our pond and find a frog worthy and capable of winning that contest. I want you to win it . . . for me. You think you could do that?"

Justin smiled. "You bet I can."

John checked his watch. "Looks like it's getting close to bedtime. Better wash up."

"Can I check the light for a few minutes?"

John smiled. "Okay, fifteen minutes. Then come inside."

"Yes, sir."

IN THE ATTIC BEDROOM, Justin lay on his bed and stared at the ceiling. The night breeze flowed through the open window. Shadows from the swaying oak tree in the moonlight danced across the walls and ceiling. The tree limbs brought to mind his drawing of the swamp, the tree, and the hideous face and the ominous threat.

He didn't doubt the undead man he'd seen in the trees was also the one who threatened to take him. Trying to decipher the strangeness of it all was impossible.

The moving shadows on the wall chilled him. He hurried to the window, pulled it down, and locked it.

A little more at ease he returned to bed. His wandering thoughts halted when he remembered his grandfather's cancer. The notion of losing Grandpa outweighed the possible threat that crept through the night.

Tears heated his eyes and chiding himself didn't stop them. Justin couldn't bare the emptiness that the loss of his grandfather imposed on his life. He hoped for a miracle. Short of that, the future looked bleak.

CHAPTER 6

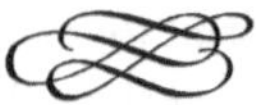

After midnight, Justin was still awake. His mind couldn't escape the grip of his grandfather's cancer. His focus on the tragic dilemma was so strong that he could no longer picture the face.

When he attempted to think of more pleasant things, like the events from previous summers he had spent with his grandparents, more tears flowed. Those moments were pleasant memories never to be relived except in his mind.

Frustrated, Justin went to the window and opened it. He was surprised by the coldness of the June night. The crisp air had hushed the crickets that normally chirped outside the house and in the pasture. It was eerily quiet.

No moths fluttered around the security light at the barn. The air was still and cold like death.

The full moon lit the lawn and barn where he could almost see everything. But the long shadows from trees and shrubs disturbed him, though he didn't understand why.

The serene night was like a smooth lake surface right before a blast of wind rippled across it.

Suddenly, Charlie broke into harsh barks and snarls near the barn. Justin figured he was chasing away a skunk or opossum near the chicken coop, which wasn't unusual. He started to shut the window when Charlie yelped and scampered across the yard. The dog whined and cried as it retreated beneath his grandfather's pickup. Then it became silent.

Justin shook his head and winced. "Skunk sprayed again? Grandma won't like that."

He lowered the window, yawned, and went to back to bed.

Justin rested his hands behind his head. More relaxed, his eyes grew heavy. A large shadow moved past his upstairs window. He bolted upright and flung off his sheet.

Being in the attic bedroom, he couldn't see how anything could just pass by his window. He hurried to the window and peered out. The window offered a panoramic view of the barn, the garden, and part of the pasture.

On each side of the window were trellises covered with thorny rose vines. Placing his face against the glass he scanned both trellises but didn't see anything.

Justin rubbed his eyes and returned to bed.

As he sat on the edge of his bed, he thought about his bike ride to Harper's Grocery earlier that day.

The Butler brothers must have gotten word that he was back for the summer because they were waiting for him in their normal hiding places. Although they tried to bully him, they never seemed clever enough to get their team effort to succeed. The only reason they attempted to pick on him was because he lived in the city and they were country boys. Justin was an outsider they didn't want around.

Clifford Butler was seven years old and sat on his bike behind a tobacco barn. Since he was the youngest, he was allowed the first chance to knock Justin off his bike. The question occurred to Justin several times: Since Clifford was so small, what did he truly expect to do if he succeeded? He certainly wasn't a physical threat.

Clifford had a three-speed bike but didn't know how to shift the gears properly, and Justin lost him in less than a minute. By then, his nine-year-old brother, James, took chase. But James was a chunky kid. Trying to pedal hard taxed his breathing quickly. He huffed and puffed as he pedaled after Justin, and soon, red-faced, he pulled off the road and stopped to catch his breath. Justin effortlessly rode on.

Over the next hill Zeke waited. He was fourteen, lean and muscular. If he actually got his hands on Justin, he could do serious damage, but his brute strength lost out to Justin's quick wit.

If Zeke had a brain, Justin reasoned, he'd have been the first one to try to catch him and have the other two brothers set a roadblock or box him in. But, as it was, Zeke was the only one left and his ten-speed was no match for Justin's TMX bike once he rode off the main road and across ditches.

That afternoon, Zeke had tried to pull him off his bike by grabbing Justin's shirt and tugging back. Justin, though, kicked Zeke's bike chain several times until the chain popped loose. Zeke had no choice but to let go and fix his bicycle.

Justin pedaled away, coasting down the hill and into the general store gravel lot. He chained his bike to the air compressor beside a Dr. Pepper machine.

He opened the screen door. The smell of boiled peanuts mixed with cigar and pipe smoke filled the air. Older men sat on a rugged church bench telling their stories and laughing.

Old man Harper smiled at Justin and placed a stack of new comics on the counter for him to look through. He chose five comics, grabbed an oatmeal pie and a Mountain Dew from the cooler. He waited for Mr. Harper to add up the total. After he paid for the items, he headed back to the door, knowing the Butler brothers were outside waiting for him.

Angry and waiting.

The Butler brothers wouldn't start a fight with him in the parking lot because Harper had stern rules for fighting or scuffling on his property. If caught, the sheriff would be called, and they'd be banned from his store. So he didn't have to worry about unchaining his bike. He'd have no incident doing that and riding away. It was down the road that he'd have to make certain they didn't do something underhanded.

As the screen door slammed shut, Justin headed down the steps. All three brothers leaned against the air compressor with their arms folded.

"So city-boy," Zeke said. "What'd you buy me?"

Justin frowned and pushed past him. He pulled the key from his pocket, knelt, and unlocked the bike chain.

"Nothing," he replied.

Zeke unfolded his arms and grabbed an aluminum bat he had hidden behind the compressor.

Justin hated bullies. He'd seen plenty of them at his city school. One thing he'd learned was that most bullies cowered down if confronted. Seeing the bat made his heart race, but whatever he did, he couldn't show fear. Bullies fed on fear and became bolder, sometimes cruder.

"What'cha looking at?" Zeke asked.

Justin smiled. "A couple of assholes, I do believe."

Justin couldn't believe the words had come out of his mouth. From the stunned expressions on the brothers' faces, neither could they.

Zeke's hand tightened on the end of bat.

James looked at Zeke. "You gonna let him get away with that?"

"You shut your mouth, James," Zeke said. "You know Old man Harper will call the law."

"No, James," Justin said, walking his bike past them. "That's not the real reason. Your big brother is nothing but a puny coward."

"He is not," Clifford said defensively.

Justin slung his leg over his bike and pedaled between them. "He's a coward. Why else does he need a bat? Can't take me without it."

James frowned and formed pudgy fists. "Get him, Zeke."

"No," Zeke replied. "Not here. Not right now."

"Why not? Is it true? Are you afraid of him?"

Zeke grabbed James' shirt with a clenched fist. "No, you idiot. Sheriff Hopkins is parked right over there."

"Where?"

Zeke motioned with a nod. James turned around quick. The patrol car was parked at the edge of the road near the top of the hill. Hopkins waved and smiled.

Justin smiled and taunted, "You girls be careful going home."

"Talk now," Zeke said in a near whisper. "I'll make you cry later."

Justin rode away. His heart pounded faster than his feet could pedal, but inside, he felt like a champion. He had stood his ground.

As he lay on the bed remembering that brief moment of triumph, he smiled and drifted off to sleep. If tomorrow came, it had to be better than today.

CHAPTER 7

Seated at the desk chair, Elias held the pinning board and studied the giant swallowtail. Mud smudged from his fingers onto the board but not the insect. He was impressed how the boy had crucified such a beautiful creature without remorse. It didn't diminish the boy's purity since it was only an insect.

Turning in the chair, he watched Justin's chest rise and fall. Elias placed the pinning board down and picked up the sharp sickle he had laid on the desk. He wiped the blade covered with dog blood onto his worn pants. The blade gleamed in the glowing moonlight that spilled through the attic window.

Elias stood and eased across the bedroom. He bent close to the boy's mouth and inhaled his breath. He wanted to slit the boy's throat and make the sacrifice tonight, but the moon wasn't full.

One more day.

Elias feared his body might not last that long. Deterioration was setting in quickly due to the summer heat. The sacrifice of the minister had not pleased his master. Searching through the night for another sacrifice would weaken him further. He had to stay close to the farmhouse until the full moon was high in the sky the following night.

He turned and went to the window. He lowered himself on the thorny trellis and climbed down.

Although he couldn't sacrifice the boy yet, he could offer something else.

~

A SHARP, cold breeze blew through the window and awakened Justin around five a.m. The rotten stench of decayed flesh appalled him.

The window was wide open, and the curtains danced in the wind. Cold fear made his body shiver. He was certain had closed the window before he drifted off to sleep.

His bedroom door was locked, so neither of his grandparents had opened the window, nor would they when the night air was chilly.

The decayed odor of death gagged him. Justin pulled his blanket above his chin and covered his mouth. Finding courage, he slipped from bed, went to the window, and closed it.

Even with the window shut the odor pierced the room. As he walked to his desk, brittle chunks of dry mud crunched underfoot. He turned on the desk lamp. A trail of moss and dried mud covered the hardwood floor from the window to his bed. The dirt fragments formed large footprints. Much larger than his own. Now he wondered if he had locked the intruder inside rather than outside.

Justin jerked open the desk drawer and grabbed his hunting knife. As he evaluated his room, he noticed more mud on his desk chair and along the side of his pinning board.

He wanted to awaken his grandparents, but they'd probably assume he had brought in the mud himself. His grandmother would then reveal his brief stint in the creek to ease his mind while not intentionally telling his grandfather

Justin brushed the mud from his chair and sat down. He held the knife tight. The glow of the desk lamp spilled across the floor but stopped short of exposing what might be hiding under his bed in the dark shadows.

Lowering himself on his knees, he cocked his head to the side to see what was underneath his bed.

Nothing moved.

All was silent.

Justin held the knife before him as crawled closer to his bed. Nothing except tiny spider webs and dust bunnies occupied the space under his bed.

He stood and dusted dirt and moss from his pajamas. He set the knife on the bed and returned to the window. He edged to the side of the window so he didn't give the perpetrator a clear view of himself. But with the lamp on, whomever or whatever had been in his room knew he was awake. He couldn't hide that, but he could stay out of sight.

Justin's mind drifted to the drawing and the threat.

"I'm coming for you."

He was now more than certain he had seen the person from the drawing in the pasture. How had this undead person materialized from the drawing and know where he lived? He didn't doubt the very being that threatened him had been in his room.

The smell of death and decay lingered. The odor had to be from the undead man.

Outside, his grandfather started his pickup truck. Justin peered through the window. Someone limped away from the deep shadows near the barn.

He started to shout a warning, but his voice would never rise above the roaring truck motor. The man stood beside the barn and watched his grandfather.

Justin changed clothes quickly, ran downstairs to the washroom, and grabbed his boots. He yanked to loosen the wet shoelaces but they were stuck in the brass brackets. He pried the boots open enough to slip his feet inside.

The truck pulled down the drive. His grandfather was going to the farmers' market. He opened the back door, but he didn't have time to catch his grandfather before he turned onto the dirt road.

Justin returned to the kitchen and opened the pantry. He took his grandfather's .22 rifle and a flashlight. He stepped outside the back door and onto the porch.

Clouds hid the moon, making the backyard even darker than the front side of the farmhouse. Tall pecan trees towered over the work sheds. The gravel path that led to the barn was dim. The security light on the barn was positioned toward the drive since visitors came to the front door.

Even though it was dark, he didn't turn on the porch light. Doing so automatically pinpointed his location to the intruder.

Gravel crunched beneath his boots as he walked the path to the barn. Justin cradled the rifle in both hands as he walked. He had used the rifle to shoot crows and copperheads. Occasionally in the winter he went rabbit hunting with his grandfather, but he had never shot the gun in the dark. His hope to make an accurate shot, if necessary, was diminished by the darkness.

There wasn't any sign of Charlie. He thought about how the dog had scampered in terror across the yard. At the time, he believed a skunk might have sprayed the redbone, but now, he knew the undead man had attacked his dog.

Charlie was dead silent.

Justin wasn't certain where the dog had hidden. Under normal circumstances, Charlie would have greeted John as he loaded bushels of vegetables onto the pickup truck, but the dog hadn't. And Charlie should have started barking at the stranger. The dog never seemed afraid of anything. Once he had stood between an angry bull and Justin to protect him. He worried about the dog and its welfare and if the dog was still alive.

A chicken squalled.

A second later, silence.

Justin took a deep breath and loaded a round into the rifle chamber. He clicked off the gun safety and took several timid steps forward. His adversary had to be in or near the chicken coop.

After seeing the undead man in the pasture he wondered if a rifle could actually kill him. He suddenly remembered the cat and ferret and their crazed eyes. In the darkness their small size gave them an even greater advantage of a surprised attack. They'd be harder targets to shoot.

As Justin stepped past the tool shed, a faint whimpering cried from behind a barrel.

Charlie.

Justin stepped closer to the dog. When he was within a few feet of Charlie, he shone the light. The dog cowered and quaked with fear. His jaw trembled. Slick blood was drying on his side. The cut didn't look too deep, but it was difficult to tell in the poor lighting.

He reached to inspect the wound. Charlie bared his teeth and snarled.

Justin pulled back his hand.

"It's okay, boy. It's okay. I'm not going to hurt you."

Charlie's nose wrinkled and he exposed even more teeth. Justin stepped back. The dog was never temperamental, but he understood that frightened, injured animals often reacted with violence, no matter how benign they were. The best he could tell, the laceration on the dog's side had come from the undead man. Charlie had threatened him and was attacked in response.

Justin stared at the dog, and then he looked toward the barn. The longer he stood there, the less boldness he possessed. He grabbed a bucket, turned it over, and seated himself a few feet from where the dog lay. Although he couldn't make himself investigate the barn, he'd stay to protect Charlie.

He held the rifle tight until the sun edged over the horizon. Birds sang and fluttered from tree to tree.

Justin looked at Charlie. The dog lay still.

"Charlie? You okay?"

Charlie's head rose in response to his name, but his tail didn't wag, and a few seconds later, he lay his head back down.

As weak sunlight shone across the barnyard, Justin walked to the barn. Since his enemy favored darkness, he probably wouldn't risk an attack in the light. That was Justin's assumption, and he hoped his was right, but if he was wrong, he'd have a better chance with the rifle in daylight.

He propped the rifle upright against the barn wall and scooped a large bucket of cracked corn to feed the chickens. When he reached for the door to the coop, he froze. A bloody handprint was smeared on the wooden doorpost. The bucket of corn dropped from his hand and spilled across the dirt.

Looking through the chicken wire, Justin discovered all the decapitated chickens in the center of the coop. A large design of strange symbols and letters were painted in a circle of blood. The artwork was spectacular, if not entirely menacing. The exquisite patterns were carefully and painstakingly crafted. A dark circle of evil energy projected from it. He wasn't certain what the symbolism represented, but he knew it was not in his best interest to step inside the circle. The person who designed this wanted him, and quite possibly had entwined a spell with the blood pattern to snare him.

Had he walked to the chicken coop before daybreak, he'd probably interrupted the man and been killed. Looking around, he didn't see any indication that the man was nearby, but he couldn't rule out the possibility with absolute certainty.

Justin didn't want his grandfather to find the chickens and the blood symbols. Going inside the fence broadened his fear of being entrapped inside the coop should the man still be around. He took the water hose and washed away the blood symbols, but left the chickens where they lay.

He decided to go to the pond to find a bullfrog for the frog-jumping contest. Maybe after he captured one, he'd have a better idea of what to do with the chickens. He grabbed the rifle and headed back to the house.

ELIAS HID in the hayloft and licked sticky blood from his hands. His spell cast, he waited. If the incantation failed, he had nightfall to look forward to. Under the full moon, he'd sacrifice the boy and gain immortality.

<h1 style="text-align:center">CHAPTER 8</h1>

*A*fter Justin placed the rifle back inside the gun cabinet, he checked on Charlie. Although the dog slept, his body quivered and kicked from obvious nightmares.

He knelt closer and inspected Charlie's wound without touching it. The cut wasn't deep nor was it bleeding. The superficial injury appeared less than the trauma Charlie experienced from the undead man's attack.

Justin let the dog sleep and walked to an outbuilding where his go-cart was kept. He grabbed a fishing net with a four-foot handle and placed it between the seats. He checked the fuel and set the choke. Once he took his seat, he turned the key three times before the engine hummed and sputtered.

Blue smoke billowed and formed a thick cloud inside the building. He patted the gas pedal several more times before the cart rolled forward. After readjusting the choke, he mashed the accelerator hard and sped down the driveway.

Justin turned left on the dirt road. He was glad the pond wasn't in the same pasture as the grove of trees where he'd seen the undead man. He drove about a quarter mile, turned into a short path, and stopped at the metal pasture gate.

The engine idled as he got out and unchained the gate. Giving a slight push, the heavy gate swung open. He drove forward about ten feet, got back out, and shut the gate. No livestock were penned in this lot, but his grandfather would be furious if he came home and saw the gate wide open. An open gate was an invitation for people to trespass and fish.

Once Justin secured the gate, he drove down the grassy pasture.

With no clouds on the horizon, the day would be bright and sunny. Even though he was still a bit apprehensive about the undead intruder, Justin had convinced himself that he was safe as long as he remained in the harsh sunlight. He never suspected he had other dangers to fear.

Since the sun had yet to rise, the frogs were more sluggish than they would be in hotter temperatures. Acting in the early morning hours, he held a slight advantage to catch a champion bullfrog with the fishing net.

Fifty yards from the pond, he shut off the engine and let the go-cart coast until the thick grass stopped its momentum. If he drove any closer, the loud motor would frighten frogs and fish deeper into the water. After the cart stopped, he took his net, a small backpack, and continued on foot.

As Justin crested the dammed end of the pond, he glimpsed the black cave opening of Devils Den in the center of a wooded area across the pond. A heavy mist hung over the trees. Long tendrils of fog serpentined down tree trunks, making the opening darker and more sinister. The blackened cave entrance seemed to draw energy into itself like black holes did in space.

The haunted cave garnered its name after several people vanished inside years earlier. His grandfather warned him to never go inside. Supposedly, from what Justin had been told, anguished cries for help echoed throughout the cave passages. Police investigations never found those who made the soft cries, so they reported the bizarre moans as nothing more than whistling wind. Although Justin fished at the pond during the summer, he had never gotten close enough to the cave to hear the voices. After his drawing, the strange visitation in his room the night before, and the brutal chicken slaughter, he held some belief that the cave legend was true and not a fictitious account.

Crows cawed in the darker recesses of the mist-shrouded woods. Beyond the cave and the rocky wall that housed Devils Den was a marshy little swamp. Dead trees scarred that area of the woods. He never collecting in that area because butterflies preferred to visit the crown vetch and clover flowers.

The flock of crows burst into flight with piercing shrieks and faded deeper into the gloomy dead trees.

Justin returned his attention to finding a giant bullfrog. Looking down, he saw a coiled copperhead at the tip of his right wading boot. He almost yelled. His attention on the dark cave had been so intense that he didn't realize he'd almost stepped right on the snake. The copperhead slowly uncoiled and slipped into the water. It swam across the water's surface for a few feet and dove out of sight.

He released a long sigh and closed his eyes. Had the snake bitten him, he might have died before an ambulance reached him. The last thing he needed was his mind to keep wandering and worrying. His careless distraction almost became a costly life-threatening mistake.

Without taking another step, Justin peered along the pond's edge for bullfrogs. The thick cattails and knee-high grass made them hard to see. The less he moved, the better chance he had of not scaring them into the water. Once spooked, bullfrogs tended to stay in the water and were unlikely to return to the pond embankment for hours.

Before he moved, he checked the grassy path for more snakes. Copperheads sought water in masses during the summer heat. If he'd seen one, others probably were nearby.

Justin took each step with trepidation. Despite the dangers, the beauty surrounding the pond was captivating. Dragonflies and damselflies performed remarkable acrobatic flights and skimmed across the water. Occasionally a largemouth bass broke through the surface and crushed a fragile insect in its jaws. Katydids and cicadas chummed in the dark forest near Devils Den.

A couple of bullfrogs croaked on the far side of the pond. Near the shallow end of the pond were three big frogs. Two were fairly large, but the giant one in the middle was bigger than the other two put together. It was the largest frog he'd ever seen. He kept his eyes on the frog as he crept toward the shallow end of the pond.

"That one," he whispered. "Grandpa will be amazed. That's probably the biggest frog he's ever seen."

When the frog trio was less than forty feet away, Justin became braver and slipped into water up to his knees. Approaching them head on might prevent them from leaping into the pond. He hoped they'd jump back into the grass and away from the pond.

As he waded within ten feet of the frogs, the two smaller frogs leapt forward into the water. He cringed and held his breath.

The massive bullfrog, more reserved and sluggish, waited for Justin to make a move.

Justin eased closer and readied the fishing net to drop it straight down on the frog. As if sensing his thoughts, the frog leapt back into the grass. The net sunk in thick mud.

"What a jump!" he said, rinsing the net in the pond. "Had to be at least four feet. I gotta catch you."

Stepping out of the mire, Justin ran across the grassy terrain. The frog sprang across the pasture with gigantic leaps. At least the frog was heading *away* from the pond. He had a better chance to catch it on the grass than in the water.

Nervously tightening his hand on the net handle, he ran after the bullfrog. Too busy keeping his eyes on the massive frog; he never realized it was jumping toward the misty side of the forest. Beyond the mist was the swamp. Pools of water and dark shade would make it hard to find the frog if it reached the swamp.

Justin ran, but the frog kept a faster, swifter pace. Each giant leap taunted and frustrated him. At the edge of the trees, the frog stopped. He raised the net up, ready to fling it over the frog, but fear suddenly seized him and he couldn't move.

Straight ahead, in the center of the swamp, was the forked dead tree he had drawn. Every detail of the tree had been captured in the drawing as though he had sat for hours carefully copying it onto the paper. Slowly he lowered his arm. The frog seemed less important.

If he'd ever seen this tree, it would have been over a couple years ago when he rode on the tractor with his grandfather to pull stumps out of the ground. He couldn't have remembered the details to the perfection he had. And yet, here stood the tree, an identical mirror image of the one in his sketchpad.

On a thick tree branch, an old withered noose dangled in the breeze. A cold, dark sensation flowed around him. Invisible vines twisted and attempted to attach themselves to his legs and pull him into the swampy mire.

Black crows with piercing red eyes stared at him. Their heated pupils radiated an evil that numbed him.

Chill bumps rose on his arms. When he finally managed to break free of their gaze, he looked down. The frog leapt away from the swamp. Justin followed but kept glancing back over his shoulder at the tree because he feared the creature in the water might emerge and come after him.

He needed to catch the frog quickly and get back to the farmhouse. After the frog-jumping contest, he'd call his parents and beg them to come get him. His fear that he'd never see them again was more than just his imagination. His gut feeling held valid proof by the evidence of the tree and the undead man stalking him. The longer he stayed with his grandparents, the more danger he was in.

~

THE BULLFROG KEPT a ten-foot distance from Justin. Every time he thought he could net the frog, it jumped. Frustrated, he ran faster, dropped the net, and missed the frog by inches. Again, it outpaced him, hopping around trees and between moss-covered rocks.

Justin attempted a different approach. Instead of panicked running, he chose to move slower.

The bullfrog sat motionless as he crept closer. He held the net low to make a side-sweep. When the frog jumped into the air, he hoped the net scooped it up. However, the frog didn't move as the net swept through the air above its body. Once the net passed over, the frog took three expansive leaps.

Justin ran after it, stopped suddenly, and shook his head.

The bullfrog had jumped into the mouth of Devils Den and disappeared into the blackness of the cave.

"No," Justin whispered with tightness in his throat and stomach. "Not in there."

He approached the cave warily. He contemplated *what* to do next. His grandfather had given him several stern warnings to never go inside the cave. Grandpa had also showed him yellow newspaper clippings about a boy that had disappeared inside Devils Den twenty years before.

However, in spite of the warnings, he couldn't ignore the bullfrog's size. The promise he had made to his grandfather was he'd win the contest. To win, he needed *that* frog. He doubted anyone had ever seen one that size. Its incredible leaps were sure to out jump any other frog.

Justin unzipped a side pocket of his backpack and got a small flashlight. He also had a larger flashlight but the batteries in the smaller light had just been replaced. He set his backpack on the ground and entered the wet, dark cave. He didn't plan to go far. He didn't need to. Reptiles and amphibians became extremely sluggish by cool temperatures. Most caves kept a steady temperature near sixty degrees, so he should be able to find the frog quickly, net it, and hurry back outside without anyone ever knowing.

Shining the light in the cracks and crevices, he didn't see the bullfrog.

Justin sighed. He didn't hear any painful cries, but nervousness overtook him as he walked further. He was more afraid of his grandfather finding out he had gone inside than he was of the voices or who pleaded for help.

His determination to find the frog made him ignore the more prominent dangers inside the cave. By the time he considered turning around, he had taken several turns in the cave's strange maze. He lost track of which direction he had taken last. His flashlight flickered and dimmed.

Justin knew he was in trouble.

CHAPTER 9

John sat on the tailgate of his truck, waiting for customers to buy vegetables at the farmers market. The Sunday morning crowd was sparse. As he watched people pass, a chill iced through his veins. Had he not been seated, he'd probably have fallen down. The sensation wasn't pain. He sensed something was very wrong. For reasons he didn't understand, he had to get home.

Quickly.

John yanked the truck keys from his overall pockets, slammed the tailgate shut, and scrambled into the driver's seat. The urge to get home brought uneasiness to his stomach and tears stung his eyes.

John drove carefully through the market parking lot, but once he hit the road, he drove like a maniac.

THE AIR inside Devils Den was damp and cool. The wet cave walls glistened. Water dripped into small blackish pools along the edge of the pathway.

Justin's light dimmed, brightened, dimmed, as he walked deeper into the cave. He tapped the back of the light several times. He assumed the light suffered more from a bad connection than dying batteries because the batteries were new. The flashlight flickered, but his burning curiosity lured him deeper into the cave.

He no longer looked for the bullfrog. The amphibian should have become too sluggish to travel this deep into the cave. It had probably squeezed into a hole that he had stepped over without noticing. On his way out, he'd look among the wet rocks and crevices for it.

The flashlight dimmed. Justin slapped the end harder than before. The light's intensity increased several seconds before fading again. He decided to turn back and get the larger flashlight. He didn't understand why his grandfather had dramatically exaggerated about the cave. Nothing he'd seen so far had proven to be dangerous. The snake at the pond had scared him worse than the cave.

The path's gradient grew steeper with each step he took, but he had not come down a descending slope. The path had been level without any deviation and now it was strangely different. The wall formations didn't look familiar, either. He wished he had marked the walls with a piece of limestone to guide him back to the entranceway. The glow of the flashlight didn't reveal any scuffed footprints left by his tennis shoes.

A cold, howling breeze flowed from the cave depths. It brushed past, chilling him. His short sleeve shirt wasn't enough to keep him warm.

Justin wondered how deep into the cave he had walked. No outside light filtered in. He was certain he hadn't traveled more than twenty yards. Turning off the flashlight, he stood in pitch-blackness. Now the darkness frightened him. Without the assurance of a quick exit from the cave, he feared he was lost. He turned the light back on and hurried up the path.

Tears of desperation heated his eyes when he came to a crossroad of intersecting paths he hadn't passed earlier. He was lost. He didn't know which path to take. If he chose the wrong direction, he'd wander in complete darkness after the flashlight eventually stopped working.

The wind swirled and moaned. Drifting in the air was the soft whispering, anguished cries of tortured souls. Their pain-filled chorus was faint and in languages unfamiliar to him.

Justin shone the flashlight down each tunnel. Shadows slinked deeper out of the light's reach. He wanted to believe the flickering light played tricks with the darkness, but he remembered the drawing, the solemn threat, and that the tree he had drawn towered outside the cave. He no longer felt alone. Something else lurked inside the dark tunnels.

The frigid air hung still, silent. Fog escaped his mouth as he contemplated which direction to take. He chose the path straight ahead and hoped he found the entrance before darkness swallowed him.

The path descended, narrowed, and turned sharp to the right. The tight crevice required him to squeeze and contort his body. Midway through the turn, he was wedged and unable to move. He sucked in a deep breath and bent slightly back, freeing himself.

Muffled, intangible moans whispered.

The corridor widened and straightened. Justin placed his hand against the wall as he walked. His feet slipped on slick, muddy rock. The small flashlight fell onto the path, bounced off a rock, and landed in thick mud further down the slope.

He wobbled to maintain his balance but the soft earth beneath his feet shifted, and he fell. His weight forced the mire to collapse and flow like a viscous mudslide. Helpless to slow his descent, he dug his fingers into the mud, clawing and grabbing fistfuls of sludge, but nothing was available to grab or slow his speed.

Justin pushed the toes of his boots into the muck but they slid as if on polished glass. He flailed his hands above his head, trying to find something, anything, which could anchor him.

Nothing.

Not even hope.

The clumps of clayish soil were like motor oil. The more he plunged his hands into the mire, the slippery they became. He passed the light, and reached for it, but it was inches from his fingertips. The four inches of thick muck carried him deeper into the dark abyss. The flow would carry him to wherever the path ended or dropped.

In desperation he reached for the jagged wall. He thrust his fingers into a stone pocket and held fast. Layers of mire flowed around him. The jagged rock cut his fingers. The lacerations burned as cool mud kissed the wounds, but he'd accept the pain rather than the possibility of plunging into a dark ravine. He had no way to know how far down the slope he had traveled. Eventually the steady flowing current would overpower his white-knuckled effort to remain stationary. The constant tug of the moving mudslide weighed heavily on his skinny arms.

Terror seized him. His stomach rumbled with nausea, as he felt more helpless than ever. Warm tears bit his cold cheeks. His arms strained to hold him in place.

Cold air hurt his dry throat as he gulped frantic breaths.

Voices echoed further down the slope. Fearful of what else might hear his frantic cries, he bit his lower lip to silence himself. He concentrated to slow his breathing because the slightest noise amplified a great distance in the cave that had somehow become a deep cavern.

Water trickled and splashed onto rocks in the chasm below. Justin feared he was only a few feet from plummeting over the sloped edge into the shallow water. The fall to the bottom would most likely kill him.

He clung to the rough rocky pocket. The dim glow of his flashlight floated on the mire toward him but just out of reach. The path was too slick to let go and crawl to it. The mud kept coming, but he couldn't figure out its origin. The light moved past him, spiraling with the mud and flowing with the current that dropped into the abyss. Seconds before the light disappeared over the ledge; it became wedged in a solid mass of rocks near the center of the path.

Only the narrow beam of faint light prevented Justin from being blanketed by darkness. Holding a tight grip on the wall with his left hand, he felt along the wall with his right until he found another deep crevice to insert his hand. He pulled himself upward and pressed his feet against the wall, alleviating some of the strain his hands and arms suffered.

His arms ached, burned. He didn't have much time before his strength disappeared, and he drifted over the ledge.

Pressing his feet against the cave wall, Justin reached with one hand, and hunted for another handhold. Finding one, he pulled himself a few feet further from the ledge. Freeing his other hand, he repeated the maneuver.

Confident he was placing more distance from the drop off; he froze when something crawled across the back of his hand. He flung a hairy spider into the drifting mud. A gooey, gummy substance coated his hand. Stuck to his hand was a large silk egg sac. Tiny spiders scuttled across his hand and up his arm.

He wiped off the spiders with a quick swipe. Their tiny, swarming legs unnerved him. Even when he was certain he had gotten rid of them, his skin still crawled. The cave became eerier.

A feathery buzzing wisp brushed the side of Justin's face. He rubbed his cheek against his shoulder; fearful something had landed on it.

His heart pounded as he imagined more spiders emerging from their hiding places and crawling toward him.

Justin had grown too weak to keep pulling himself up the sloped path. The mass of rocks where the light was stuck might support him if he reached them. But if he missed, he'd have no second chance, but he had no other choice, either. He was too tired to hang on much longer. Once he lost his grip, he'd fall over the ledge anyway.

He had to take the risk.

Justin pushed off the wall with his hands and feet like he was kicking off the side of a swimming pool. He turned, flung his arms into the mire, and did a couple shallow breaststrokes. The vicious ooze slowed his strokes, making swimming difficult. But he accomplished enough to get to the center of the sloped path. The overpowering sludge carried him to the immobile object in the mysterious stream. The mass he had thought were rocks wasn't, but he clung to them like a lifeline anyway.

After gaining a stable position atop the unmoving mass, he grabbed the flashlight, rubbed the mud off the lens cap, and focused the light on the anchored object beneath him. To his horror he clung to a dead man's carcass. The abrupt fright that seized him almost caused him to let go.

No flesh remained on the man's face, just deep holes where his eyes, nose, and mouth had been. The jaw hung open with the memory of the man's final scream.

A rusty chain wrapped around the crumbling ribcage. The chain lodged with the corpse's chainmail. A silver dagger protruded through the mail into where the dead man's heart had once beaten.

Justin adjusted his stance, and the man's brittle bones powdered, dissolved, and slid. He grabbed the chain. The crumbling body broke free of the binding chain and drifted with the mud over the ledge.

Justin's sore hands burned as he used the chain to pull himself to his feet. Mud and mire flowed around his boots. The mud's resistance made walking difficult, but slowly, step-by-step, he pulled himself up the ascending corridor. A strange light flickered higher in the distance. In what seemed an eternity, he made his way to the top.

Instead of returning to the level crossroads, he discovered the chain fastened to a castle rock wall. The black wall was thick, solid. The rocks were colossal, the mortar thin. Three lit torches licked the foggy air with hisses as their fire vaporized the mist.

Chained to the wall were four impaled skeletons sheeted beneath thick spider webbing. These men had suffered agonizing and brutal deaths. Their remains stated a stern warning not to trespass further.

Justin couldn't understand how a castle wall closed off the path that had led downward. The narrow gate behind the skewered humans was not the route he had chosen. Entering the gate possibly held the same end result for him, as it had for the spiked men.

A death filled with pain and agony.

But Justin had nowhere else to go. He doubted the gate led back to his grandfather's farm. That path had disappeared.

The only alternative was to repel down the sloping stream of mud and hope the rusty chain held his weight without snapping. Should the chain support him, his next dilemma was whether or not the chain was long enough to reach the bottom of the ravine.

A damp stagnant breeze flowed through the open gate. The torch flames danced in the stirring wind. The impaled skeletons' narrow eyes glowed crimson red. Masses of spiders climbed the webbing, spun silken balloons to catch the wind and drifted upward, toward him.

Wailing voices whispered in the air. Pleading cries begged for mercy.

Justin held the chain tight and stepped back. Mud oozed around his feet, attempting to pull him with it.

Bats chirped and flitted from crevices.

As he carefully backed down the slope, his hands throbbed and burned. Warm blood leaked through his clenched fists.

Guttural growls echoed through the open portal. Justin glanced at the gate. Huge yellow eyes peered through the darkness.

He hurried down the slope, hand under hand, step-by-step, until his feet nearly slipped at the edge. He grabbed the chain hard, ignoring his pain.

The flowing mire smacked rocks and water below. He anchored the heels of his boots against the rock ledge. He freed one hand, flipped on the flashlight, and shone it into the blackness below. The light didn't illuminate the bottom.

With the flashlight pointed upward, Justin dropped it into the ravine. The light grew smaller and smaller, fainter and fainter, as it plummeted. The flashlight vanished but he never heard it splash. The drop seemed endless. The light might have landed on a soft pillow of moss that prevented an echoing sound.

Growls raged at the top of the corridor near the castle wall.

There was no going back up. He feared the unknown of what might be in the chasm below, but he needed to find another cave exit. His grandfather needed him, and he needed his grandfather. If Justin never found a way out of the cave, his grandfather would worry himself sicker, and possibly increase the rate of his deteriorating health. Constant worry weakened one's immune system. And in his grandfather's case, the cancer would grow stronger and become the victor. He had to get out before his grandfather discovered he was missing.

Justin's hands hurt, but he lowered himself off the ledge and down the chain. The lacerations on his hands felt like blazing fire melting his skin as the links passed through his fingers. He winced and cried as the rusty chain bit into his flesh without mercy.

He slowed his descent by pressing the chain between his boots. His boots caught a knotted set of links and abruptly stopped him.

Without light Justin couldn't examine the damage his hands had endured, but his right hand hurt worse than the left. Holding his weight steady with his boots, he cautiously removed his right hand and blew it. The coolness of air diminished the pain slightly, but he had to continue down. He ached all over. He wasn't sure he'd be able to repel much further. Even if he ignored the pain, his strength was nearly gone.

Justin pulled the handkerchief from his back pocket and wrapped it around his bleeding, right hand. As he tightened the cloth the pain lessened.

Exhausted, he took the chain in his right hand. He didn't have any idea how much further down he had to go. He was tired and thought about just letting go. Giving up seemed such an easy thing to do, but his grandfather's words came to mind.

"The McKnights' are fighters. When problems arise, we don't run from them. We stand our ground and do our damnedest to win."

Justin smiled and nodded. Taking a solid grip on the chain with his wrapped hand, he placed his left hand over it. He looked down and said, "Thanks, Grandpa."

The chain passed through his hands again, snagging and ripping the handkerchief without any further damage to his hands. In a few seconds, his feet touched moist ground. He let go of the chain and sat back against a mossy rock. He closed his eyes and took several deep breaths. He wanted to sleep, but the wailing cries were closer and prevented him from relaxing. Reality cued him that dangers lurked nearby. He couldn't see the danger, but its sinister presence was manifested in the sorrowful cries.

John drove across Cumberland Lake. Heading for the farmhouse, the growing urgency that something was wrong made him drive faster. The only other thing that had ever caused him such apprehension was when his doctor called and scheduled an office visit to talk about his blood tests and X-rays. The long drive to the doctor's office entertained John's mind with various scenarios, but even the horrible news of cancer that day was mild compared to what presently dug fear into his soul.

He couldn't explain why this cloud of dread overshadowed him, but he remembered that his mother had a sixth sense with premonitions that seldom concluded as false alarms. He had experienced a few similar episodes in his life, but nothing that compelled him to action. His first impulse was that Justin was in trouble.

John shifted gears as his truck climbed the steep highway. Ahead of him was a slow pickup towing a fishing boat. John mashed the gas and attempted to pass. As he veered into the oncoming lane, a row of speeding vehicles headed right at him. He swerved back behind the boat and cursed under his breath.

He yanked a hand towel off the seat and wiped sweat from his brow. His speed dropped as he waited for the last of the oncoming traffic to pass. Once the lane was clear, he gunned the engine and drove around the truck and boat. Although he was able to increase speed, he wasn't able to drive as fast as he wanted. To make matters worse, a quarter mile later, he stalled behind another truck hauling a small yacht.

"Dammit!" he shouted and tapped the horn.

Oncoming traffic increased, leaving John to suffer the long wait of cresting the hilltop. He gripped the steering wheel tight. As the roadway leveled, the driver pulled his truck and yacht off the road and turned into a campground.

Tears and sweat stung John's eyes as he sped homeward.

The morning air was stagnant and hot. John unbuttoned his shirt, looked ahead at the empty highway, and shook his head with regret that he was probably too late.

CHAPTER 10

When Justin awakened, a bright blue light glowed around him. He wondered how long he had slept. The blue light shrank into a small dot and vanished in a blink.

He sat up and listened. Water cascaded down the cave wall and splashed into a deep pool. Rubbing his hands together, he felt no blisters or cuts. No pain.

Justin crawled closer to the water. In the pitch-blackness he was no better off than a blind man. He didn't want to fall into a water pool and risk not being able to get back out.

At the water's edge, Justin cupped handfuls of water and drank. The water was sweet, cold. When he quenched his thirst, he wiped his hands on his pants. Still no pain but his skin was sticky and moist. He wiped them again, but they still didn't feel dry. He itched all over.

His feet ached with each step he took. His boots pinched his toes like they were several sizes too small for his feet.

The waterfall splashed and mist filled the air. Within the sound of cascading water, the pain-filled voices echoed like whispers in the breeze. Turning in the direction of the cries, Justin followed the underground stream; being careful that each step forward was on rock, not water. Cave pools could be over ten feet deep. Should he fall in, without light, he might tread water for hours and not find the edge to pull himself out.

The rock path ascended into spiraling carved steps. Rushing water

61

cascaded down the steps. As he rounded two sharp, narrow coils of stairs, the splashing waterfall became fainter while the voices steadily grew louder. The final step left him standing at the entrance of a large room.

Light flickered along the far wall. Justin stopped walking and listened, fearful of what used the light source. Hissing sounds filled the air. He eased along the path in a crouched walk, occasionally looking behind him, worried that he'd be grabbed from behind.

Large wooden sconces were mounted in wall crevices. The fiery torches blazed and hissed as water dripped from overhead icicles. The cave floor gleamed with white snow and blue ice.

Justin shivered. He wished he had a long-sleeved shirt or a jacket. His breath formed tiny clouds as he exhaled. Hugging his arms, he tried to get warmer.

He edged along the path quietly, looking for any sudden movement from a hidden attacker or creature. The wailing cries increased in volume, and then dropped silent. Along each side of the path were barred cages with prisoners inside. The fear in their eyes turned to curiosity as they gazed at him. As far as he could see, no guards were posted.

Justin stopped between the first two cages. The ice-covered iron bars tightly enclosed the strange prisoners. The cramped spaces forced them to hunch over or rest on their knees in their own filthy waste and urine.

Justin covered his nose with his shirt and cautiously stepped further down the narrow path. At the corner of one cage set a pile of cured animal hides. He grabbed one and draped the rancid fur around his shoulders. For some warmth, he'd tolerate the odor.

He squinted while searching the room. The torchlight didn't offer ample lighting. He wished that he had kept the flashlight because he worried that somewhere in the shadows someone other than the prisoners was watching his progress.

Worse than their living conditions were the captives' odd deformities. Leaking yellow and green pustules covered their bodies. Some had no hands. Others were missing their fingers, feet, or legs. Several prisoners had only one eye. Their empty sockets were crudely sewn shut. Every captive was missing at least one appendage. But *none* of them caged near him were human.

Piles of skulls and bones lined the walls. Incomplete skeletons covered with icy cobwebs hung shackled to the wall. Death had saved them from further torture.

Justin looked into the face of one prisoner. Her wide eyes stared absently. Her mouth motioned words but no sounds came forth. He feared walking any further. Whoever, or whatever, had imprisoned them could just as easily take him. But going back to the underground stream was simply a dead end. No hope of escape existed from where he had come. Even if he wanted to climb the chain to the higher cavern ledge, he wasn't tall enough to reach it and finding it in the darkness was impossible. Going forward was his only option.

A short man gnashed his teeth and struck the bars of his cage with his fists as Justin stepped in front of it. His braided, heavy white beard flowed to his knees. Although imprisoned the threat was enough to make Justin jump back. The man was almost as wide as he was tall with thick muscular arms, chest, and legs. His body looked powerful, but his aged, wrinkled face indicated his defeat.

The prisoner was a dwarf.

When the man opened his mouth, only wordless grunts gurgled in his throat. His thick hands wrapped around the bars. He pushed against them to no avail.

At first Justin thought the dwarf wanted free in order to kill him, but the dwarf's blue eyes expressed concern, *not* hostility. He released the bars and pointed to the direction Justin had come. He pointed his stern finger again and again with a nod of his head indicating the boy should leave and leave *quickly*.

Justin reached for the dwarf's cage door, but the dwarf shook his head and grunted. In the cage next to the dwarf, a thin man said, "He's warning you to go back. The Spellmaster will arrive soon. It's best you leave before he appears. There will be no hope for you if you don't. You'll be doomed like we are."

Justin frowned. "I don't understand. Why doesn't he speak?"

"The Spellmaster has silenced his mouth with a spell."

"Who is the Spellmaster?"

The white bearded dwarf dropped to the ground and cowered, hiding his eyes behind his hand.

Seconds after the words escaped Justin's lips, a man stood before him wearing black robes, hood, and a cape. His gray beard spiraled to his ankles, and his green serpent eyes narrowed and focused on Justin.

Justin had never seen pupils so black and evil. The gaze was frightening and yet, hypnotic. It was as paralyzing as a mouse seeing a snake. He was afraid to run, to move, or breath.

The Spellmaster's staff, long and as black as obsidian, bore red eyes that stared and blinked from each knotted ridge in the wooden cane. The eyes studied him with as much intent as the aged wizard.

Justin stepped back to turn and run, but his feet meshed to the floor. Iron bars grew from the ground like saplings and encaged him.

The Spellmaster walked three steps, raised his hands while chanting an unfamiliar language, and vanished. All the prisoners lay on their cell floors with their eyes shut tight. Their bodies trembled.

CHAPTER 11

Sheriff Hopkins drove his brown SUV patrol vehicle down the one-lane dirt road that led to Hope Chapel on the bluff overlooking Cumberland Lake. Two county cars were already at the scene, and Hopkins was to meet his deputies there.

The forest shielded both sides of the dirt road. Heavy dew dripped from the leafy canopy with enough intensity that it looked like rain. Hopkins turned his windshield wipers on. The blades swept away dew and leaf debris.

Hopkins slowed to a stop where the concrete culvert met the road. He pushed a button and lowered his side window. Something had cut a swath through the saplings, leaving a path of bent and shaved twigs along the upper edge of the culvert. For a moment, he thought the trees had been bush-hogged. But upon closer inspection, he noticed more trees were bent than cut through.

He stepped from his SUV and crouched at the side of the road, studying the tire marks that had left the road. He pushed the tip of his cowboy hat up and frowned. Midway down the hill, he noticed the housing of a busted headlight on a tree branch. Just a few feet away on the concrete was a pool of transmission fluid and black motor oil. A mangled muffler lay trapped between a large rock and a fallen tree. Burnt leaves smoldered but no major fire had occurred. He had no doubt that a car rested at the bottom of the water.

Hopkins stood and readjusted his hat. His long, lanky figure produced a shadow that cut across the dirt road. The morning sun flashed off glittery glass on the road ahead of his SUV. As he studied the shattered glass, the blue-green tint and color of glass indicated it had come from an automobile.

He opened the door and climbed into his SUV. He'd alert his deputies to investigate the accident after he met with them at the church.

When Hopkins pulled into the church parking lot, Eugene Bailey—the County Coroner—talked to the deputies. A state police officer talked to a man whose pale face was stricken with fear and worry.

Hopkins stepped out of his vehicle, adjusted his hat, and walked toward his deputies. He smiled his uncanny George Strait smile in an attempt to ease the tension. He was often teased about his remarkable resemblance to George Strait and that if ever a look-alike contest occurred, he'd win it hands down. Regrettably, he couldn't sing a lick, and he didn't listen to country music. On two different occasions at the county fair, people visiting from a neighboring county insisted on an autograph and scoffed when he declined. He attempted to inform them that he wasn't the country music star. They walked away disappointed but not angry. In spite of the confusion, Hopkins' polite demeanor gifted him with never making any personal enemies.

Hopkins extended his hand to the coroner. "Morning, Eugene. What happened?"

Eugene pressed the rim of his oval-lens glasses against the slender bridge of his nose. His narrow face made him look like a weasel. "Cold-blooded murder, Sheriff."

"Who?"

"Pastor Ledbetter."

"Seriously?"

"Afraid so."

Hopkins looked at the grim faces of his deputies. They nodded.

"Where's the body?" Hopkins asked.

"Around the back of the church," Eugene replied. "Kind of odd. His car isn't here though."

Hopkins nodded. "I believe his car was run off the dirt road about a quarter mile from here. Went down the ravine into Cumberland Lake."

"Want us to go check it out?" Deputy Shannons asked.

"Yes," Hopkins replied. "Just to make certain it is his car."

Eugene motioned Hopkins to follow. "I'll show you where Ledbetter is."

"Okay," Hopkins said.

Eugene grabbed the sheriff's arm as they walked. "I hope you've not eaten yet."

"That bad?" Hopkins asked.

"Worse than you'd ever imagine," Eugene said in a cold whisper.

A chill ran through Hopkins' body. Homicide wasn't rare in this part of the state, but brutal murder wasn't something he expected to encounter while he held the Sheriff's Office.

The coroner led the way around the church. He stopped before they rounded the corner and said, "Brace yourself. Believe me, you cannot unsee what you're about to witness firsthand."

Hopkins stepped around the church and stopped walking immediately. He never had the chance to fight the sudden nausea that dropped him to his knees. He vomited.

"Sorry," Eugene said. "I tried to warn you."

Hopkins wiped his mouth with the back of his hand and winced.

Ledbetter was stretched between two trees. His hands were staked above his head against the trees with metal spikes. Because of the awkward angle his hands were positioned, both his shoulders had popped out of socket and were dislocated. His feet dangled about two feet above the ground. Ledbetter's head slumped slightly forward. Blood covered his chin and saturated a wide crimson circle down his shirt. His tongue had been cut out.

"This is more than just murder," Eugene said. "It's a ritualistic killing."

Hopkins took a deep breath and walked closer to the corpse. "What makes you suggest that?"

Eugene pointed. "Careful where you step. There are blood patterns covering the leaves and grass. Strange symbols. Not certain what religion they represent, so I need some photos to take back to the lab for research."

Black flies circled and buzzed around Ledbetter's body. Ants licked at the blood drops on the leaves and grass. Carrion beetles crawled across the ground and on Ledbetter's rigid body. The sickening smell of decomposition hung thick.

Hopkins stared in disbelief and shook his head. "Was the pastor dead or alive when he was butchered?"

"Judging by the amount of blood on his clothes, I'd say he was staked to the trees while alive. Probably had his tongue cut out while he was alive, too."

"But why?"

"No clue for that yet, Sheriff. But, murders like this don't have to have an exact motive."

"But Ledbetter was a pastor. I've never heard anything bad about him."

Eugene shrugged. "Do psychopaths need a reason?"

"No, but this is one of the last regions I've ever expect to see something like this."

"Evil can nest anywhere," he said. His shrewd eyes narrowed.

Hopkins nodded. "Whatever did this, houses evil. Don't you think so?"

"The body is presented in a ritualistic manner, almost crucified. Perhaps someone believed sacrificing a pure person endowed them greater power?"

"Eugene, best to my knowledge we still live in the Bible Belt. It's unlikely we have any cults in this area."

"I understand, but parties responsible for crimes like this don't rightly advertise their presence, either."

Swarms of black flies with sticky feet landed on the trees around the staked hands, looking for places to deposit eggs while drinking body fluids as decay set in.

"Agreed," Hopkins replied, brushing away flies with his hat. "Who found him?"

"Bill Greaves. He's the man with the state trooper."

"He just *happened* upon this?"

Eugene straightened his glasses. "He came to air out the church before the members arrived for Sunday School. He found Pastor Ledbetter before he did anything else."

"You have a possible time of death?"

"Working on it, but my best guess is this happened Friday night after the revival service. I'll know more after a few lab tests."

Hopkins looked at Ledbetter and shook his head. "He's hung like that for two days?"

"Not quite that long. I will let you know."

Hopkins nodded. "Okay. I'll leave you to . . . this. I'll talk to Mr. Greaves."

Eugene gave a solemn nod and pulled out his digital camera. "I'll take as many pictures as possible of the blood patterns and body, but I'll need help getting Ledbetter down from the trees."

"Tell me when you're ready, and I'll help."

"Thanks."

∼

BILL SAT on the concrete picnic table when Hopkins approached. The state trooper had left with the deputies to inspect the accident scene. Hopkins wondered if the car at the bottom of the ravine was Ledbetter's and if so, what had forced the car off the road? And if Ledbetter had been driving, how did he get back to the church?

"Morning, Bill."

Bill nodded, but his eyes were filled with dread. His face was ashen white, and his hands shook. He kept wringing them together like he was washing them under a faucet.

Hopkins tipped his hat back. "What time did you find the pastor?"

"About a half hour ago."

"You usually come here this early?"

Bill shook his head and refused to make eye contact. "No, not usually, but today was supposed to be hot, so I decided to open the windows for a bit. These old churches get musty after a few days of heat and no air circulation, so it's good to let the morning breeze through. But, I never unlocked the door."

"Why not?"

Bill frowned and rubbed his chin. "The place didn't seem right."

"What do you mean?"

"The church seemed . . . darker. The smell of death. I heard noises behind the church. Something in the trees. That's when I discover Pastor Ledbetter's body. A flock of crows flew away. I think they were pecking his scalp before I spooked them."

"Were you at the revival service Friday night?"

"Yes, sir."

"Any people here you didn't recognize? Strangers?"

Bill slowly shook his head. "No, just our small usual crowd. Didn't have any visitors. Great message though. Pastor preached his heart out."

"Any church members have bad feelings toward the pastor?"

"No. We all got along quite well."

Hopkins looked at the ground and said, "Did you happen to pass anyone walking on the road when you drove here this morning?"

Bill shook his head. "No. I didn't see anyone or any cars, either."

"Any way you can reach parishioners and cancel church this morning? You don't want any others seeing him."

He nodded and pulled out his cell phone. "We have a prayer chain. I'll get that started."

"You do that, Bill, but be discrete. I'd hold off on telling them about how he died. Just inform them that there's been a tragic accident until we find out more information."

"Sure, I understand."

"The less news that gets out about this, the better opportunity we have to find the murderer."

Bill hit a number on his phone, briefly informed the person that church services were canceled and asked them to pass the message to the next on the list. After he put his phone in his pocket, Hopkins placed a hand on Bill's shoulder. "Maybe you should head home. I'll call you later when I find out more."

Bill stood. His eyes became distant. He said, "How could anyone do something so gruesome and evil?" He never waited for Hopkins' reply. Instead, he answered the question himself, "The devil's afoot."

Hopkins watched Bill get in his car and drive away. He peered around the side of the church. Eugene was too busy taking forensic pictures of the crime scene to even suggest taking Ledbetter's body down from the trees. He was relieved to not have to move Ledbetter yet. He dreaded when they did. Seeing the carnage already bothered him enough for weeks, but actually having to pull metal stakes from a dead man's hands would trouble his mind for a lifetime with unlimited nightmares to come.

Some mossy debris on the concrete pavilion floor caught his attention. As he knelt to examine the clumps of mud and moss, he realized the debris outline a path of bare footprints. Whoever had left them was a very large individual. He followed the path to the grass and into the gravel lot where they vanished.

Hopkins got into his SUV and drove to meet his deputies. He needed to focus his attention on something else. Anything that might help him forget the tragic murder.

Even though the hour was early, the morning was sticky and hot. He turned on the air conditioner and loosened his collar. As much as he tried, he couldn't drive the image of Ledbetter's mutilated body from his mind. Like Bill, he wondered what twisted person or persons had tortured and killed a country preacher.

Hopkins pondered the way Ledbetter's body had been fastened between the two trees. The corpse hung at least two feet above the ground. His hunch was that there wasn't any way one person was responsible for the murder. The footprints implicated a large person had been there, but one man, even a very muscular man, couldn't possibly hoist Ledbetter that far off the ground and nail him between the trees. Eugene had suggested that Ledbetter was alive when he was staked. If alive, he would have fought his assailant. That made it even less likely one individual performed the task. Even an unconscious person would be impossible to place into the position Ledbetter died.

As the SUV crept along the dirt road, the quaint area Hopkins had grown up in and called home seemed tarnished by evil. He had never expected such a crime to occur in his county. Once the tragedy hit the local gossip chain, he had little chance to quash people's fear. The only thing to help eliminate such a panic was to catch the murderer.

Hopkins slowed to a stop. The broken pile of glass sparkled. Partly hidden in a patch of honeysuckle at the edge of the road was Ledbetter's bible. Getting out of his vehicle, he studied the deep tire grooves where Ledbetter had almost left the roadway and veered sharply back onto the road. Even after the patrol cars had passed through, he was able to see the driver's struggle to keep the car from leaving the road.

Ordinarily, such bizarre weaving indicated a drunk driver, but he didn't believe Pastor Ledbetter had been drinking when he left the church. The autopsy would probably support his suspicion. Ledbetter had probably been fighting off his killer while trying to keep the car on the road.

But why take the preacher back to the church? A ritual of some sort or perhaps mockery?

Hopkins took a handkerchief and picked up the bible, careful not to place his fingerprints on the leather. Blue-tinted shards were embedded in the leather. He took a gallon Ziplock bag from his vehicle. Right before he slid the bible into the bag, something else caught his attention. A jagged, yellow fingernail was snagged in the leather, too.

He smiled.

DNA.

Lab analysis and a computer data search might just reveal who the murderer was.

Hopkins zipped the bag shut and placed it on the passenger seat.

A few minutes later he parked behind the state patrol car. He stepped to the edge of the steep embankment and looked down. The two deputies were heading back to the top. Their slacks were soaked to the knees. The state patrolman walked about fifteen feet ahead of them. He carried a piece of the rear bumper with the car tag still fastened on.

Hopkins slid back his cowboy hat and wiped sweat from his brow. "What you have there?" he asked.

Officer Winston held up the bumper. "Found this wrapped around the side of a tree."

"You call in the tag number?"

"Yep. Car belonged to Pastor Ledbetter."

Hopkins shook his head.

Deputy Shannons stopped to catch his breath about one hundred yards from the top of the ravine. Although he wasn't severely obese, he carried about a good fifty pounds more than his frame deserved. His tan shirt was damp with sweat. Panting, he said in a half-shout, "Car's not all the way under. It lodged in a shallow pool, but it will take some work for a wrecker to get to it."

"May have to wench it from a four wheel drive," Hopkins said.

Officer Winston made the last few steps up the path and joined Hopkins on the dirt road. "That car took a hell of a beating. Had it not hit the water, Ledbetter would have burned to death."

"He might have preferred that instead of what he endured."

Winston winced. "You saw the body?"

Hopkins nodded. "As sheriff, there's no way to avoid it."

"Yeah, it comes with the territory of our jobs. I've seen a lot of bad accidents on the highway. A lot. But never anything like what happened to Ledbetter."

"I know."

"I could understand if it was a drug deal gone bad," Winston said. "Or someone messed up on meth and lost all their sense of reason. But a pastor?"

"There aren't words to describe my shock. I found swerving tire marks back about a hundred yards where Ledbetter was apparently fighting off an attacker while he was driving."

"So the killer was in his car?"

Hopkins nodded. "That's my assumption."

Winston looked back down the ravine. "Why not just kill the pastor where the car crashed? Why would he take him back to the church on foot?"

"I've been wondering the same thing. I guess he wanted to make a point by killing him close to the church. I don't know."

"You think it was personal?"

Hopkins shrugged. "I really can't say. Eugene found symbols drawn in blood under the body. He's taking pictures to see if he can find their meaning. He believes it was a ritual killing."

Deputy Shannons stepped beside Hopkins and Winston. He swallowed hard to stop panting. "No other car tracks here?"

"Nothing fresh," Hopkins said.

"So he walked back on foot?" Shannons asked. "Carrying the pastor?"

"I believe so."

"Damn."

Winston loosened his necktie. "Perhaps we should comb the road back on foot ourselves. Maybe see if we can find footprints along the edge of the road."

Shannons nodded. "Deputy Meeks and I could do that."

Hopkins said, "You two go do that, and I'll pick you up in a while and bring you back to your vehicles."

Shannons and Meeks started down the dirt road toward the church.

"I found some footprints under the pavilion. Large ones," Hopkins said. "I don't think he was wearing shoes."

"You think there was only one murderer?" Winston asked.

"I can't see one person hanging Ledbetter between two trees."

"Any weird cults around here?" Winston asked.

Hopkins frowned and shook his head. "Just a lot of country, bible-believing folks. Never seen anything that proved otherwise."

"I'd post an APB but without having more evidence to go on, I don't know if that would do us any good."

"I have a feeling that whoever is responsible is still nearby," Hopkins replied.

"Why?"

"Bill Greaves told me that he didn't see any strangers at Friday night's service. He also didn't see any cars that he didn't recognize or pass anyone on the road this morning."

Winston shook his head. "A vagrant on foot just passing through?"

"No, not necessarily. He could have used a boat. These inlets allow people to drift to the bank all along the lake's edge."

"I didn't think about that." Winston headed to his car. "I'll drive to the marina and look around. If I find anything of interest, I'll radio you."

Hopkins nodded. "I have to see if Eugene's ready to lower the body."

"Need any help?"

"I think we'll manage with the four of us."

Winston offered a grim smile and nod, but the look in his eyes indicated he was thankful Hopkins had passed on his offer. He closed the door and drove away.

Hopkins got into his SUV and rolled down his window. His life would no longer be the same after today. But the day was early and more unexpected tragedy was coming. Hopkins' ideal world was about to be challenged in ways he had never imagined.

CHAPTER 12

*A*s John topped the hill on the dirt road, he noticed the go-cart parked near the pond. He stopped, opened the gate, and drove through the pasture and parked beside the go-cart.

"Justin!" he shouted as he stepped from the truck and slammed the door. His echoing yell was the only response that replied. "Justin!"

John closed his eyes and took a deep breath, hoping to calm his heart. His stomach tensed with nervous fluttering. Despair claimed him.

He looked through Justin's belongings behind the go-cart's seat. The net Justin always carried was missing, so he expected the boy was trying to capture a bullfrog for the contest.

John took the frog-gigging stick from the go-cart and eased around the pond. Justin was an excellent swimmer, but John's first instinct was to circle the pond and look in the water. Even some of the best swimmers drown. Accidents happened. And some bizarre urge warned him that his grandson was in dire danger.

Dragonflies darted and skimmed across the pond's surface. Frogs jumped into the water with each step John took. In ten minutes he had circled half the pond before he noticed a deep indentation in the mud that only a fish net could leave behind. Next to the spot was Justin's boot prints heading into the grass and toward the swampy edge of the pasture.

John followed a path of bent grass and clover until he reached the bog.

"Justin!" he yelled again.

No reply.

Scuffs in the dried pine needles indicated hurried footsteps that were headed to Devils Den's entrance. John picked up his pace.

Terror gripped his chest when he found Justin's backpack on the ground in front of the cave. He leaned into the entrance and shouted Justin's name again. After the long, steady echo ceased, John sat down on a large rock and shook his head.

How many times had he warned Justin to never go inside? More than a hundred, he was certain.

John unzipped the backpack and searched through the contents until he found a large flashlight. With his heart hammering he entered the cave for the first time in twenty years. He felt dizzy and realized he was breathing too hard. He leaned against the cool cave wall and took slower breaths to prevent hyperventilation. Once he gained control of his breathing he followed Justin's footprints along the damp cave floor.

"Justin!" he shouted.

Several bats darted from their perches and flew deeper into the cave.

"Where are you?" he asked with tears in his eyes.

The cave's darkness swallowed him. He peered at the narrow path ahead of him, desperately following his grandson's footprints. After he made his second turn in the path, he was horrified. A solid rock wall blocked the path. Not a cave in. A rock wall.

For a moment, John thought had taken a wrong turn. The flashlight revealed he had *not*. Half of Justin's last footprint was visible. The other half disappeared beneath the wall. It was as if the wall had been set into place after Justin walked past.

"Impossible," he whispered. But knowing the history of Devils Den, he knew it was possible.

His deepest fear came with the fact that he'd probably never see Justin again.

CHAPTER 13

opkins parked in the church parking lot. He met with his two deputies under the pavilion. Both were studying the large footprints on the concrete.

Hopkins asked, "Did you find anything?"

Shannons nodded. "We found footprints as large as these in a couple places. Probably the same person. Barefoot, too. But why would anyone traipse around this neck of the woods without shoes? Especially at night. I mean, poison ivy, snakes, briars. I value my feet."

Hopkins smiled. "I agree. It's strange. Anything else?"

"Ledbetter had to have been alive when he was brought back to the church."

"Why is that?"

"We only found a few drops of blood here and there. Maybe he had a busted nose or a gash on his forehead from the car crash, but there aren't large amounts anywhere along the dirt road."

Eugene joined them at the pavilion. "I've taken all the photos and evidence I need. It's time to take Ledbetter to the morgue."

Hopkins eyed his deputies. Their eyes revealed as much uneasiness as his did about the situation and what they had to do.

Hopkins shook his head and said, "Come on, men. Let's get Ledbetter to a better place. That's no way for him to be."

Shannons nodded without saying a word. His face paled, and he shoved his hands in his pockets as he turned and headed for Ledbetter's corpse.

Hopkins faced Eugene. "How do we take him down? Those spike heads are wide. Ledbetter's hands are wedged tight."

"I think I have a crowbar in my van," Eugene replied.

"That will crush his hands," Hopkins said.

Eugene shrugged and nodded. "I realize that, but it's really all we can do. A hammer will mangle his hands worse. We don't have time to get a blow-torch and hope we can cut through the spikes without incinerating his hands. His hands won't be visible in a coffin anyway."

Shannons looked at Hopkins. His face was pasty white. "I'll go get the crowbar, Sheriff," he said as he bolted away.

Hopkins knew his deputy couldn't stomach what they had to do. He hadn't eagerly volunteered to get the crowbar. He was running to get out of view while he vomited in private. Hopkins didn't blame him. He wanted to do that same, but he maintained control. If he had eaten a large breakfast, he doubted he'd kept anything down. Since he was in charge, he didn't want to appear weak.

Hopkins rubbed his eyes. "Did you bring the body bag?"

"In the van," Eugene replied.

"You expect us to carry his bloody body to the van without it?"

Eugene straightened his glasses. "No, I'll go get it. With the details of the crime scene I got carried away with making certain nothing was disturbed. Be right back."

Lib stood on the porch when John parked his truck in the driveway. She held an empty clothesbasket in her hand.

"Have you seen Justin this morning?" John asked with a quaking voice.

"No, dear." She frowned. "He drove off in the go-cart this morning. He's probably at the pond."

"The go-cart is, but he's not."

"Is something wrong?"

"Lib, he's gone."

"What?"

"Justin's gone. He went into Devils Den."

The clothesbasket dropped from her hand, spilling clothespins across the porch. "Surely not, John. He knows not to go in there. He's never disobeyed us."

"I know. But he did go inside. I followed his footprints until they vanished."

"You lost sight of them?"

"No, Lib. They just *stop*. Half his footprint is under a massive wall of rock."

"Oh God, you mean it caved in?"

"No."

She took his hand. "Come inside and sit down. I'll fix you some coffee and you can explain what you did see."

"I can't. I have to find him."

Even though tears brimmed in her eyes, Lib forced a small, hopeful smile. "We'll find him."

John grabbed the phone.

"Who are you calling?"

"The Sheriff's Office."

"I'll make some coffee."

John read the sheriff's department number off the emergency phone number pad fastened to the wall and quickly punched the numbers on the phone.

When the dispatcher answered, he said, "This is John McKnight. I need to speak to Sheriff Hopkins, please. It's an emergency. What do you mean he's not in? Can you get in touch with him? Good. Please tell him my grandson is missing. He's lost inside Devils Den. I can't find him."

His hands shook when he placed the phone in the cradle.

"Is he coming?" Lib asked.

John wrung his hands and feebly shrugged. His face was pale and his eyes filled with worry. Tears forced him to blink several times to stop their flow. He sat at the head of the table and wiped his eyes.

"I just don't understand what possessed Justin to go into that cave," he said. "He was supposed to catch a bullfrog for the contest."

Lib took a coffee mug from the cabinet and poured some coffee. She handed John the mug as she sat in the chair beside him. "He's a boy that loves to explore. Jack did the same thing when he was that age."

John shook his head. "He *never* went inside that cave. *Ever*."

"At least not that he told you."

John's jaw tightened. His eyes narrowed. "Are you saying that he did?"

"No, but see how upset you are?"

"I'm not mad, Lib."

"You sound angry."

John took a sip of coffee. "I'm not mad. I'm just scared to death about Justin. Jack never set foot in that cave. I'm certain of it."

"I don't think Jack did, either. But if he had, he'd never have told either of us. He knows how much you hate that cave."

"That wasn't his reason. Donnie was the reason he never stepped near that cave."

A tear etched down Lib's cheek. "I know. I have tired to force that from my memory."

"I've tried, too. For the most part I hadn't given it much thought until today."

"Donnie disappeared how long ago?"

"He's been gone at least twenty years."

She folded her hands on her lap. "Jack was barely fourteen. I don't know how he ever got past it."

"I don't either. Donnie was his best friend in school. They went everywhere together. When he disappeared inside Devils Den, it terrified Jack."

"Every night," Lib said. "When I told him goodnight, he insisted I keep his bedroom door open and the hall light on."

John nodded. "That's about the time Jack started showing interest in the insurance business. I believe he was searching for some type of assurance or maybe a form of protection."

"He hardly left the house, studying all your policy pamphlets."

"I believe that's where his obsession for the insurance business began," John said. "You know I tried to get him to come with us to Devils Den to look for Donnie. He never would."

"It was awful. People searched for days and never found Donnie."

"I kept looking for weeks after the search team gave up."

Lib squeezed his arm. "I remember. But the fear of the cave isn't the same for Justin as it was for Jack. With the scary movies that boy watches on television our warnings would sound like legends or ghost stories. Kids today are numb to real fear."

John released a long sigh. "I suppose you're right. Justin probably thought he'd go in and look around and be home well before me."

He got up and opened a drawer. He grabbed a pack of cigarettes and pulled one out. He struck a match with a shaking hand.

"I thought you were quitting," she said.

"Lib, please, not now."

With a look of disappointment on her face, she shook her head. "The cancer, John, you promised me."

He nodded. "I know, but I'm stressed. I feel so tightly coiled inside that I might snap. A cigarette will calm me. One won't make that big a difference with the cancer anyway. It's already there."

Instead of arguing her point, she changed the subject. "Should we call Jack?"

"I'll let you do that."

"Shouldn't you talk to him?"

John grabbed his rifle and headed for the front door. "No, I need to get back to the cave in case Justin has come out or I hear him calling for help."

Lib followed him outside. "But the sheriff . . . ."

"Tell him where I'm at. He can meet me there," John said as he pushed open the screen door. Hard dried mud crunched under his boot. "Where'd the hell did this mud come from?"

"I think Justin must have tracked that across here this morning before he went to the pond."

John knelt and looked at the tracks. He shook his head. "No, Lib. This has moss mixed in it. There's no moss around our farmhouse and barn. There is a lot in the swamp."

"Are you sure?"

"Yes, why?"

Lib frowned with concern. "I swept up a pile of it in Justin's room this morning. I haven't had a chance to sweep the porch."

"Don't sweep it. Not yet."

"Why?"

John pointed at the tracks. "These footprints are too large to be Justin's. Plus, whoever left them wasn't wearing shoes."

"You think it's a connection to Justin's disappearance?"

He nodded. "Very possible. I'm sure Sheriff Hopkins will want to see this. I'm going to see if I can find Justin around the cave. The longer he's gone, the more danger he'll probably be in."

"Okay, John. Please be careful."

"I will."

CHAPTER 14

Jack sat in his office when Lib called. "Hello. McKnight's Insurance. How may I help you?"

"Jack, I tried to reach you at your house," she said.

"Rita and I have been here since breakfast, Mom."

"You're working on Sunday?" she asked.

"Just catching up on some paperwork. You doing okay? I bet Justin is keeping your hands full."

Lib didn't reply. Her uncontrollable sobs prevented her from speaking.

"Mom, what's wrong?" Jack asked.

"Justin."

"Is he okay? What happened?"

"He went inside Devils Den. Your father hasn't been able to find him."

Jack placed a hand over the phone. "Rita, pick up the phone. It's Mom. Justin is missing."

Rita's eyes widened as she rushed to her desk and grabbed the phone.

"Mom, are you sure that he went inside?" he asked.

"Your father found his backpack outside the cave and followed his footprints as far as he could, but they just disappear."

Jack's heart raced. His hands shook. For a few seconds he didn't take a breath. He was numb inside. Sweat crept across his brow.

Rita noticed his shock and said to Lib, "Have you contacted the local police?"

"Yes, the sheriff is on his way to investigate."

Jack sat on the edge of his desk and ran a hand through his hair.

"Lib," Rita said. "We're leaving now. We'll be there as quickly as possible."

Lib cleared her throat, but her voice remained shaky and shadowed by tears. "Okay. You be careful. If we find him before you get here, we'll call your cell."

"Yes, please do. We're on our way. See you soon."

Rita hung up the phone. Jack's face was pasty white. His eyes were distant.

"Honey, are you okay?" she asked.

"It's returned."

Rita frowned. "What?"

"The thing that took Donnie."

"Didn't Donnie get lost inside?"

"That's what they finally wrote in the missing report."

"And that's not what happened?"

Jack wiped sweat from his brow.

"Jack, do you know what happened to Donnie?"

He replied with a gentle nod, but he refused to make eye contact.

"Why didn't you tell anyone?"

He closed his eyes. His jaw shook as he fought his inner fears.

"Jack?"

His mouth moved, but no words came.

Rita took his hands into hers. "Tell me, Jack. Why didn't you tell anyone what really happened?"

"Because it would take me too!" He stood. His eyes widened. "If I told anyone, he would come back and take me."

"He? Who?"

Jack covered his face with his hands. "I don't know. He, it, was a living corpse. His body reeked of decay. He looked dead, but he was strong. *Alive*. He took Donnie. I tried to stop him, but I . . . he yanked Donnie from my grasp."

Rita wrapped her arms around him. "Oh, Jack. I'm so sorry."

"I wanted to save Donnie. I really did." Jack's body shook with painful sobs. Tears flowed. "I wanted to help him, but I wasn't strong enough."

"It's not your fault."

"And now, he's returned. He's taken our son."

"No, dear. We're going to find Justin. I know we will."

Jack shook his head. "Not if it returned. That cave is cursed."

"Come on. We're going to go find Justin. I'll drive."

As they headed out their office door, Bob took a step back. "I didn't expect you two here this morning."

"We may be gone a couple days," Rita said. "You mind keeping an eye on everything?"

"Sure," Bob replied. "What's wrong?"

"Justin is missing."

Bob looked at Jack. "I'm sorry. I'll make certain everything runs smoothly while you're gone."

"Thanks," Jack said.

"Not a problem. Please keep me posted."

Jack nodded. His mind drifted back to the day Donnie disappeared. The hideous face of the evil man that took his best friend haunted him. Now Justin was gone. The demon that had plagued his teenage years had his son. To get Justin back he'd have to find a way to overcome the paralyzing fear that incapacitated him twenty years earlier and confront, perhaps kill, whatever lurked inside Devils Den.

SHERIFF HOPKINS MET Lib on the front porch. She showed Hopkins the large footprints.

"I'm glad you hadn't swept them up yet," Hopkins said. "One of my deputies will measure and photograph them."

"Okay."

"So John's at Devils Den?"

She nodded and said, "Please help him find Justin."

"Don't worry," he said. "We're going to find him."

"I hope so."

He offered an encouraging smile. "I promise. We'll search every inch of that cave if necessary. We'll find him."

JOHN TURNED on the flashlight as he stepped into the dark opening of the cave.

"Justin!" He shouted.

The name echoed over a dozen times without a reverberating reply from Justin.

Fighting tears of desperation, he thought about how Justin had looked after he was told about John's cancer. The boy was crushed. He wished their last evening had been one of joy, and not his dismal revelation about his cancer. John wanted nothing else but to find his grandson and wrap his arms around the boy.

"I'm going to find you," he whispered.

John took a deep breath and sacrificed his safety to find his grandson. As he walked he pictured different scenarios as to why Justin had entered the cave but none justified sound reasoning. Justin had no valid reason to enter the cave.

The bright light revealed Justin's boot prints. John was careful to plant each step where he had walked before. He didn't want to disturb his grandson's footprints. He was certain Hopkins would insist on seeing the boy's path as well.

Again he came to the cave wall that cut Justin's last step in half. It didn't make sense.

"How?" he wondered aloud.

He placed a hand against the cold, wet rock. Without stepping from his previous path, he shone the light across the floor. Justin's path was one direction. He hadn't turned back at any point. But the wall was there.

John heard movement. Faint voices filled with pain.

"Justin?" he whispered.

John stood still, holding his breath. The voices faded.

Right as he turned to head back, a bright light stung his eyes.

"John? That you?" Hopkins asked.

"Yes."

"I'm coming to you. Stay put."

"Careful. Just walk where my footprints are and pay close attention to Justin's. Maybe you can figure this out."

When Hopkins reached John, he knelt closer to the floor to inspect Justin's boot print.

"It just vanishes."

John nodded. "I know."

Hopkins rose and pushed back his cowboy hat. He traced the wall with the light. "Seems a solid wall. Nowhere for him to have climbed over or gone around."

"I've been trying to figure it out."

"I know it's been years since I've been inside this cave, John, but I don't remember that wall being there."

"It wasn't."

"You used to be able to walk an hour along this path without stopping."

"That's right. You should still be able to."

"It's not a cave-in."

"That's what I told Lib."

"Any reason why Justin came inside?"

"No. I've told him all his childhood to never set foot in here."

A small cloud of fog escaped Hopkins mouth as he exhaled. "This place has always been eerie."

"Every since Donnie disappeared."

"I remember when you had the church picnic outside."

"Twenty years ago."

"Time flies."

John nodded.

"Okay, John. Let's get out of here."

"What are you going to do? Do we need to blast the wall?"

"First, John," Hopkins said as he led the way back to the cave entrance. "I'm going to have my deputies get out here and search the outer area of the cave, just in case Justin slipped out through another opening."

"There's no other way in or out."

"With caves, John, sometimes there are."

John stepped out into the woods behind Hopkins. "I suppose."

"And, second, we're going to get a geologist out here to look around. Maybe he can study the rock formations and see how Justin got around that wall."

"When can you do that?" John asked.

Hopkins glanced at his watch. "I can make a few calls, but since it's Sunday, it will probably be morning before one can come out here."

John shook his head. "No, Sheriff, that's too late. Justin cannot stay the night in there. It's too dangerous."

"I understand your concern, but finding a geologist that's available might take a few hours and depending on where he lives, he'd have to travel a few more hours to get here. It will be dark then."

John looked at the dark cave with tears in his eyes. "I knew I should have sealed that cave off years ago. The only reason I never did was because I hoped that somehow Donnie would find a way out."

"You can't blame yourself for Donnie or Justin. Kids are kids. They explore and sometimes do dangerous stuff. I did. You probably did, too."

"Yes, but I could have prevented this."

Hopkins put a hand on John's shoulder. "Trust me. We're going to do everything we can to find him. In fact, we're going to issue an Amber Alert, call the newspapers, everything."

"Amber Alert? Why? He's not been taken. He's lost." John's face was pale, his eyes haunted. He appeared seconds away from passing out.

Hopkins pointed to a large rock near the cave entrance. "John, perhaps you should take a seat there."

Without questioning, John sat down.

"When I stopped by your house, Lib showed me those footprints on your front porch. We found near identical ones at Hope Chapel earlier today."

"So?"

Hopkins took off his cowboy hat and squatted to be eye-to-eye with John. "Pastor Ledbetter was murdered at the church."

John rose to his feet. "What?"

Hopkins nodded. "Easy, John, sit down. Someone killed him."

"But why?"

"That's what we're trying to figure out."

"But you found similar footprints?"

"On the pavilion, there were large bare footprints outlined by mud and moss."

John frowned. "How did the preacher die?"

Hopkins sighed. "Without going into specifics, it was gruesome. Worst thing I've ever seen."

"And you think this person has Justin?

"No. I am not making that assumption yet. Not until my deputies make print comparisons. Once they do, we'll go from there."

John attempted to stand, but he wobbled and dropped back down on the rock.

"Are you okay?" Hopkins asked.

"I'll be fine. I'm just tired."

"We need to get you home."

"No. I need to be right here until Justin is found."

Hopkins pointed toward the open pasture gate. "There's one of my deputies now. He can look after things. You need to get home, eat, and rest."

"There's no way I can rest."

"I know. But try. Let me give you a ride back to the house."

"Thanks, but I can drive. I probably do need to eat, but I'll be back later."

"One of the deputies will be here. Should Justin show up before you get back, we'll call you."

John offered a smile that didn't match the pain in his eyes as he headed for his pickup.

CHAPTER 15

*R*ita drove with determination. While Jack struggled with past fears, her motherly, protective instinct had kicked in. Her son was missing and regardless of what it took, she'd do everything necessary to get him back.

She vaguely remembered Donnie from middle school. Jack had mentioned his disappearance a couple of times when they fished at the pond near Devils Den. His reluctance to go into detail about the incident kept her from pressing him on the issue. But today, she'd seen the horror in his eyes unlike anything he'd ever shown before. Whatever had taken Donnie still terrified Jack.

"Justin was right," Jack said.

"Right about what?"

He sighed. "You remember when we had the flat tire the other day?"

"Yes."

"We both heard this awful sound in the woods. Something I've never heard before. I don't have any idea *what* made it."

"So?"

"When Justin was about to get into the car, he was scared to death."

Rita frowned. "About what?"

"He told me that he was afraid that he'd never see us again."

Rita chewed her bottom lip as tears moistened her eyes.

"It was like he knew something was going to happen."

"He has a big imagination. With us working all the time, it's what he does. He uses his imagination to cope with our absence."

"But this was different."

"How? A premonition?"

"Possibly, but after all this time," Jack said. "I never thought it would return. I have no idea how it would still be alive."

Rita gave him a side-glance. "What exactly did you see?"

Jack slightly shook his head as he thought. "I believe it was a man. A big man."

"You said that he was like a living corpse."

"Yes."

"That's so absurd. Are you sure that's what you actually saw?"

"Rita, it sounds crazy, but you know me. I am not one to make stuff up."

She nodded. "I know. You barely have a sense of humor."

He responded with a wry grin.

"Well, it's true," Rita said. "You've wrapped us so deep in this insurance business that we don't have time to enjoy life or take Justin on summer trips. He's wanted to go to nature museums, but we never have time. If we lose him because of this . . . ."

"I'm sorry. You're right. I've put the business first for too long."

"Tell me about more about the man that took Donnie. What makes you think he would have come back for you if you told authorities?"

"He told me he would."

"And if you chose to come back with a lot of people, how would he do that?"

"I was a kid, Rita. Twelve years old."

Rita nodded. "I know, but you just abandoned your friend? That easily?"

"No. Not easily. He had both of us. His huge black hand was wrapped around my throat. I couldn't breathe. I thought I was going to suffocate. I crapped my pants. Okay. It was *that* terrifying."

"How did you escape?"

"He wore a bone necklace. I'm not certain but it looked like it was made out of bones from human fingers. I yanked it from his neck and noticed a scar around his neck. When I dropped the necklace, his eyes widened and he released me. He gasped for air. He seemed weaker without the necklace. Donnie almost broke free, but the man grabbed the necklace. Once he possessed it again, Donnie couldn't fight him. I ran and didn't look back."

"Any kid would," she said softly.

"I know you don't believe me."

"Hon, I know you're telling the truth. I just want to know what we're up against and how we're going to find Justin."

"That's all I remember."

"Call your mother. Let her know we're about a couple hours away."

He dialed the number while she kept a hard stare on the road.

~

JOHN ATE a sandwich and drank a large glass of tea while sitting in his recliner. Afterwards, he drifted to sleep and awoke when the phone rang.

Jostled, he sat up, looking at his watch.

Lib hung up the phone. "Jack and Rita are a couple hours away."

He rubbed his eyes and stood. "Lib, why'd you let me fall asleep?"

She gave a small smile. "You were so exhausted. You needed to rest."

"I *need* to help the police officers find Justin. It'll be getting dark soon."

"Hopkins called a half hour ago and said that they're still searching."

"They still haven't found anything new?"

"No."

"I'll go see how things are going."

"Don't get in their way."

He shook his head and mumbled under his breath as he walked out the door.

John opened the truck door and Charlie hopped into the cab. John knew how much the dog loved Justin, so he thought taking the dog along wasn't a bad idea. He hoped the dog picked up Justin's scent and could track him down. It was worth a try.

When John stopped on the other side of the pond, he was surprised to see a Lexington Television News van in the pasture. Female news reporter, Misty Waters, stood beside Hopkins outside the cave while interviewing him for the evening news. Her long brown hair ruffled in the wind.

Several deputies walked along the woods searching for clues.

John eased his truck closer to the news van. With his window rolled down, he caught the last of the interview before the cameraman shut off the camera. Misty lowered her microphone, stepped closer to Hopkins and said, "So there was a murder near here over the weekend, too?"

Hopkins nodded. "We discovered the minister's body this morning."

With a concerned expression she said, "Can you give me some of the details?"

"Sure."

As she took out a pen and notepad, he explained who had been murdered and where, but he didn't go into detail about how the murder was carried out.

"Any connection to the McKnight boy's disappearance?" Misty asked.

"I hope not, but we don't know yet."

Hopkins noticed John sitting in the pickup. "That's John McKnight," he said as he pointed. "Justin's grandfather."

John opened the truck door. He and Charlie got out as Hopkins and Misty approached. The smell of Jasmine perfume drifted on the breeze.

Hopkins made quick introductions.

"You brought your dog?" Hopkins asked.

"Yep. I'm hoping that Charlie can find Justin."

Misty scratched the dog behind the ears. Charlie's tail wagged.

Hopkins shrugged. "That's a great idea."

"Charlie and that boy are inseparable most of the time."

"Really?" Misty asked.

John nodded. "Yeah. It's odd the dog wasn't up here when I came home. I never found any dog prints around the mouth of the cave, so for some reason he didn't follow Justin to the cave."

Misty rubbed the dog's neck and pulled back her hand. "What happened to his back? He's been injured."

John looked where she pointed. A long thin laceration covered the dog's back and side. Gnats gathered on the dried blood.

"I have no idea," John said, inspecting the cut. "He might have got caught in barbwire."

Misty said, "John, do you have a recent photo of Justin? So we can put it on the air in case someone has seen him?"

"Sure," John replied. "Lib has plenty of them. That's our farmhouse up on the hill. Just stop by and ask her."

"I will, John. Thanks." Misty smiled and turned to Hopkins. "After we get Justin's photo, our crew will head to Hope Chapel to film about the murder."

Hopkins nodded. "State police and forensics are there, so you'll have to film from a distance."

"That's not a problem," she said. She smiled and headed to the van. "If I have any further questions, is it okay to call you?"

"Of course."

When she got in the van, John said, "I believe she likes you."

Hopkins blushed. "I doubt she'd be interested in a country sheriff."

John frowned. "Why would you say that?"

"A woman as pretty as she is and with the career she has, she has bigger ambitions than settling down here."

"People can report news anywhere," John said.

Hopkins shrugged. "Maybe so, but I'd bet that she'd like to be an anchor on one of the major news networks."

"You'll never know if you don't ask her."

Hopkins smiled. "Right now, I don't have time to worry about it. We have to find Justin."

The dog followed John to the mouth of Devils Den. Charlie's ears drooped and his head lowered. He sniffed the cool air drifting from the cave. A few seconds later, he chuffed and sniffed the ground around the rocks.

Hopkins rubbed the dog's ears. "I believe you're onto something. He might actually be able to pick up Justin's scent.

John took a step into the cave and patted his leg. "Come on, Charlie. Find Justin."

The dog's tail wagged. His ears perked. He took a step closer and the wind of the cave gushed out and swirled around them. The dog's tail stiffened. A low guttural growl came from the back of his throat.

"Easy, boy. What is it?" John asked.

The dog's tail dropped and curled between his legs. He whined. John grabbed his collar and tried to lead him to the cave. Charlie resisted and jerked free of John's grasp. The dog snarled. Spittle formed at the edges of his mouth and sprayed the air. The dog sensed something they did not.

Then, as quickly as his courage beamed, it faded. The dog turned and bolted through the woods, across the pasture, and headed to the farmhouse.

"I've never seen him act like that," John said.

Hopkins frowned. "You don't suppose there's a bobcat in the cave?"

"I doubt it. Besides, Charlie's not afraid of a bobcat. He ran one out of the yard before and killed it."

A black cat darted from the cave's mouth. It scampered through the trees and toward the swamp.

"I'll be damned," John said. "Charlie can kill a bobcat, but he's afraid of a puny black cat?"

Hopkins laughed. "There are some people who harbor similar fears."

John slowly took a seat on the large rock outside Devils Den. "You still haven't found any useful evidence."

Hopkins looked away. "Not yet, but it will be on the news tonight and on the front page of the Lexington papers in the morning. I'm still trying to contact a geologist. I will be making more calls soon. Deputy Shannons will be staying out here half the night. Deputy Meeks will take over around three a.m."

"I'll stay with them," John said.

"You don't have to."

"I want to."

"I understand."

Hopkins stepped back to the cave entrance and said, "You know, this place brings back memories. I've not been inside Devils Den since I was about eighteen. That was with Ben. When's the last time you've seen him?"

"Ben? Lib's brother?" John shook his head. "We've not seen him in a long time. At least six years, I'd say."

"Does he still live out on Boykin's Hollow?"

"As best I know, he owns the entire hollow now."

"He *owns* it?"

"He bought everyone's estates along that road but left them empty."

Hopkins frowned. "That's odd."

"It's like driving through a ghost town."

"Where'd he come across that kind of money?"

"Not sure. He's not taught as a botanist for years."

"Maybe he won the lottery?"

John shrugged. "That's possible. I've wondered about it at times. If you drive up the hollow, all the houses are deteriorating with 'No Trespassing' signs posted everywhere."

"Did he finally get married?" Hopkins asked.

"No, not that we've heard. We drove out to his place around Christmas to surprise him. He wasn't home. He must have been horseback riding because the stable was empty and his saddle was gone."

Hopkins frowned. "Does he ride often?"

"He rode across country once, so he says. You know how he tells tales. But, I believe he was telling the truth. He likes exploring dangerous places, too. He spent more time in this old cave than he did with his parents when he was a teenager."

"He loved being in there, but me, not so much. I went inside a couple times, but the cave had a way of twisting reality for me."

"Ben could probably draw a map from memory of all the twists and turns in there."

Hopkins' eyebrows rose. "We really need to get in touch with him then. He'd be the best help in finding Justin since he knows the cave so well."

"That's true," John said. "But Lib and I haven't a clue how to reach him."

"He doesn't have a cell phone?"

"No. I doubt that his home phone is even working. He's been difficult to find."

"Tell you what," Hopkins said. "You go back home and see if Lib can contact Ben. While you're doing that, I'll find a geologist who can be up here at daybreak."

John looked at Devils Den and surrendered a nod. "I can do that."

"If you're able to find Ben, there's a greater chance of rescuing Justin before morning."

"That would be great."

Hopkins watched John walk to his truck. Taking out his cell phone, he pulled up the Internet and searched for a geologist close to the area. If Ben couldn't be located to help with the search and rescue, Hopkins had no other alternative in discovering what had happened to Justin.

Eugene examined Ledbetter's corpse. All evidence concluded the preacher had died Friday night around ten o'clock. He had died a slow, torturous death. The agony must have been horrendous. Not only had a symbol been drawn in blood on the ground, but the killer had also carved similar patterns on Ledbetter's chest and back.

Since Ledbetter didn't have a wife or any immediate family in the area, Eugene had his assistant attempt to locate next of kin.

Eugene draped the white sheet over Ledbetter's body, pushed his tray into a morgue cooler, and shut the door. He returned to his desk at the far end of the room. A pile of photos was spread across the desktop.

Three specific sets of symbols had been drawn. One was on the ground and two on Ledbetter's body. However, he couldn't find conclusive interpretations online, but he did find that most of the symbolism tied directly to voodoo or a religion that had evolved from voodoo.

Each artistic pattern coincided with a particular stage in Ledbetter's anguish. He needed to find a way to decipher their meanings. If he could, they might find the man who had sacrificed Ledbetter before he killed someone else.

CHAPTER 16

*D*r. Frank Meadows sat in his recliner as he watched the evening news. Details of a missing boy in a cave caught his interest. When the news went to commercials his phone rang. He muted the television.

"Hello?"

"Dr. Meadows?"

"Yes."

"You're the state geologist?"

"Yes, sir," he replied, a little less politely, wishing the caller would get to the point rather than tier his conversation like someone preparing to eat a seven course meal. "And you are?"

"Sheriff Hopkins from Cider Knoll, Kentucky."

"How might I help you?" Meadows replied, in his former friendlier tone.

"We have a boy who is lost in Devils Den."

"Yes, just watched that on the news. Not to belittle this, but that's one hell of a name for a cave."

"Yes it is."

"Why name it that?"

"You have to know the area, Dr. Meadows. A lot of religious and superstitious people came up with that name. Some believe the cave leads straight to hell and demons torture people inside."

Frank laughed.

"I know it sounds funny, but really it's no laughing matter. About twenty years ago another boy vanished inside. His body was never found."

Frank's laughter ceased. Cold chills shot up his back.

"And why do you need me?"

"We need someone with your experience to evaluate the geological structure of the cave."

"I see."

The news came back on. The caption read, "Pastor Murdered Near Cider Knoll."

"Could you possibly come out first thing in the morning?"

"Did you say you were from Cider Knoll?"

"Yes."

Frank scratched his beard. "A boy is missing and a pastor was also murdered there?"

"I'm afraid so. Not a typical thing for this part of the state."

"But you don't have a connection between the two?"

"No. Nothing like that."

Frank replied, "Why do you need me to evaluate the cave? I mean, are there drop-offs or a cave-in?"

"It's hard to understand unless you've seen it yourself, but half of the boy's last footprint is underneath a cave wall."

"You sure he didn't climb over this wall?"

"No. The wall is tight with the cave ceiling and adjoining walls. It's a dead end. I've been in the cave years ago. I can tell you that the cave shouldn't end where it currently does."

Frank rubbed his chin. "You have my interest, but I don't know that anything I can do will help."

"We're hoping you might find something we're overlooking."

"I can be there at dawn."

"Thanks."

"Don't mention it."

Frank hung up the phone. For a moment he thought about calling back and not going, but he thought about his son with his ex-wife in Nevada. He'd be devastated if his boy was missing. He glanced at his son's photo on the wall. His heart ached. He hadn't seen Timothy since December and wasn't certain he'd have time over the summer.

He opened a Kentucky map and spread it across the kitchen table. Devils Den was in an area he often wished to explore. But children vanishing without a trace made him leery of what else might be inside. Although he wasn't a religious man, he understood strange things existed in the world that had no explanations.

Having worked for five years as a geology professor in Nevada, Frank was intrigued by the geology of the Appalachian region where he now lived. The rock diversity was completely different due to the glacial retreat centuries before. Many highways also cut through small ridges, which exposed the earth's sedimentary layers and eliminated the need to take core samples. With the mountainsides accessible, he saved immense time by not having to dig down through the layers. All he had to do was climb to the stratum he wished to evaluate.

Excessively skinny, he had been tagged with the nickname, Scarecrow, in Nevada. Thankfully, the name had not followed him to Kentucky. And even though he ate like a horse, he was never able to gain weight. Medical doctors told him his metabolism was high, and he burned off calories about as quickly as he consumed them.

Being thin gave Frank added advantages when spelunking. He could squeeze into tight spaces that most people could not. With this in his favor, he might be more beneficial in the search for Justin.

Frank grabbed his pack and started sorting through his caving supplies. Once those items were in check, he'd gather his excavation gear in the garage. And his gun.

JOHN RETURNED to the entrance of Devils Den. He picked up long, dead branches and placed them in a pile. As he gathered more, Hopkins approached from the swampy area of the forest.

"What are you doing?" Hopkins asked.

"Building a fire. The sun will be setting soon. I'm camping here until we find Justin. I'd hate for him to come out and not see me waiting."

Hopkins grabbed some branches and helped. "Were you able to contact Ben?"

"No. Lib tried several times. His phone is disconnected."

"I have a bit of good news," Hopkins said with a smile. "A geologist will be here first thing in the morning."

"You think he can help?"

Hopkins shrugged. "I believe he can. Besides, we don't have any alternatives."

"We could drill a hole through that wall."

"That could be risky. That's why we need the geologist to study that wall's foundation. If we just start drilling, we risk a cave-in that might endanger the rescuers. Besides, we don't know for certain if Justin is inside the cave."

John frowned. "I'm telling you that he's in that cave."

"I know that's what his footprints indicate, but I also know that caves can have many passageways. Should Justin have stumbled onto a different route, he might come out a mile or more away from here."

John took his lighter from his pocket and attempted to light the woodpile. "Maybe so, but I can't stand that he'll be underground all night."

"Maybe I don't recall Devils Den as well as I thought I did. I remember that cave passage went more than a mile when I explored it with Ben."

John looked up. "It should."

"But the trail barely goes fifteen yards."

"I know."

"That wall isn't the result of a cave-in. That's easy for anyone to determine."

"What's the name of the cave?" John said. "It's called Devils Den for a reason. It's haunted or something evil possesses it. Something took Justin and blocked our access to get him back. For all we truly know, it just might lead to the mouth of hell."

Hopkins glanced at the cave. "You believe the rumors?"

"I'm starting to," John said, turning his attention to the woodpile again.

"Me, too."

Frustrated by the wind, John said, "Damn fire won't start."

Hopkins picked up a handful of dead leaves and placed them under the smaller branches. John lit them and a gentle fire slowly rose. He snapped tiny dry twigs and placed them on the flames.

"John, the best thing for you to do is be at home with Lib. You know she'll stay up all night worrying about you."

"Jack and Rita should be arriving soon. She won't be alone."

"John . . . ."

A defeated expression crossed John's face. "I feel like I'm letting Justin down."

"No, you're not. We'll find him. But until we're certain of the cave's stability, we cannot go any further into the cave. Even using heavy equipment to drill through that wall is dangerous, if we don't know how sturdy the ceiling is."

The sun slipped below the ridgeline and dusk strangled the last of the fading light. The fire blazed and crackled. Bats flittered out of Devils Den to prey on night insects.

Headlights at the pasture gate caught John's attention.

"Who is that?" Hopkins asked.

"Jack and Rita."

A couple minutes later the car parked next to John's truck. Rita got out and jogged up the hill to the fire. Jack was seconds behind with Lib.

"Where's Justin?" Rita asked. "Is he still inside?"

Hopkins nodded.

"Why aren't you searching for him?"

"It's more complicated than that."

"Why?" she asked, her hazel eyes reflecting the firelight, giving her stare an ominous glow.

"There's a wall blocking the way," John said.

Lib hugged John and whispered, "How are you holding up?"

"Best as I can."

Jack stared at the black cave mouth with uneasiness.

"I don't understand," Rita said. "What do you mean there's a wall?"

John and Hopkins explained how the cave *used* to be and how it was now.

"A geologist will be here in the morning."

"Morning?" she said. "That's not soon enough."

"That's what I keep saying," John said.

"Give me your flashlight," Rita said.

Hopkins unfastened one from his belt and hesitantly handed it to her. "I can't allow you to go inside alone."

Rita flipped the light on and glanced at Jack. "Come on. Let's go."

Jack's eyes widened. "I can't."

"Never mind," she whispered, shaking her head. She looked back at Hopkins. "Sheriff, will you show me what you're talking about?"

He took the flashlight and nodded. "Just follow behind me. We don't want to contaminate Justin's prints. They are key evidence."

When they reached the wall, Hopkins showed her Justin's last footprint and that there weren't any crevices above or at the sides of the wall where Justin might have squeezed through.

Rita pressed her hands against the cold rocks and placed her ear to the wall. "No one's heard him yell for help?" she asked, fighting tears.

Hopkins shook his head. "No."

"What do we do?"

"We wait until the geologist says that it's okay to drill through the wall. Trust me; I'd have already done that. But a cave-in would delay the search even more. We'll do everything to find Justin. I promise."

Rita turned and stormed for the cave entrance.

She suddenly stopped and faced him. "You need to talk to Jack," she said.

"Why?"

"Because he saw what had taken Donnie that night."

"Really?"

She nodded. "That's why he won't come inside Devils Den."

"I'll talk to him."

"What he'll tell you doesn't sound believable, but I believe he's telling the truth."

Outside the cave, Hopkins called Jack aside. Jack shared the information he had told Rita, and although Hopkins would love to dismiss it as nonsense, the conviction in Jack's voice validated his sincerity. The entire time they talked, Jack never took his eyes off the cave entrance and when he walked away, he kept an eye over his shoulder as he returned to the campfire, as if something might rush from the cave and take him. The fear in Jack's eyes was genuine. Hopkins had been around enough people to know that. He wondered what they were actually up against, and whether adorning the cave with the name, Devils Den, signified more than mere coincidence on the part of superstitious people or were they about to face more hideous abnormalities?

Undead men kidnapping children. The sacrificial offering of a pastor. Strange symbols painted in blood. He needed to call Eugene to see if he had discovered the meaning of the strange symbols.

Hopkins introduced Jack and Rita to Deputy Shannons. Afterwards, Hopkins got in his SUV and drove to the Sheriff's Office. He wanted to research Donnie's disappearance records from twenty years ago. Perhaps there were clues other officers had missed that might aid them in rescuing Justin. His discoveries would present unsettling news that even he and John weren't aware of. Things that made Devils Den a more treacherous landmark than legends ever hinted about.

AFTER DUSK, Elias shoved the loose hay off his body and crept to the large loft window that overlooked the farm. The moon edged over the horizon, much larger than normal and hauntingly yellow and bright. Time was fleeting for the sacrifice to be done properly. He needed the boy. Justin.

Elias flicked crawling maggots off his decaying skin. Piles of fly eggs embedded in the loose folds of his skin. He reeked of death.

Watching the attic window, he waited for the boy to flip on a light, but the room remained dark, empty. Little activity stirred around the farmhouse. The place seemed abandoned.

A minute before he descended the ladder to inspect the house, a car pulled into the drive. The bright headlights forced him to cover his eyes. The old woman stepped out of the house and quickly got into the backseat. The car retreated down the drive. The car traveled several hundred yards up the dirt road, turned, and entered the pasture on the other side.

Elias' curiosity stirred. He hurried down the ladder with the sickle in hand and staggered to the house. Peering through dark windows, he looked but saw no one. No voices or sounds. A low growl rumbled in his throat.

The near full moon rose higher. He had to find the boy.

The landscape darkened but with the moon rising, Elias didn't have much time to see where the car had gone without being revealed under the light of the moon. He hobbled quick steps, crossed the road, and squeezed through the strands of barbwire.

A small fire brightened the edge of the woods. Several people sat around it, but not Justin. He hurried as fast as his aged body allowed, making a beeline toward the trees near the swamp, not far from his sepulcher. Without the boy's sacrifice this resurrection was doomed.

Into the dark woods Elias moved clumsily from tree to tree. His body grew weaker. Death and defeat were settling over him. Exhausted, he leaned against a dead oak and took several deep breaths while trying to decide what he must do.

From thick underbrush the black cat exited and mewed. A second later, it darted into hiding. Elias pushed off the tree, moved to the next one, rested, and then slinked into the shadow of another tree. Soon he came the large massive tree where he had been hung over a century before. Rage burned inside his chest.

How fitting, he thought. To die near the same tree where he had nearly died well over a century before.

The ferret and cat stood at Elias' feet. He glanced at the glowing campfire near the front of Devils Den before sitting on dry hemlock needles. His familiars darted into the darkness to serve as his eyes while he rested. Perhaps they'd find Justin before the moon rose overhead.

~

AFTER DEPUTY MEEKS replaced Deputy Shannons, Jack and Rita fed the campfire more dry branches while John and Lib slept in the car. No amount of coaxing could get Justin's grandparents to go home and sleep. They wanted to be nearby when Justin was found.

Deputy Meeks sat on a log near the flames and yawned. His eyes were heavy. He opened a thermos and poured some coffee.

"Want some?" he asked them.

"Sure," Jack said, holding out his Styrofoam cup.

Meeks filled the cup.

A horrible screeching sound echoed from the dark woods near the swamp.

"What was that?" Jack asked.

Meeks stood, pulled his gun, and shook his head. "I'm not sure."

Rita rose to her feet and took a step to follow, but Jack grabbed her hand.

"You two stay here," Meeks said.

The deputy turned on his flashlight and placed it against the side of his gun as he moved. Twigs snapped and dead leaves crunched as something scampered further into the woods. Meeks picked up his pace with his finger tight on the trigger. Nervous sweat saturated his underarms and trickled down his face.

Since they still had no clue who had killed Pastor Ledbetter, Meeks believed he might encounter the murderer. After all, evidence indicated the preacher's murder had occurred after dark, possibly by a vagrant but definitely by a psychopath.

The flickering campfire faded as Meeks walked past the cave entrance and along the rugged path between dead trees. The ground became wet. The stagnant smell of the swamp drifted in the air.

He turned the flashlight back and forth, scanning across the path and brittle underbrush. Leaves and debris were kicked and tossed into the air to his left. He swung the light in that direction. Golden eyes glowed in the light. He took a step back as he tried to discern what stared at him.

A ferret.

It chattered and slipped into the brackish water.

Meeks exhaled, lowering the gun. Relieved that a rooting animal had magnified his fear, he clicked the gun's safety.

The smell of death drifted on the wind. Sour breath brushed the hairs on the back of his neck. He never had time to turn or defend himself.

An arm slipped around his neck. Before he could fire a round or scream, rusted metal tore a rugged gash across his neck. The deep lash severed his juggler vein and vocal chords. Warm blood gushed out. The deputy's neck slumped forward. His gun dropped to the ground.

Elias pulled the officer's body into the swampy water and tugged him to the tree on the moss-covered isle. He had expended valuable energy, but he needed to hide the body. He didn't have time to properly sacrifice this man. Justin must be nearby. Otherwise, the rest of his family wouldn't be huddled around the fire. Perhaps the boy had gotten lost in the cave.

He remembered the one young man he had taken inside the cave the last time he had resurrected. If he could get past Justin's family, he could explore the cave and find Justin. Judging by the moon's fullness, he had tonight, or at the most, one more night to offer the young man.

CHAPTER 17

MARSHALL JACKSON ARRIVED at his office with the morning newspaper tucked beneath his arm. He smiled at the receptionist as he unlocked his door. He set his coffee and paper on his desk.

Marshall was a massive man—six foot, six inches and two hundred fifty pounds of rock hard muscle. He had been effective as an agent and solved cases that would have gone cold had it not been for his mule-headed attitude. He was prone to spend hours dissecting the tiniest detail to find clues no one else noticed.

With his enormous size and his deep, theatrical booming voice, questioning a prime suspect was his strongest attribute. Adding a frown to back his threatening tone, most hardened criminals he interrogated were reduced to tears. Necessary information spilled from them in seconds.

He once lost his temper with a kingpin's thug. The man harbored information about the whereabouts of a senator's kidnapped daughter. The ruffian's defiant attitude angered the bear inside Marshall. Marshall slammed his fists through a solid oak desktop rather than tear the man's head off.

Broken, splintered pieces of wood covered the floor and the suspect dropped to his knees, disclosing all the relevant information Marshall had asked. An hour later, the girl was rescued and ten men were arrested.

That occurred thirty years prior when Marshall was in his prime. He was now more reserved, settled, and eagerly awaiting retirement. Modestly graying with sparser hair, he looked forward to lazy days on his pontoon boat when he could fish from dusk to dawn.

On the wall behind him was the only picture he had of his hard-working, tenant-farming father. In the aged photo, Marshall was eight years old. He rode on his father's shoulders as he guided the single plow behind an old gray mule. Shirtless and covered with sweat, his father's chiseled muscles reminded him of the rigorous labor his father endured to provide for Marshall and his ten siblings. Harder times.

Marshall sipped his coffee and scanned the top headline: "**Boy Missing in Cave and Pastor Murdered—Cider Knoll, Kentucky.**"

He said, "Bingo."

Marshall adjusted his glasses and pushed the intercom button.

"Ms. Banks," Marshall said. "Get a helicopter ready for me. There's an urgent matter in Cider Knoll, Kentucky that requires my immediate attention."

"Yes, sir," she replied.

Marshall opened a filing cabinet drawer and pulled out a leather bag. He unsnapped the clasp. The old leather book and newspaper clippings were neatly placed into their proper files. He set the bag on his desk and read through the paper once more. Twenty years had passed and this was the last opportunity he had. Elias had returned. Although Marshall had never met Elias, he knew the man well. He wondered how much power Elias had gained from sacrifices and dark magic.

He had almost stopped Elias twenty years ago. But his counterattack missed its mark and Elias escaped. Ordinary weapons were useless. Marshall's years of investigation revealed that only magic could defeat Elias. This time, Marshall was prepared. There would be no more chances after this confrontation.

Destroying Elias would be easier if Marshall solicited the aid of the only man better trained for this mission than he was. But he couldn't invest any more time searching for Ben Whytten. For the past ten years, Ben was untraceable. A phantom. According to records the man had vanished without leaving a paper trail. No credit card usage. No phone calls. Nothing.

It was as if he never existed.

Ben was an inaccessible asset.

Regardless, Elias had to die.

Today.

5:30 A.M.

Dr. Frank Meadows pulled into parking lot of Roma's Diner in Somerset. He craved a big breakfast and a large cup of coffee before he researched the *haunted* cave walls. But he also stopped because he noticed the Sheriff's SUV parked there. Several pickups with boat trailers lined the outer edge of the lot.

Dawn was breaking the horizon as Frank opened the diner door. A lot of elderly men and women sat at tables drinking coffee and spreading gossip. A sign greeted him with the message: "Seat yourself."

Frank looked across the diner until he found the only uniformed officer in the place. Hopkins sat at the bar, sipping coffee from a large ceramic mug. His empty breakfast plate set before him.

"Sheriff Hopkins?" Frank asked.

Hopkins turned and smiled. "Yes, sir."

Frank extended his hand. "Dr. Frank Meadows, the geologist you called."

"Grab a seat and order breakfast. I'll buy," Hopkins said, shaking his hand.

"Oh, that's not necessary."

"I insist."

The smell of fresh coffee, fried bacon, sausage, and pancakes prompted Frank to order immediately. A shapely waitress scribbled his order on her notepad and smiled.

"Glad you got here early," Hopkins said. "I should have told you to stop here."

"I saw your vehicle."

"We've no new information from my deputy. Seems most of the McKnight family camped outside the cave last night."

Frank nodded. "I don't blame them. I brought my gear. I will get some samples, and if there's any way to climb around that wall, I have my spelunking ropes and ties."

"Maybe you can find a way. Justin's grandfather is torn up over this. It is weighing heavy on him."

"Anything like this happen before?"

"Like I mentioned on the phone, we had another boy vanish twenty years ago around this date. I went back to the office last night to review his missing records. A couple dozen volunteers searched the area for about two weeks before concluding that they weren't going to find him."

Frank shook his head. "That's hard to handle."

"It is. However, I dug further. Forty years ago, two teenagers disappeared in that area, too. Almost forty years to the date."

Frank's eyes widened. "Damn. So this is a recurring event?"

"It seems that way. I'd have looked at reports for sixty years ago, but a fire destroyed all the records in the old Sheriff's Office."

"Any clues as to what's behind this?"

The waitress brought Frank's breakfast and coffee.

"Enjoy," she said with a smile.

Frank smiled back.

"Jack McKnight told me some information last night that I had not heard before. Pretty disturbing."

Frank mixed his sausage, eggs, and hash browns into the center of his plate. He took a huge bite and quickly followed with another. He had barely swallowed before taking a third forkful and stuffing it into his mouth.

Hopkins stared at Frank in amused bewilderment.

Frank realized his bizarre eating mannerism had stopped the sheriff's delay in disclosing more information. While chewing, Frank mumbled, "Go on."

Hopkins explained the strange zombie-like man Jack described. Although Frank continued eating, his enthusiastic appetite wasn't as ravaging as seconds before. Chill bumps prickled his arms and fear shadowed his eyes. He set his fork beside his plate and swallowed his food.

"You think this man is responsible for Justin's disappearance?" Frank asked, blowing steam off his coffee.

"It's a far reach. We're talking about a sixty-year time span with an abduction occurring every twenty years in between. The man Jack had seen should have rotted away by now. I can't see how he could still be alive."

"That would be my thinking," Frank replied. "If you believe in such possibilities, which I don't. I'm a scientist. I'd have to have valid proof."

"I'm not a scientist, and I have a hard time accepting this as fact. However, if you had seen the sincerity in Jack's eyes as he spoke, he definitely encountered something horrible. The man had actually pried Donnie from his grasp and vanished into the darkness of Devils Den."

"The pastor that was killed," Frank said. "How far did that happen from the cave?"

"By road, a good five miles. Through the forest, one, maybe two, miles."

"Could the same person be responsible?"

Hopkins nodded. "There are large footprints at both locations that seem to belong to the same person."

"But you're not certain?"

"We're waiting for forensics to compare mud samples and the embedded tissue samples. They found flakes of dry skin in the mud."

Frank finished eating and pushed the plate forward. The waitress returned and Hopkins took the tab slip and headed to the cashier.

"Best we get there soon. Don't think John will remain patient much longer," Hopkins said.

"I'll follow behind you."

"Sure," Hopkins said, taking his change from the cashier. "But I need to make a quick stop beforehand."

6:30 A.M.

MARSHALL LOOKED at the hilly countryside as the helicopter flew over. Glancing at the pilot, he said, "How much longer?"

The pilot looked at his watch. "Within a half hour we should be landing."

"You have the coordinates for the cave area?"

"Yes, sir. We should be able to land in the pasture if the ground is level enough."

"Good."

Marshall studied the notes in his journal. Looking at a calendar, then his watch, he whispered, "I hope I get there in time."

～

JUSTIN SHIVERED beneath the smelly animal hide. No matter how tight he wrapped the fur around himself, he couldn't get warm. Besides freezing, his aching hunger gnawed inside is gut.

His skin itched and for a while he thought that he was having an allergic reaction to the animal hide. The flickering light that shimmered faintly from the sconces wasn't enough to see his skin clearly, but it was bright enough to see that he had developed a mottled rash. Had he brought his pack he'd have a lighter and matches to make a modest fire for warmth and a brighter light source.

Justin rolled his pant leg up. More mottling. He rubbed his fingers across the raised bumps. No pain. No real discomfort, other than the persistent itching. He'd toss the hide off except he wasn't dressed for icy temperatures.

While most of the other prisoners slept, the few that were awake moaned or softly cried. Justin watched the icy path between the cages, hoping a guard carrying food or water might pass by. Even if one did, he doubted he'd trust eating whatever rations they offered. His desperation made him hope that the wizard returned and granted him a chance to plead his case.

He thought about his family and wondered if he'd ever see them again. He assumed his grandfather had found the go-cart and his backpack at the mouth of the cave by now. He had no doubt his grandfather was furious for his disobedience. Regardless of the giant bullfrog, Justin should have respected the warning and not gone inside the cave. He wondered if he'd ever get back to the surface and leave this strange world behind.

Too many things occupied his mind for him to sit and cry. Besides, crying didn't change the situation. He was still locked inside the cell. Tears couldn't help or erase the past mistakes he had made.

Through the dim lighting Justin analyzed each of the cages closest to him. The prisoners' amputations concerned him. This wasn't *just* a prison. It was a vast torture chamber. He wondered why so many were being held prisoner and mutilated.

Justin thought of the picture he had sketched and the strange man appearing the next day. What he had imagined was only a drawn nightmare had manifested into reality. The undead man had come to take him as he had promised. In his room. With Justin no longer at his grandparents' farmhouse, he wondered if this man would harm them.

For a moment he entertained the idea that his troubling sketch had somehow been a divination to warn of imminent danger. If he possessed such an artistic gift, shouldn't a similar drawing have shown his imprisonment?

Justin curled into a fetal position, pulled the fur tight around him, and hoped he'd fall asleep and reawaken safe and secure in his attic bedroom. However, when his slumber ended, he'd discover his world had altered. Fate controlled a sick sense of humor. He had a slim chance that anything he remembered would ever return to its former state.

CHAPTER 18

*H*opkins pulled into the tiny gravel lot at Harper's Grocery. Frank parked beside him.

The Butler brothers sat on the dusty wooden porch. Their bikes lay on the gravels. They were eating MoonPies and drinking Dr. Pepper. Although the boys occasionally caused trouble, they were destined to become much worse if someone didn't intervene. Especially Zeke.

Zeke was becoming a man, but if his father and stepmother kept their overbearing tirades geared toward him, he'd probably spend most of his life in prison. Zeke's life was hard, and his father's constant verbal abuse made it a living hell. After Zeke's mother died giving birth to him, his father blamed him for her death. His stepmother resented Zeke because he wasn't her son. The more they railed at him, the harder he picked on his younger brothers and other kids like Justin.

Hopkins had graduated with Zeke's father, Thomas, but they had never been close friends. He had confronted Thomas twice about how he treated Zeke and once had Human Resources pay the family a visit.

Physical abuse was easier to prove than verbal abuse. Thomas displayed a wonderful charismatic personality to the county workers. After a half hour he had convinced them that not only was he a perfect father, but he was a wonderful, caring individual. Because of his splendid deception, no actions were sought to remove Zeke from the home.

Hopkins knew it was only a matter of time before he'd have to intervene. His biggest fear was that his intervention might force him to break laws he was sworn to uphold.

He closed the SUV door and leaned in Frank's open window. "Be right back. I want to get some food and drinks for everyone at Devils Den."

Frank nodded.

As Hopkins neared the front porch of the general store, the Butler brothers looked up and watched his approach. Nervousness weighed on their faces. They were up to something.

He didn't offer a smile as he came closer. He stared directly into Zeke's eyes. The young man quickly looked away.

"What kind of trouble are you planning this morning, boys?" Hopkins asked with a slight grin.

"None, Sheriff," Zeke said. His face paled as he slowly slid a baseball bat behind him. "We're just sitting here."

Hopkins folded his arms and placed one foot on the step next to Zeke's leg. "Are you waiting for someone?"

They shook their heads. "No."

Hopkins stared toward the road and said, "I suppose Justin usually rides up here this early, doesn't he?"

Zeke refused to make eye contact. "I guess, but he normally only comes up here on Saturday."

"But you're hoping he'll show today, aren't you?"

"No, not really," Zeke replied.

"Why do you have the bat?"

"We were going to play baseball in a little while," James said.

"Baseball, huh?" Hopkins said with an even smile. "Where's your ball and gloves?"

James looked at Zeke, hoping his older brother had a quick reply, but Zeke stared at the porch and then he looked at the gravel lot. "We're going to hit some rocks. James lost our baseball last week, so we didn't need our gloves."

Clifford frowned and scratched his head with his chubby fingers. "James didn't lose the ball. It's in the laundry room on top of the washing machine."

Zeke glared at Clifford.

"I'm going to tell you something," Hopkins said, staring at Zeke. "You may not like Justin because he lives in the city, but if I ever see you threaten him with a bat or any other weapon, I'll lock your ass in jail. You understand?"

Zeke nodded. His eyes widened. "We didn't bring the bat to hurt him. I just wanted to scare him."

"That's not the point. Never ever treat *anyone* like that."

"Yes, sir."

"I don't suppose you watched the news last night."

"Our TV doesn't work," Clifford said.

"Well, you boys need to get home where it's safe. Justin won't be coming here today. He's missing."

Zeke stood. "Missing?"

"What happened?" James asked.

Hopkins shook his head. "Justin went inside Devils Den yesterday. We can't find him."

Zeke exchanged glances with his two brothers. Fear settled in their eyes.

"Why'd he go in there?" Clifford asked. "Everyone knows the bogeyman lives in there."

"Did you search the cave?" Zeke asked.

"As far as we could. There's no sign of him." He pointed to Frank in the truck. "That man will explore the cave and see if he can find Justin. He's an expert on cave systems and geology."

"Do you think someone took Justin? A kidnapper?" James asked.

"Possibly. Pastor Ledbetter was killed Friday night."

Tears filled Clifford's eyes. He tugged the back of Zeke's tank top. "Let's go, Zeke. Let's go home. I don't want the bogeyman to get me. Let's go."

Zeke frowned and yanked his shirt free of Clifford's grasp. "Don't be a big baby, Clifford."

Hopkins frowned. "I suggest you all get to your home immediately. We don't know who killed the pastor, and he's still on the loose. The quicker you get home the better."

The brothers hopped on their bikes and pedaled away.

Hopkins walked inside Harper's Grocery.

"Morning, Sheriff," Mr. Harper said. "Any luck finding Justin?"

Hopkins shook his head. "No, not yet."

"Bunch of folks met up here earlier, got some supplies and headed out to John's farm to help look for him."

"I thought it looked empty in here this morning."

Harper nodded. "I'm thinking about closing shop and going out there myself. I only see Justin on Saturdays, but he's a hell of a great kid."

"That he is," Hopkins replied. He grabbed a couple of cases of Mountain

Dew and a few boxes of snack cakes. "I just feel like a failure that we've not found him yet."

"You're not a failure. You just haven't succeeded yet."

Hopkins pulled out his wallet.

"Those you buying for yourself or for folks helping search for Justin."

"For the volunteers."

Harper smiled and shook his head. "You're money's no good then. Take them on up. As soon as I lock up, I'll be up there, too."

Hopkins smiled. "Thanks."

As FRANK FOLLOWED the sheriff's SUV along the dirt road to Devils Den, he couldn't help but mentally survey the terrain. His apprehension for venturing inside the cave had subsided while he occupied his mind with other geological formations along the way. However, when they drove across the pasture and stopped, the ominous dark entrance taunted him. The darkness seemed to move, as if it breathed and called to him. He'd never experienced such a sensation.

Four people sat around the glowing embers of dying campfire. He assumed them to be the parents and grandparents of missing boy.

Before Frank emerged from the driver's seat, he considered turning his truck around and speeding for home. He found no shame in cowardice, if it was his life in jeopardy. But these people needed help finding a young man. He couldn't ever hold his head with pride or look anyone in the eyes again should he desert this family.

Reaching into the back of his truck, he removed a dusty duffel bag and slung it over his shoulder. He unsnapped a side compartment. His gun was tucked between two three-ring binders. He let the pouch cover fall back over the compartment but didn't snap it shut. He didn't know if he'd need quick access to the gun or not, and he wasn't about to take that chance.

Frank caught John's feeble gaze. The distraught look and hopelessness in his eyes informed Frank how essential his geophysical testing of the cave walls might be to find Justin. He needed to measure densities, magnetism, and any anomalies that existed.

Hopkins approached and walked beside him. At the campfire, the sheriff made quick introductions. Afterward, he looked at John and said, "Any idea what time Justin entered Devils Den?"

John looked at Lib with a questioned expression. She said, "I heard the go-cart start up between seven and eight yesterday morning."

Hopkins looked at his watch. "Ok, he's been missing nearly twenty-four hours. We have to act fast." He turned to Frank. "You have your gear ready?"

"Yes."

Looking around, Hopkins asked, "Where's Deputy Meeks?"

"We don't know," Rita said.

Jack pointed. "We heard some strange noise near the swamp about an hour before sunrise. He went to check it out."

Hopkins clicked his radio transmitter. "Meeks, do you read me?"

No answer. No static.

Nothing.

"Did either of you go see where he went?" Hopkins asked.

Jack and Rita shook their heads.

"He never yelled for help or fired his weapon," Jack said. "I just assumed he was still investigating the area. Besides we don't have a gun and didn't know what we might encounter if we went looking for him."

Hopkins nodded and hurried down the path. "Frank, go figure out what you can about the cave wall. I'll be back in a few minutes."

Frank watched Hopkins disappear into the dead trees near the swamp as he stepped closer to Devils Den. He shuddered. A cold, dank breeze spilled from the cave. For a moment, he thought he heard whispering voices. Looking around, he wondered if anyone else had heard it.

He slid his hand into his pack until his fingers touched the gun. With renewed boldness he walked into the cave.

Turning on his flashlight he followed Justin's footprints until he came to the wall. He was dumbfounded to find the last footprint exactly like Hopkins described. He laid the duffel bag down and scanned the ceiling and the adjoining walls. He couldn't find any cracks or openings where a boy could squeeze past, but he noticed something Hopkins had not. The wall was composed of a rock much different than the other two walls. Although it was hard to decipher under the glow of a flashlight, he was able to tell a difference in its composition.

Frank removed a small pickax from the duffel bag. He swung a hard, sharp blow. Sparks flew but he failed to breakaway a chunk of rock from the wall. The spike end of the pick bent.

"Damn," he said.

Turning the flat end around, he swung again with the same results. His pickax didn't flake or chip any fragments loose, but now the pickax was destroyed.

Frustrated, he started his diamond-tipped core drill. The bit spun and whined. Adjusting the water level, he eased the bit against the wall. The bit wailed as metal attempted to bore into the rock. Seconds later, the bit stalled. Smoke billowed from the little motor and the chuck lost grip. The tip of the bit snapped, leaving the power tool useless.

"What the hell?"

After Frank flipped the power switch off and the broken bit ceased spinning, the eerie cries and moans he had heard earlier now drifted from beyond the wall. He stuffed his tools into the bag and zipped it. From the side compartment he grabbed the gun. In the other hand he flashed his light down the path. The voices became louder. He leaned back against the wall and slumped down in the corner with paralyzing fear. Although he didn't see anything, he knew he was no longer alone.

~

HOPKINS STOPPED WALKING when he discovered the large pool of blood that coated dry pine needles. Meeks' gun lay on the ground. The loss of blood was too much for someone to survive. His deputy's body had to be nearby.

He shook his head in disbelief, stooped down, and picked up the gun with his handkerchief. The safety was still on.

"Damn, never got a shot off."

"Dispatch," Hopkins said via transmitter while watching the swamp. "Contact Deputy Shannons and all other available officers. Send them to John McKnight's pasture where Devils Den is. We have a deputy missing. I believe he's dead. Over."

"Copy that."

He followed the blood trail to the black swampy water. Two narrow lines of needles were mangled and swept aside where Meeks' feet had been dragged. The path had blood splotches. Whoever had killed Meeks had dragged him into the water. At the edge of the bank was a large bare footprint in the mud. Hopkins tucked his deputy's gun into his belt and pulled his own. The footprint had to belong to the same person. No coincidence. They were dealing with a serial killer.

Hopkins studied the trail and tried to see the forest line on the other side of the swamp, but the massive tree in the center of the water prevented a clear view. He couldn't tell if the perpetrator had emerged from the water or was hiding behind the tree.

Near the tree, large bubbles broke the water's surface. Hopkins released the safety and waited for something to emerge near the tree. He hoped that whoever or whatever had hidden Meeks' body and possibly taken Justin would reveal itself so he could kill it.

Ripples edged across the water and slowly reduced in strength. Once they disappeared, the swamp was dead and still.

Hopkins listened for movement in the wooded area. Crows cawed. Insects chummed. In the far distance the familiar sound of a helicopter approached. Within a minute the low-flying chopper passed overhead. It was barely a few feet above the treetops.

FBI was painted across the sides and the underside of the chopper.

He holstered his gun and turned to see the helicopter hover and descend to a flat area of the pasture. He didn't know why the FBI had been notified, but he was thankful for their help and possible insight.

As Hopkins walked to the smoldering campfire, the chopper blades slowed and a large man dressed in a dark suit stepped out. He ducked his head and jogged out of the blades' perimeter.

"Who's that?" John asked.

Hopkins shook his head. "I have no idea."

Marshall carried a briefcase and hurried to meet Hopkins.

"Sheriff," Marshall said, extending his huge right hand. He towered over Hopkins and his hand seemed to swallow the sheriff's as they shook hands. He smiled and said in his deep voice, "I'm FBI special agent Marshall Jackson."

"Sheriff Hopkins."

"Good to meet you."

Hopkins frowned. "You're here because of the missing teenager?"

"That's *part* of the reason I'm here."

"The murder?"

Marshall smiled. "The murderer. I'm here to stop him."

Rita stepped closer. "You know who did it?"

"I'm more than confident who the perpetrator is. It's a matter of finding and stopping him before he disappears again."

"Do you think he's hurt Justin?" she asked.

"I cannot answer that, but I do know if the boy's missing, this man is probably the person responsible."

"Oh, God," Lib whispered.

Hopkins removed his hat and wiped sweat from his brow with his shirt-sleeve. "I have an officer missing. I believe he's dead."

Rita gasped.

Jack's face was pale.

"What makes you think he's dead?" Marshall asked.

"Come with me," Hopkins said. As Marshall followed, Hopkins turned to John and the others. "You folks just stay here."

"No argument from me," Jack whispered as he glanced at Rita. Worry creased her brow.

Hopkins said, "How do you know who is responsible for the murder?"

Marshall shrugged. "I've researched him for years. I almost caught him twenty years ago."

"Twenty years ago? That's when Donnie disappeared inside Devils Den."

"Yes. Unfortunately, that young man was sacrificed. The man respon-sible escaped without a trace."

Hopkins stopped walking.

"Donnie was killed?" he asked.

Marshall nodded.

"How do you know that?"

"The man who killed the pastor offered Donnie as a blood sacrifice."

"You have proof of this?"

Marshall sighed. "None that I can show you."

"Then how do you know?"

"That's something I'll explain to you later."

Hopkins glanced to the campfire where the others stood. Jack sat on the large rock, staring at the ground. His face hung emotionless. "Jack McKnight was Donnie's best friend. He was there when Donnie was taken. But what he says is a bit absurd."

"Why is that?"

"He believes the man was a walking corpse."

Marshall nodded. "In a manner of speaking, yes, he is."

"But how?"

"It will take time to explain. Time that we don't have right now."

"Okay."

"But Donnie wasn't the only one killed that night."

Hopkins frowned. "What? I checked the records. There aren't any murders reported. Just Donnie's disappearance."

"Three others died. Trust me, I know."

Hopkins tapped his transmitter. "Check the files for the night Donnie disappeared twenty years ago. I need the names of three people killed that night."

"On it," the dispatcher replied.

"I've known about Donnie's disappearance for years," Hopkins said. "I don't recall any people murdered that night."

"I doubt you'll find records listed for them."

"Why?"

"That's something you should ask the former sheriff."

"You think Sheriff Douglas covered it up?"

"If your records don't account for the murders, he probably did."

"He had no reason to cover them up."

"To prevent panic in this county, he might have."

The baking sun grew hotter, making Hopkins wipe more sweat from his brow. "I checked the records forty years ago and two teenagers disappeared then, too."

"I know. More murders, too."

Hopkins shook his head. "I found the abductions, but no murders."

"Douglas held the sheriff's office then, too."

"Why would he . . . ?"

Marshall walked past and asked, "Where did your deputy disappear?"

"Right up here," Hopkins said, hurrying ahead of Marshall.

Hopkins stopped at the congealing pool of blood. Marshall studied the bloody needles for a moment and then he glanced at the massive tree in the center of the swamp.

"Do you see the noose?" Marshall asked, pointing.

The frayed noose swung in the breeze.

"I'll be damned," Hopkins said. "No, I never noticed that."

Marshall gave a grim smile. "One hundred forty years ago. *That's* where this all started."

"What?"

"They tried to kill him, but he survived."

"They hung him and he lived?"

Marshall nodded. "He's still alive."

Hopkins eyed him. "You're beginning to sound as farfetched as Jack."

"Perhaps you underestimate the truth in Jack's recollection."

"I suppose I don't want to believe it's possible."

Marshall chuckled. "None of us want to believe such a nightmare exists. However, we must act fast if we wish to end it."

"You think Justin's still alive?"

Marshall shrugged. "If I had to place a bet on it? I'd say that he is. The boy is probably destined to be Elias' final sacrifice. Otherwise, your deputy would never have been attacked."

"Elias? So you know his name?"

"I do. Once he sacrifices Justin, we've lost all hope of stopping him."

"Since you know who he is, how does he continue to elude you?"

"I will impart more information as soon as I investigate the area. I promise." Marshall walked along the edge of the swamp and stopped near a patch of shrubbery. He pointed at the shrub. "What do we have here?"

Hopkins knelt and pushed back the branches. A bloody, half-eaten rabbit lay in the leaves. He took a stick and pulled the animal carcass out.

"It's a dead rabbit," Hopkins said. "I can't be certain, but I'd say a person chewed the raw flesh. Animal tears would be more jagged."

"I agree," Marshall said, looking closer. "This kill is fairly fresh, so the culprit is still nearby."

Hopkins opened his mouth to speak, but a loud scream echoed from the cave.

"What the hell was that?" Marshall asked.

"Dr. Frank Meadows. He's in the cave."

"Hurry," Marshall said, pulling his gun.

CHAPTER 19

*J*ustin shivered beneath the filthy fur. He peered through a slit in the hide. No guards had passed by. No outside movement, other than scurrying rats feasting on a prisoner's carcass. Their tiny eyes glowed red in the flickering torchlight.

Neighboring prisoners moaned or cried softly as starving rats bit them and then darted away when the person moved. Troubled by the thought the rats might mistake him for their next meal; he sat up and looked around. He feared the wizard might return at any moment. But he hoped someone brought him food. It had been hours since he had eaten.

His stomach growled.

Hanging in a metal basket at the top of his cage was a loaf of stale bread that hadn't been there earlier. Magically, it had appeared. Like a timid mouse Justin reached and quickly snatched the bread. Fearful that others might not have food and they'd cause a commotion upon seeing his, he tucked the loaf under the fur and waited.

The other cells had baskets with fruit or bread in them. A few prisoners ripped and tore bites of bread with their teeth like starving animals. Their feral eyes revealed how much of their sanity was gone.

As Justin ate, he noticed a prisoner's face disfigured by knotty tumors. The deformed flesh made him think of his grandfather. He wondered what cancerous growth might look like *inside* his lungs as it slowly killed him. Warm, salty tears leaked from Justin's eyes, but he never uttered a sound.

He chided himself for not listening to his grandfather. He needed to free himself and find his way back to the surface. Whether or not he made it home, he had to escape, or he'd lose appendages, too.

Devils Den was far worse than his grandfather had deemed it.

Justin swallowed the last bite of stale bread and wished he had water to soothe his scratched throat. None appeared.

A wintry breeze swept through the prison. He rubbed his arms to combat the chill. His skin felt different. Little ridges and bumpy layers covered him. His arms were mottled like his legs. When he looked at his hands, he gasped. Webbing had formed between his fingers.

In a corner of his cell a bottle materialized. Hoping it contained something to quench his thirst, he popped the cork. He sniffed the bottle. The vapor was harsh, pungent. His eyes watered.

"Don't drink it," a man whispered.

Justin caught the gaze of the prisoner in the cell across from his. The human never blinked. His cold callous stare was frightening. Long, silky strands of hair flowed around the man's shoulders.

"What is it?" Justin asked, pulling the animal hide tighter.

"Drugged wine. Drink it and worse than this might happen to you." He pointed to his left arm. It was amputated at the elbow.

Justin sniffed the wine again. He corked the bottle and tossed it on the floor. "Thanks for telling me."

"What's your name?" the man asked with a thick accent.

"Justin."

"I'm Drake. Where are you from?"

"Cider Knoll," Justin replied.

"Not familiar with the place. How did you get here?"

"Devils Den."

Drake frowned. "What?"

"It's the name of the cave I entered. I was unable to find my way back out. How did you get here?"

"I was spelunking in Gouffre Berger Cave in France. Heavy rains flooded the cave and swept me away. When I came to, I was here."

"How long ago was that?"

"A week. Maybe ten days."

"How did you lose your arm?"

"The wizard. After a day in this cell without a drink, I was parched. When I found the bottle of wine, I drank it. I never suspected it was drugged. When I awakened, my forearm had been removed."

"Why did he cut off your arm?"

"Best I can tell he's a necromancer. Rather than sacrifice a mortal, he dissects prisoners and offers their body parts in exchange for magic. The more suffering he inflicts, the stronger his magic."

"Why does he need body parts for magic?"

"Necromancers raise the dead. That requires a lot of magic. To be granted such power, blood and flesh must be offered as sacrifice."

Justin looked at the dozens of prison cells. "Looks like he has enough people to raise an army."

Drake nodded. "Probably. We're like livestock. He harvests our body parts until we die."

"Has anyone escaped since you've been here?"

"No," he replied. "The lucky ones are the skeletons chained to the wall."

"Looks like their luck ran out."

Drake shrugged. "They don't suffer anymore. That's better luck than the rest of us."

Justin eased closer to the bars of his cage. Little clouds drifted from his mouth as he exhaled. His teeth chattered. On the surface the summer weather was blistering hot. Being thrust into an extremely cold climate without time to acclimate was painful and made him miserable. As he repositioned the animal fur across his shoulders, it slipped from his grasp and dropped to floor. He reached to pick it up.

"Step into the light where I can see you," Drake said.

"Why?"

"Please. Just do it."

Although light was minimal from the torches, a small section of Justin's cell was better lit than the rest of it. He stepped into the corner.

Drake's eyes widened. "Why don't you use your power to release us?"

"What powers?"

"You're a Rana. You have great strength and magical powers."

Justin frowned. "I don't know what you're talking about."

"A Rana is a mystical shaman. A frogman. A race believed to be extinct."

"I'm human."

Drake laughed. "You're not human. I don't understand why you're even in the cage."

"I'm human. Not a . . . Rana."

Justin looked at his hands again. The webbing was thicker with less space between his fingers. His mottled skin did look and feel like the skin of a bullfrog.

"The wizard," Justin said. "He changed me."

Drake bellowed a long, deep laugh. "Never. He'd be no match for . . . . Wait. You really were human, weren't you?"

"Yes."

"Of course you'd have to have been when the wizard caged you. His magic is weaker than a Rana. He couldn't have imprisoned you in these cages. He certainly can't hold you in one."

"I don't know how to get out."

"Grab the bars and test your strength."

Justin placed his hands around the bars and tugged. To his surprise the bars bent slightly. He exerted more strength and stretched them far enough apart to squeeze through.

"See?" Drake said.

Justin nodded.

"Now, let me out."

He started to, but then he wondered whether he could actually trust this individual. His story almost sounded true. Almost. The one thing that troubled him was this man knew too much about the wizard and the Underworld to have come from the surface. Drake may have witnessed the wizard amputating a prisoner's appendage, and perhaps that was the reason for his missing forearm. But, no one from the surface would have learned about a Rana during a few days of captivity, not if it was an extinct race.

Justin turned to walk away. His boots pinched his toes. He slipped off one and stared in disbelief at his froglike foot. He tugged off the other boot. Although the cave floor was white with snow and ice, he was surprised that his feet didn't feel any cold or further discomfort.

"Justin," Drake said. "Don't leave me here. I can show you the route out."

"If you were from France, you wouldn't know what I've become. That's not something anyone outside this realm or wherever we are, would know."

Impatience reflected in Drake's dark eyes. He pulled back his hair and revealed his pointed ears. "You're right. I'm not from France, but I'm the best hope you have to get out of here safely."

Justin couldn't deny that. He grabbed two bars of Drake's cage and pulled them far enough apart for him to get out.

"Appreciated," Drake said.

"We should help some of the others get free, too."

"No."

"We can help them escape."

Drake shook his head. "Most of these prisoners aren't able to walk.

Others are mentally unstable, and I imagine many were murderers before their eventual capture."

Justin studied his hands and wondered what his face looked like now. Had it transformed as well?

"This way," Drake said, crouching as he walked through the rows of cells.

Justin followed and whispered, "So where are you really from?"

"Woodnog. An Elven village not far from this cave."

A prisoner grabbed Justin's pant leg. Her mouth whispered a strange language. The pleading in her eyes was understandable. She wanted released, too. As much as Justin wanted to help her, her handicaps would slow their progress.

"So you don't believe the wizard transformed me into a Rana?"

"No."

"Then why would I change? Especially if it's a rare and magical species."

"You'll soon learn, dark and strange things happen in the Underworld. No place is without danger. Highwaymen lurk between every town. Wizards and warlocks battle to rule kingdoms."

"Drake," a prisoner seethed. "How'd you escape?"

Drake paused for a moment, stared at the imprisoned elf, and kept walking.

"Who is that?" Justin asked.

"Don't mind him. Let's go."

"Wait!" the elf said. "You can't trust Drake. He'll kill you the first chance he gets."

Justin turned. Although both elves were covered in filth, they held a stately aura every bit as regal as he imagined an elf had. Even their desperation hadn't tainted their elven status.

The elf extended his hand. "Don't let him deceive you. He and I were exiled from Woodnog. We were banished to the swamps to die."

Justin looked at Drake. The elf's eyes shimmered with evil darkness. In an even tone, Drake said, "Let's go."

"Why were you banished?"

The imprisoned elf continued, "For planning a revolt against Woodnog and their human guardians. Drake killed two guards before we were netted and taken captive. I'm surprised they were as merciful as they were. They should have killed us."

"I should have killed you, Stiles." Drake hissed.

"As I should you." Stiles gave Justin a stern stare. "Beware, he may kill you."

"Enough," Drake said, breaking a wine bottle and rushing at Stiles.

Before Drake reached the cell, Justin forced open the bars and tripped Drake. Drake stumbled forward, and Justin shoved him into the prison cell and pulled the bars into place. He ran without looking back. Blood would be shed, and he didn't want to witness the outcome. He had already caught Drake lying, so he couldn't trust the elf to bring him to safety. And Stiles had been partners with Drake. He had to believe they were both thugs with their own best interests at heart.

The sound of rushing water caught his attention. Ice and snow covered most of the cave floor, but the underground stream moved steadily. He hoped the waterway enabled him to get to the surface. Caves were generally formed from running water, so the source should have a way in and out. He only needed to follow it.

Justin hated the thought of wandering aimlessly through the cave alone, but he couldn't discern whom to trust. Tortured individuals seldom recovered from trauma and placing his trust in a deranged stranger was more dangerous than walking alone.

"Help me," a man with a red beard and long hair said. "Please."

Justin studied the man's face. The prisoner was minus an eye. The open socket was filled with blood and pus with the consistency of soft candle wax. A dried line of blood streaked the man's cheek. The eye had been taken recently.

"You're headed to the stream?" he asked.

"Not certain where to go."

"Release me, and I swear by the gods I'll help you."

Prisoners nervously moved in their cells. Loud wails and shrieks erupted from the area where Justin had been caged.

"Hurry, if you want my aid. The wizard has returned."

Justin looked down the path. The wizard stood with his back to him. He could turn and see him at any moment. He had no time to debate whether he should release the man or fend for himself. Staring into the man's one pleading eye, Justin surrendered to his compassion and helped the man escape.

Seconds later, a bolt of harsh yellow light flashed past them.

"Run to the stream and jump in."

Justin ran. The roaring, rushing stream was within a few yards. He could see the swirling water. Closer. Faster he moved. Mist rose from the stream. He jumped.

The wizard's second blast of fiery light struck Justin in the back and propelled him forward. The impact knocked the air from his lungs, and he dropped into the water, stunned. His fingers tingled, and he couldn't move his arms or legs. They were useless. Swimming was impossible. The swift current sucked him down through a tunnel. Water encapsulated him.

Without air, he feared he'd drown but a strange thing occurred. He wasn't struggling to hold his breath. In fact, he didn't have the sudden urge to want to breathe. Then he thought about how bullfrogs could jump into a pond and not surface for long periods. His transformation into a Rana seemed to have empowered him with a similar breathing capacity.

Justin had no control over where the water directed him. After spiraling several twists and narrow turns, he buoyed up. His limp body floated atop the shallow water. The one-eyed man grabbed him and pulled him ashore.

"We're safe," he said. "You did it."

"I can't move," Justin whispered. "I'm numb all over."

"It's okay. Give it a few minutes. I'm certain the feeling will return."

"You're sure that we're safe?"

"Don't worry. You rescued me. I'll make certain you're protected."

"Thanks. Who are you?"

"Belfry."

"I'm Justin."

The earth beneath Justin crumbled. Skeletal fingers stretched upward, rising, until hands of bones wrapped around his ankles. The cave floor vibrated. More living skeletons pulled and clawed their way to the surface. Their eyes glowed ruby red and were piercingly wicked. Their teeth and bones rattled.

Belfry pried the fingers off Justin's ankles, but living skeletons surrounded them.

Seconds later, the necromancer appeared before them.

Justin blinked helplessly.

CHAPTER 20

*H*opkins reached the front of Devils Den about fifteen yards ahead of Marshall. John, Lib, and Rita stood outside the opening, but Jack had not moved from where he sat on the rock. Jack nervously looked at the cave but made no attempt to stand. His fear outranked his curiosity, or perhaps, he relived the day Donnie had disappeared in his mind.

Marshall clicked off the safety of his gun and entered the cave.

Hopkins flipped on his flashlight, following behind. "Frank? Where are you?"

"Here!" he shouted.

"Scan the light along the walls," Marshall said.

As Hopkins stepped into the darkness with the light on, Marshall looked for anything moving along the edge of the walls.

Nothing.

The sheriff and Marshall hurried to the geologist, scanning the walls with the flashlight as they approached. Frank sat cowered in the corner, holding his pack as if he could hide behind it. His flashlight was on but lay on the ground beside him.

"What is it?" Hopkins asked. "Did you see him?"

Frank shook his head. "No."

Marshall leaned down and placed a hand on Frank's shoulder. "What *did* you see?"

"Nothing."

Hopkins glanced at Marshall.

"I didn't *see* anything," Frank said, clearing his throat. "It's what I *heard.*"

"According to John McKnight, the voices are part of the reason for the cave's name," Hopkins said.

"No, it wasn't the cries for help," Frank said. "I heard that and assumed they were caused by the stirring wind passing through the lower chambers of the cave. This voice was grim and low. Right at my ear. I swear it was loud enough that the person should have been standing right beside me. He told me to leave or he'd kill me. When I turned, I saw no one, but a large hand wrapped around my throat. I felt it but didn't see it. I screamed before its grip tightened. Then it was gone."

"Here," Marshall said, extending his huge hand. "Let's get you outside."

Frank grabbed his hand. With a swift yank, Marshall pulled Frank to his feet.

As they walked to the cave entrance, Hopkins asked, "What do you make of the wall that blocks the path?"

"Hell, it destroyed two of my best tools. The rock is harder than anything I've studied. I can tell you this. It isn't the same type of rock as the two adjoining walls. And without a sample to take to a lab, I doubt I'll be able to tell you what it is."

"I'd suggest using dynamite if Justin wasn't lost inside," Hopkins said.

"I doubt dynamite would make a dent in that wall," Frank replied.

Frank stepped out into the light and took a deep breath.

Rita looked at Hopkins. "What happened?"

"Anxiety attack," Frank whispered as he headed for his truck.

She asked Hopkins as Frank got out of earshot. "Did he discover anything to help us find Justin?"

"No. Not yet."

"Mrs. McKnight," Marshall said in a gentle tone. "We're going to find your son."

"You believe he's still alive then?" she asked.

Marshall looked at Hopkins and then at her. "Yes. I believe he is."

"Good. Please find him."

Marshall smiled. "That's why I'm here."

The news van drove down the pasture and parked behind John's pickup. Misty Waters and her crew hurried to the cave. She looked at Hopkins and smiled. "Any new discoveries?"

"Nothing positive. I'm missing a deputy now. I'm afraid he's dead."

"Dear God," she whispered.

Panic set in the McKnights' eyes.

Dust billowed behind a line of cars and trucks on the dirt road. One by one the vehicles slowed and turned into the pasture. Deputy Shannons' patrol car led them.

"What's going on?" John asked.

"Mr. Harper told me that some volunteers were coming," Hopkins replied. "They want to help search for Justin."

Misty smiled. "We brought some volunteers from Roma's Diner, too."

Marshall said, "This is a great idea. Elias won't risk being seen. Besides, his agenda is during the night under the light of the moon. Just have your deputy organize them in groups of two or three."

"So you believe they'll be safe?" Rita asked. "We've lost enough lives already."

"I know," Marshall replied. "But he shuns sunlight. Everyone should be fine."

Hopkins spoke to Shannons and asked him to group together search teams.

Tommy walked up to John and said, "I've come to help find Justin."

"He'll be right proud of that," John said. "I know I am."

"Why did he go into Devils Den?"

John shook his head. "I honestly don't know, son. He came out here to get a bullfrog to put a whopping on yours."

"Once we find him, he'd best get a good one. Mine's hard to beat."

John ruffled Tommy's hair.

Frank joined Hopkins and Marshall. He took a long drink from his canteen. After he screwed the lid tight, he said, "Is there anything more you need?"

Hopkins tipped back his cowboy hat. "You aren't giving up, are you?"

"No. But I don't see a way to get through that wall."

"How about if we bypass it?" Hopkins asked.

"What are you suggesting?"

"Well," Hopkins said, walking down the path beside the outside cave wall. He pointed. "What if we drilled a large hole on the other side of where that inner wall is?"

Frank grinned. "That might work."

"Tell me what kind of equipment you need, and I'll make the calls to have it delivered. Do you have a rope I could use?"

Frank nodded and pulled a rope from his bag. He said, "Give me a few minutes and I'll make a list for you."

"We'll be at the swamp, looking for my deputy. Just follow this path."

"Sure." Frank said. He grabbed a notepad and pen.

As Marshall and Hopkins walked back to the swamp, Marshall asked, "There is a person of interest I need to ask you about."

"Who?"

"Ben Whytten."

"Ben? Why him?"

Marshall paused in step. "You know him?"

Hopkins nodded. "Of course. He's John's brother-in-law. We were talking about him yesterday. He knows this cave better than anyone."

"That's precisely why I need to find him."

"That will be a problem."

"Why's that?" Marshall asked.

"John hasn't been able to contact him in more than six years. No one else has seen him either."

"Exactly the same problem I've had. He seems to have vanished without any trace at all."

"Is he a person of interest because he knows his way around Devils Den?"

"That's part of the reason."

"There's more?"

"He's the reason I was unable to stop Elias last time."

Hopkins frowned. "He interfered?"

"I don't think he intentionally did so. He was also trying to stop Elias but didn't know I was doing the same thing."

"What happened?"

Marshall shrugged. "That's why I want to talk to him. I don't know what he did, but he weakened Elias's power so much that Elias fled. He was gone. When I pursued Ben to confront him, he disappeared, too. That was the last time I have seen either of them."

A trio of crows perched on the branch above the noose. The peering red eyes studied them. One cleaned its beak on the limb.

Hopkins and Marshall stopped at the edge of the swamp. The thick tree canopy cast dreary shadows around the pool. Lingering morning mist drifted through the trees. Insects and birds played a strange melody and hushed quickly at their arrival.

Hopkins unraveled the rope. "Too many people have vanished here without explanation."

"I agree. Even after we stop Elias, I want to know what Ben knows."

Standing near the path where Hopkins believed his deputy had been dragged, he handed the knotted end of the rope to Marshall. "You look as powerful as a bull. Hold this for me. I want to get to the tree in the center of the swamp to see if my deputy's body is there. I don't know how deep this water is."

Marshall nodded. "No problem. If you start to sink, I'll pull you out."

Hopkins placed his right foot into the black, stagnant water. The thick mossy bottom sucked his foot and held fast. As he placed his next step, his right foot sank another six inches. He fought to pull his foot out to take another step. An acrid smell worse than sulfur permeated the air.

"Dammit," Hopkins whispered as he pulled his foot free of the mud and lost his shoe. He reached through the thick sphagnum moss and felt around until his found it. He yanked his shoe from the water and poured out water and strands of moss. Shaking his head, he flung it to the bank.

Marshall laughed.

Before Hopkins pulled his other foot free, he was more careful. As he slowly lifted his leg, the stubborn mud released its hold without stealing the shoe. He rinsed away the sticky mud and leaf debris, then tossed the shoe near the other one.

The next few steps were easier, but the swampy water was now waist-deep. The moss congealed around him like Jell-O as he sloshed forward. Fortunately, this was the deepest he had to wade because the bottom ascended to the gnarled tree. Its thick roots wrapped the isle firmly, making the earth beneath his feet more solid.

When Hopkins stood on the mound near the tree, he noticed large drops of blood on the green mossy carpet.

"See anything?" Marshall asked. His voice boomed and echoed through the swamp. The crows cawed in response but didn't flee from their perch.

"Blood," Hopkins replied.

He edged around the tree cautiously, looking for snakes while hoping to not find the corpse of his friend and colleague. Seeing no snakes or a body, he moved to the opposite side of the tree.

Mosquitoes hummed in his ears. He swatted them away.

He discovered more blood was on the ground.

A large hollow opening was at the base of the tree. Flies swarmed. Seeing the brown slacks and shoes, his stomach tensed. Meeks had been crammed down the hole. He couldn't see anything above his deputy's belt. The hole was too dark.

"Found him!" Hopkins said. Remorse filled his soul as he contemplated the best way to get the body out of the tree.

Marshall didn't have to ask if the deputy was alive. He knew Elias' mentality. Elias had killed the man.

Hopkins dropped to his knees and reached into the dark hollow tree. He grabbed Meeks by the ankles and positioned his legs. He heaved backward and pulled. Standing, Hopkins tugged again and as he backed up, he freed Meeks from the hole.

Meeks' eyes were wide, frozen in death. His throat had been slit, but his body wasn't covered with decorative carvings like Ledbetter. The majority of blood had been washed away when his body was pulled through the water. Strands of sphagnum were stuck to his face, arms, and drying clothes.

Hopkins lowered Meeks' legs to the ground. With a gentle sweep of his hand, he closed the deputy's eyes. He plucked away moss and debris from his deputy's face.

Meeks was only twenty-four years old, and had been a deputy for over a year. He hated to tell Meeks' parents about the death of their only son. Whatever Marshall knew about how to stop Elias interested Hopkins more than ever. He'd do what was necessary to destroy this *undead* person, if that was truly what was responsible for all the events since Friday.

Hopkins tapped his transmitter. "We need the coroner. Immediately."

"Copy that."

Hopkins rolled the wet socks off his feet and quickly plucked several black leeches off his ankles. Looking at his watch, he estimated a good half-hour before the coroner arrived. Eugene was always prompt, but even he couldn't get there any faster than that.

He looked at Marshall and said, "Coroner's on the way."

EUGENE DISCONNECTED the call after dispatch told him he was needed at the McKnight farm near Devils Den. He grabbed his equipment and camera. Still unable to decipher the symbols carved in Ledbetter's body, he assumed the same person who had killed Pastor Ledbetter probably murdered Deputy Meeks, too.

The elusive murderer held other bizarre secrets as well. The fingernail that Hopkins had found wedged in the bible leather entertained more mysteries than Eugene ever expected. No DNA records in criminal file database matched. Worse was that the aged fingernail dated back more than one hundred and twenty years.

"Impossible," he told the people at the lab. When they informed him the tests had been run several times, he demanded to see the data reports. After reading them, he still had difficulty believing the data, but each test was conclusive with the same end result. No errors had occurred in the dating process.

The fingernail was well over a century old.

What exactly roamed the countryside and *how* were they going to kill it?

FRANK SURVEYED the side of the mountain wall that housed Devils Den. He had measured the inside distance of the path to the wall and walked the same length down the outside trail to pinpoint where they could blast another opening. While he did this, his hands shook and sweat soaked his shirt. He still felt the lingering tightness of invisible fingers around his throat. Although he hadn't seen anyone, he didn't doubt for a second that the verbal threat and attack was real. The only reason he never fired his gun was because he was uncertain of the cave's structure and stability. Any loose overhead rocks might have crashed down on him had he fired a single round. However, he was certain if he had actually seen what gripped his throat, he would have shot, cave-in or not.

Under ordinary circumstances, his fear would have forced him to flee the area and never look back. But Sheriff Hopkins had called him out in front of the McKnights and an FBI agent. How could he run after that? Besides, the sheriff could easily report his cowardice to state officials. If he did, Frank would probably be asked to resign his position or be the laughing stock of the Geological Society. And his former nickname—Scarecrow—was nowhere near as bad as the names or labels his fellow colleagues and students would place on him then.

Frank had half-heartedly laughed at the thought of a haunted cave when Hopkins first called. But the wall that had somehow appeared and now blocked a well-worn path proved something mystical and paranormal, perhaps even *magical*, validated the theory that Devils Den was indeed haunted or possessed by dark powers. The wall seemed impenetrable after destroying his best tools.

So the sheriff's peer pressure to test his courage wasn't the only reason Frank decided to help continue the search for Justin. His curiosity was eating him. As a scientist he *needed* to know where that wall had come from and what its composition was.

The challenge lay before him. He wasn't about to back down.

CHAPTER 21

The small battalion of armored skeletons encircled Justin and
Belfry. Belfry sat on his knees near Justin's head. The skeletons
moved closer. Some held swords and shields, while others wielded two-
handed axes.

The wizard raised his staff above his head and mumbled an incantation.
The whites of his eyes turned ink black. The red eyes in his staff glared.
Bluish-white sparks glowed from the wizard's fingertips as the staff
absorbed his magic like a conduit, magnified it, and transmitted the power
back into the wizard.

The elf had misinformed him about a Rana's powers being stronger than
the wizard's. If they truly were more powerful, he wouldn't be paralyzed.

"Do something," Belfry whispered.

"I told you. I can't move."

"You're a Rana. Your magic doesn't require movement. Think it!"

Justin focused on his own hands rather than a direct attack on the aged
wizard. The wizard's seasoned wisdom should sense power sent against
him by a novice and easily cast it aside, only to retaliate with a fervent
vengeance.

Prying apart the steel prisons bars let him know he had phenomenal
strength but as far as what other powers he had, he was uncertain. He had
no training and no idea how to draw upon magic, but he did have strength.

"Thief," the wizard said. "You dare enter my prison and let this drudge free? What purpose does he serve you?"

Justin concentrated on his hands, and his fingers began to twitch. His hands rose and formed fists. The hold the wizard had cast upon him weakened.

The wizard took his staff in both hands and outstretched it before him. He levitated three feet off the ground.

Justin pushed himself to his feet. A fiery burst of strength poured through his muscles. He rushed the nearest skeleton and shoved his fist through the warrior's sternum. Crunching bone splintered. The skeleton fell to the ground in two halves, dropping a shield and sword.

Justin grabbed the shiny shield, spun, and sliced the head off the next skeleton. The wizard was a few yards away. He believed he could stop the wizard, but more skeletons dug their way out of the ground, replacing the two Justin had demolished, becoming obstacles to slow his attack.

Laughter roared from deep inside the wizard. The staff eyes glowed a fevered red, filled with hatred and lust for destruction. Justin felt the warmth of their resentment as they focused on him.

Justin battered another skeleton with the back of the shield, scattering the bones into a cloud of dust. With an upper sweep of the shield, he disassembled another skeleton. Before the bones collapsed, more fingers emerged from the soil, slowly pulling another fleshless minion into battle.

A bolt of blue-white light shot from the staff. Justin blocked the blast with the shield. Belfry took the sword, swung, and split the skull of an advancing skeleton. As the skeleton dropped to the ground, two move clawed their way out of the dirt.

"Get back to the stream," Belfry said.

"I can stop the wizard."

"You know how?"

"No."

"Then we swim further down the channel."

Justin frowned. "Why?"

"Unless you can immobilize him, it's our only option. We're too close to his throne of power. For each skeleton we destroy, two more replace it."

More than two dozen skeletons blocked the short distance between Justin and the wizard, which was over twice the number that had encircled them before. He had enough strength to destroy them, but was he fast enough to reach the wizard before they doubled in number again? The thought occurred to him that the wizard could keep using the skeletons as a distraction and cast a deadly spell his direction.

He slung a skeleton out of his way and ran to the stream where Belfry stood. Belfry faced him, nodded, and dove into the water.

Behind Justin clattering skeletons rushed with their weapons raised. The wizard turned a hundred eighty degrees in the air to face him. His black eyes narrowed. Blue fire shot from the eyes of the staff. Justin jumped into the stream and the strong current sucked him away. The blue bolts of light struck the cave wall. The explosion dropped heavy boulders into the water, blocking the tunnel where Belfry and Justin vanished.

Even if Justin wished to come back this direction, the rocks prevented it.

Forever.

CHAPTER 22

The wizard—the Dark Chancellor—returned to his throne of skulls. His frustration burned through his hands and into the dark staff. He had thought the Rana had invaded his dungeon to drain his magic and steal his staff, but after inspecting his cells, only two prisoners were missing.

Belfry and the boy he had recently imprisoned.

Telepathically, he held council with his staff that enslaved the Ten Sages of Vylan. When he had caged the boy, he had not detected anything except fear. No magic. No power. He certainly didn't sense the presence of a rare Rana in the midst of his prison.

He recognized the boy as the one Elias wished to sacrifice, which was the reason he captured him. Elias was close to succeeding in his pursuit to gain immortality, but the chancellor's meddling destined Elias' failure. The Dark Chancellor never expected Elias to survive one hundred forty years. None had succeeded before him, and if the Dark Chancellor had his way, Elias wouldn't either. He'd keep the boy hidden from Elias.

Without immortality, even magic couldn't prevent Elias' century and a half old body from deterioration. Elias' alacrity to sacrifice the boy would keep him searching until it was too late to find a suitable alternate. Elias' failure was one less problem the wizard had to deal with.

WHILE HOPKINS WAITED with his deputy's corpse, Marshall went with John to get an aluminum raft. Crossing to the tree was difficult enough for Hopkins. The older, skinnier coroner didn't possess enough agility to get across. Besides that, Hopkins didn't want the body to be soiled by the muddy swamp water a second time. It not only made the autopsy more difficult, but it wasn't something he wanted his conscience to dredge up later. Meeks deserved a proper burial with honor and dignity.

He glanced at his watch.

11:35 a.m.

~

MARSHALL HEAVED the small aluminum raft from John's shed where the go-cart had been stored. Layers of dust and cobwebs added an extra pound to the boat's weight. The stench of death gagged Marshall. He held his breath as he set it outside the shed door.

"Something's dead in there," he said.

John closed the door. "Probably rats. I put poison out a few days ago to keep the pests from getting into the feed."

"I've not seen one of these since I was a boy living in Alabama," Marshall said, carrying the raft to the truck. "I fished carp and catfish along creeks in one. Hell, I'd sink this with one foot now."

John wiped sweat from the back of his neck with a handkerchief. "I almost forgot I even had it."

Lib stepped to the door with a pitcher of iced tea and a stack of disposable plastic cups. "Do you mind taking this to the volunteers."

Marshall slid the raft onto the truck bed and smiled. "Happy to."

She brought him the tea and cups and said, "Where you staying tonight?"

He frowned. "I've not made any plans yet. Probably find a hotel room nearby."

Lib laughed. "That'd be a good drive. I'll prepare our spare bedroom for you."

"Ah, now," Marshall said with an embarrassed smile. "Ma'am don't go to any trouble for me."

"No trouble at all. It's the least we can offer in return for you helping find our grandson."

Marshall smiled and nodded. "Thank you."

"She'll have us a big dinner ready this evening," John said. "Cooking keeps her from worrying."

"I hope you find Justin will before then," Lib said. "He's probably starving to death."

"We're going to find him," Marshall said.

~

ELIAS HELD the sharp sickle as the large man struggled with the raft. Weak and drained from the heat and the long walk through the woods, he barely had time to squeeze behind the barrels of dog food so Marshall didn't see him. Killing the deputy and hiding the body exerted far more energy than he could afford to lose. He'd never survive attacking the large man. And even if he won, he'd lose what little stamina was necessary to perform the final sacrificial rites to gain immortality.

Time favored Justin, not Elias.

But Elias refused to accept defeat. With everyone aiding in the search and rescue for the boy, Elias hoped they found him soon. He was too weak to waste time hunting. He'd let them do the difficult work, but he didn't understand how Justin had vanished so easily. Even Elias' familiars couldn't find the boy's scent. It was as if magic had swept the boy away.

After the shed door closed, Elias took a deep breath and slowly exhaled. He nibbled bits of scattered dog food on the floor while maggots fed on his decaying body. His smell no longer bothered him. He had grown used to it.

When Elias channeled his spirit to attack the geologist inside the cave, he noticed a barrier that blocked the path that wasn't there twenty years earlier. The path was now sealed off. Everyone's interest focused on finding Justin inside the cave. He pondered the same question, as did the others. How did the wall get there?

Once the pickup truck drove away, he peered through a slit in the wall. The old woman entered the house, allowing the screen door to slam shut, but she didn't close the inner house door. He smiled. A screen door was a thin barrier even he could get through in his poor condition. His hand tightened around the sickle as he rose from behind the barrels and walked to the shed door.

Elias pushed the door open. The glare of the overhead sun made him wince. He had to hurry across the driveway to prevent the sun from doing further damage to his withered flesh.

~

As John turned his truck through the pasture gate, Eugene followed behind in the Coroner SUV. John drove across the pasture and into the dead woods surrounding the swamp. After he parked, Marshall took the raft out of the truck.

He placed the raft on the black water, and steadied it as Eugene climbed in. Marshall handed Eugene the rope. Hopkins gently tugged the boat to the isle. Hopkins extended his hand and helped Eugene out.

"What happened, Sheriff?" Eugene asked as he straightened his glasses.

Hopkins removed his hat and sighed. "While Deputy Meeks was on watch, they heard a noise. He was killed over there." Hopkins pointed. "And then the killer brought him to the tree and dumped his body in the hollow opening."

Eugene knelt beside the deputy's body. As he inspected the man's slit throat, he asked, "Any blood designs left behind?"

Hopkins shook his head. "No. I don't think he had time. He seemed to want to hide the body quickly."

"I'd guess he died right before sunrise. Rigor mortis is just now setting in."

"That's around the time Meeks left the McKnights and headed this direction."

Eugene looked in the hollow tree and shook his head. "Nothing else really out of the ordinary. But for his throat to have been slit, there's very little blood."

"There's a large pool of blood on the bank over there."

"Let's get his body to the truck before this heat causes him to bloat," Eugene said. "I'll take him back to the morgue. Such a shame."

"The whole situation is," Hopkins replied.

"Do you see any tombstones near the tree?" Marshall shouted.

Hopkins exchanged glances with Eugene. The coroner frowned and walked back to the hollow part of the tree. He took a long stick from the base of the tree and stepped to the edge of the water. A section of the swamp rose higher than the rest. Using the stick like a small rake, he pushed aside a mass of sphagnum moss. A jagged piece of granite poked a couple inches above the black water.

A crude gargoyle was carved at the top, but they didn't see a name engraved.

"This looks like it could be a gravestone," Hopkins said.

"There should be six of them," Marshall replied.

"Six? If there are, they're underwater," Eugene said. "How'd you know?"

"I'll tell you in a while. But twenty years ago, this area was bone dry."

They placed Meeks' body in the raft. Eugene climbed in and positioned himself beside the corpse. Hopkins found a thick heavy tree branch and tied one end of the rope to it. He flung it hard and it landed on the bank near Marshall's feet. Marshall pulled the raft back across while Hopkins waded behind and steadied it so Eugene wasn't tipped over.

John backed the Coroner SUV closer to the swamp to save time. Eugene opened the rear doors and took a black body bag from a side compartment. After they placed Meeks inside the bag and zipped it shut, they placed him on a gurney inside the SUV.

As Eugene closed the rear doors, Hopkins asked, "What did you find out about the blood drawings?"

Eugene shook his head. "Nothing yet. The only similar markings I've found online are Voodoo drawings from the nineteenth century. Nothing more recent than that."

Marshall's eyebrows rose. "What kind of drawings?"

Eugene pulled his digital camera from his pocket, clicked through the photos until he found one, and showed it to Marshall. "I have blown up pics of these at my lab. Much better detail."

Marshall looked at Hopkins. "This confirms that we're definitely looking for Elias."

"You're certain?"

Marshall nodded. "Yes. That's his artwork."

"Do you know what the symbolism stands for?" Eugene asked.

Marshall glanced at his watch. "How about we break for lunch? I'd like to look at the larger photos. If the message is the same as previous ones, I believe we can find Justin's whereabouts and stop Elias before it's too late."

"Eugene," Hopkins said. "Get Meeks' body to storage. Marshall and I will catch up with you."

Eugene nodded, climbed into the SUV, and drove through the dead trees.

"Let's see what supplies Frank needs before we head out."

Jack and Rita watched Frank as he hit the outer wall with a sledgehammer. The rock broke away in chunks. Sweat covered him. His white T-shirt clung to his skinny body. He looked a few minutes away from passing out.

John parked his pickup near the trio and Hopkins got out.

"How's it going?" Hopkins asked Frank with a slight grin.

Frank wiped sweat from his brow with the back of his forearm. "At least *this* rock breaks."

"So you think that spot is past the wall on the inside?"

"It should be. I walked the distance inside and measured it. I'm fairly certain the impenetrable wall is about five feet back to the left."

Hopkins tipped his cowboy hat back. "I can get someone out here with a jackhammer and backhoe to save us valuable time. Since it's an emergency, I think we can have those tools within a half hour."

Frank picked up a bottle of water and chugged it down. Gasping after he finished the bottle, he said, "That would be great."

Hopkins looked at Jack and Rita. "You two need to go get some lunch. We have about thirty people searching the woods, and there's nothing we can do inside the cave until we've made a new opening. Deputy Shannons will give you a call should they find Justin before you get back."

Jack looked at Rita. She nodded.

"But," she said. "We're coming back just as soon as we eat."

"I understand. I'd do the same thing. But with this heat, you need to keep food and water in your system. Doesn't take long to dehydrate and have a heat stroke."

Misty Waters finished talking to a volunteer. Noticing Hopkins, she smiled and headed his direction. Her smile faded as she watched the Coroner SUV drive away.

"You find Deputy Meeks?" she asked.

He nodded. "He's dead."

Misty looked away. "I'm sorry."

"Me, too. He was a good man to work with." Hopkins said. "There's not much more we can do until the heavy equipment gets here." He looked at Marshall and John. "Let's go get some lunch and look at those photos Eugene has."

Marshall nodded. "Sounds good."

"What photos?" Misty asked.

"The blood symbols left behind where Ledbetter was killed."

"What kind?"

"Ritualistic," Marshall replied.

"You mind if I tag along?" she asked.

Hopkins gave Marshall and Frank a questionable glance.

Marshall smiled. "Ma'am, I don't mind at all, but what we'll discuss you might not believe."

"I won't know until I hear it."

"That's true, but don't say you weren't forewarned," Marshall said. Looking at Hopkins, he added, "And while we're at it, see if you can contact Sheriff Douglas. I'd be interested in why he covered up those murders."

Hopkins nodded. "I would, too."

Misty shook her head. "Things keep getting stranger."

Marshall smiled. "Young lady, you don't know the half of it."

"I'm afraid I might not want to know," she replied.

"Again, you've been forewarned."

CHAPTER 23

The underground stream broadened into a harsh river. Justin discovered he could swim and dart through the water like a bullfrog since he evolved into a Rana. Seeing underwater wasn't difficult, either. His transformation gifted him with a third eyelid. A nictitating membrane, he recalled from one of his biology labs.

As the current flowed down and around, he clung to rocks on the side of the channel wall, kicked off, and burst through the water with incredible speed. Belfry, however, could not. He was at the mercy of the current as it battered him against the rocks.

Justin didn't know how far the underground river went before Belfry could come up for air. Justin didn't feel the need to breathe. He was sustaining his oxygen content as well as the bullfrogs around his grandfather's pond when he frightened them into the water. It was an odd sensation to be underwater and not have a fear of drowning.

The stream current spiked downward, slamming Belfry into another rock. A huge air bubble floated from his mouth and his body went limp.

Justin swam harder to catch Belfry. Before he reached him, the channel gushed out the side of the mountain and they dropped with the waterfall into a shallow pool.

Justin waded to Belfry. The dwarf didn't move. He looked lifeless. Justin swam and pulled Belfry ashore beneath dense trees. Belfry's chest rose and fell gently.

Looking around, Justin wondered where they were. The evergreens were massive, blocking the grim gray sky. Faint flickering lightning flashed through miniscule slits in the thick canopy, providing brief bursts of strobe-like light. Thunder rumbled a few seconds later.

The gushing waterfall spilled into the dark swamp. Thick low-growing deciduous shrubs provided dense undergrowth beneath the moss-covered trees. Strange birds squalled. Insects chummed. A constant hum rang in the background with the other noises.

Flashing lights blinked like lightning bugs, only much larger, and deeper in the shadow-rich swamp.

Justin nudged Belfry.

Belfry coughed and water spewed from his mouth. Justin helped him into a seated position against an evergreen.

"Are you okay?" Justin asked.

Belfry opened his eye and shook his head. He blinked several times until his vision cleared. He nodded and placed a hand to his forehead. "I'll be okay."

Justin looked around nervously. "Where are we?"

"The Swamps of Woodnog," Belfry replied.

"Scary place."

Belfry nodded and cleared his throat. "Dangerous territory."

"This is where the two elves said they were banished."

Belfry laughed. "They were to be executed here by bounty hunters, which would have been a better fate than the one they have now."

Justin looked where the waterfall spilled from the mountainside. The drop was over three hundred feet. "How did they get from here to the prison?"

"The swamps are filled with bounty hunters and thieves. The outcasts turn on one another. Perhaps someone traded the two elves to the wizard in exchange for their freedom. Or someone traded them for a spell scroll or to have a curse removed. You'll learn quickly that there are few people you can trust out here."

"All I want is to get home soon," Justin said, sitting down. "My grandfather has cancer. I want to spend as much time as possible with him."

Belfry placed a hand on Justin's arm. "Perhaps this is fate and good fortune that you wound up here."

"How can this be good?"

Belfry smiled. "You're are in a world ruled by magic. Trinkets, spells, potions. There are numerous things you might obtain that can heal your grandfather of his ailment. Seek it out and you'll find it."

"Woodnog. Is it a safe place to go?"

"Depends on your purpose."

Justin studied his mottled frog skin. "I want to find someone who can change me back and get me home. Do you believe that's possible?"

Belfry slowly stood. He shrugged his thick shoulders. "We won't know if we don't go see."

Thunder echoed.

Raindrops fell hard, splashing a pelleting rhythm along the trees, shrubs, and water channels in the swamp.

"How far are we from their town?" Justin asked.

Belfry shrugged. "At least a day? Not quite certain. The swamp has few landmarks to guide you. Could take a week or more if we accidentally walk in circles. Even longer if we have to dodge rogue bandits."

Belfry extended his hand to Justin and helped the frogman to his feet.

"We best get going," Belfry said. "Should complete darkness fall on us, we'll be dead being out in the open. Easy targets. We must find a shelter above the water and away from the roads."

"Roads? There's nothing but water trenches."

"Some of these trenches are patrolled. But since they are waterways, it makes it difficult to discern which are travelled most."

Water sloshed where the trees clung to deeper shadows.

Belfry grabbed Justin and spun him around against the thick tree trunk. He placed a finger to his lips and shushed him.

"A party approaches," Belfry whispered. "Be quiet and follow me, quickly."

Justin nodded. Belfry ducked low and cut through the thick shrubs.

Not knowing what moved through the waterway, Justin followed him. More than anything, he wanted to go home, but now he feared he'd never get out of this strange place. He wondered how his grandfather was and if he'd survive the cancer, or die sooner from worry. He also wondered if he'd survive to see his family again.

CHAPTER 24

Marshall rode shotgun in Hopkins' SUV. Misty, John, and Frank sat in the seat behind them.

"Are the blood patterns left at Ledbetter's body similar to the others you'd seen twenty years ago?" Hopkins asked.

Marshall shrugged. "I need to see the enlarged photos before I can be absolutely certain."

"Based on what?"

Marshall opened his briefcase and removed an aged leather book. "Information kept in this journal."

Hopkins glanced at the worn, cracked cover that desperately needed treated with mink oil. Strange occult symbols were faintly etched across the front.

"What is that?"

"This is Elias' diary from the 1800s," Marshall said.

"How'd you come across that?" Hopkins asked.

Marshall stared out the window. "I doubt you'd believe me if I told you."

"Try me," Hopkins replied.

"Family heirloom."

"What?"

Marshall nodded. "Elias is my great-great grandfather."

Misty slid forward in her seat. "You want us to believe that the person responsible for Pastor Ledbetter and Deputy Meeks' murders is your great-great grandfather?"

Marshall turned in his seat to face her. "I told you this would be difficult, if not impossible, for you to believe. But, I assure you, it's the truth."

Misty slinked back in her seat and shook her head. "That's impossible. He'd be what, over one hundred and twenty years old?"

"Closer to one hundred and eighty years old, Ms. Waters," Marshall said.

"But how?" Frank asked. "How could anyone live that long?"

"He is a Bokor," Marshall said. "A voodoo priest who practices black magic."

John frowned. "His magic has kept him alive this long?"

Marshall replied, "Yes. But at a cost. According to his journal logs, he must sacrifice someone who has a pure soul every twenty years for a total of one hundred and forty years."

"And he also survived a hanging," Hopkins said.

"That's when his evil manifested," Marshall said. "His soul thirsted for vengeance so he pledged his allegiance to a dark being and in return he'd receive immortality. Thus, the sacrifice of an innocent person every twenty years."

"What happens in between those sacrifices?" Misty asked.

"He lies dormant."

"He hibernates?" Frank asked.

"In a sense, yes," Marshall replied.

Hopkins gave Marshall a side-glance. "So this book is how you knew there were gravestones near that tree?"

"Yes."

"Do you think he lay dormant in one of those graves during his absence?" Hopkins asked.

"It's possible."

"Then why didn't you kill him in the grave?"

"If I had this journal earlier, I probably could have. As it is, I came across this a few months ago. My eldest aunt passed away and I found this hidden in her attic. It was buried in a crate full of old books handed down to her by her mother. I doubt she ever looked at it."

Hopkins frowned. "But you could have come out here before this all started. Before Ledbetter was murdered."

"My calculation was off." Marshall sighed. "The way I figured, my dates were off by one twenty year cycle. I thought when Elias abducted Donnie and sacrificed him that he had succeeded in his goal. It wasn't until Justin disappeared and the newspaper reported the pastor's murder that I knew Elias hadn't succeeded. This has to be the final time. We have to stop him now."

"Not to sound farfetched," Frank said. "But could he be responsible for that wall blocking the path inside Devils Den?"

Marshall shook his head. "No. But magic is involved."

"Magic's the one thing I'd never have taken into consideration," Frank said, looking at Misty.

She smiled and whispered, "Me, either."

"Why don't you think he's responsible for the wall?" John asked.

"He'd never trap Justin where he couldn't get to him. The deputy's murder is a sign that Elias is desperately searching for Justin."

"If not Elias, who placed the wall?" Hopkins asked.

"That's a mystery for us to decipher."

Hopkins turned off the highway and onto a dead end paved drive. White plank board fences flanked both sides of the drive. The drive separated into two lanes divided by a grove of tall oaks. A luxurious white farmhouse with an attached side building nestled against a rolling grassy hillside.

"Why are we here?" Marshall asked.

"This is where the coroner lives," Hopkins replied.

Frank scooted forward to get a better view. "I thought we were meeting him at his office."

"His office is the large building next to the house."

"Isn't that a bit creepy?" Misty asked. "Having a morgue connected to your house?"

Hopkins laughed. "That's the general consensus in our county, but Eugene doesn't have many friends."

"I can see why," Frank said.

"His job is his life."

Frank tried to ease the tension of their situation and added, "Of course, he could throw one hell of a Halloween party in the morgue."

Hopkins shook his head and looked at Frank in the rearview mirror. "He's pretty popular around Halloween."

"No doubt," Misty said.

Hopkins parked his SUV near Eugene's vehicle.

Eugene slid open the glass door and motioned them to come inside. He seemed overeager to welcome visitors, which was a sign of his loneliness.

Marshall entered the Coroner Office first. He tucked the leather journal under his arm.

"Here, Marshall," Eugene said, eagerly pointing to a table. "I set the photos out for your evaluation."

"Thanks." He flipped through the yellowed pages with a delicate touch in spite of his huge fingers. Hopkins stood beside him with keen interest. John watched from across the table where he could see the book without getting in Marshall or Hopkins' way.

The book was filled with drawings, symbols, and incantations. The massive tree with the noose was drawn on the first page, symbolic of the genesis of his quest for immortality. A crude stone altar was on another page. One page showed the proper places to insert a knife to kill with minimal damage. Other pictures detailed how to collect the most blood from a fresh killed corpse. Near the end of the book, Marshall found a page with symbols drawn. The same symbols as left on the ground and on Ledbetter's body.

"That's the strangest ink I've ever seen," Hopkins said.

"It's dried blood."

"He used blood for ink?"

Marshall nodded. "His own."

Eugene closed the door that stored Meeks' body. He removed his latex gloves and adjusted his glasses as he peered around Hopkins to see the pages.

"Interesting," he said. "He used his own blood to preserve his incantations. Perhaps he believed that embodied the spells with greater power."

"That's a possibility," Marshall replied.

Eugene gently lifted the book up and touched the leather binding. "That's an odd coloring for leather."

Marshall cocked his head to the side. "Yes, it is. That's probably because he used the skin of his first human offering."

Misty's eyes widened. "Seriously?"

"I'm afraid so. On the seventh page he details the process of how he cured the man's hide."

"Excuse me," she said, placing a hand over her mouth and rushing out the door.

"Did he ever have a soul?" Hopkins asked.

"Filled with venomous evil, Sheriff."

Hopkins studied the picture with the symbols again. "So, what's your interpretation?"

Marshall turned back several pages and counted them. "This is the seventh set of symbols, so I have to assume this is the final sacrifice."

Hopkins looked at the intricate detail of the symbols, as did Marshall. They compared them with Eugene's photos.

Each stroke and brush was identical in every aspect.

Misty stepped back into the room. She was pale.

Hopkins frowned and glanced at Marshall. "He recalled this from memory?"

"I guess so. I had the book."

"Better memory than I could hope for," Hopkins said.

"You mentioned he was a Bokor?" Misty asked, looking through her notes. "In this part of Kentucky and the time period, where would he have learned such magic?"

Marshall folded his hands and said, "Elias came to America on board a slave ship. The ship stopped in a port on Haiti where more slaves were traded. It is here I assume he learned the magic from another slave aboard the ship."

"And the hanging?" Hopkins said. "Was he lynched for escaping or something?"

"No. He and his family had escaped and traveled the Underground Railroad, but that wasn't the reason he was hung. His own family members hung him."

John leaned against a cold metal table to steady himself. The trauma of all the events and the information fatigued him. His hands shook. Misty grabbed a chair and brought it to him.

"Here, sit down," she said. "You don't look well."

"I'm okay," John said, dropping onto the chair. "I'm very tired."

Eugene said, "Why did they hang him?"

"From his sister's journal I discovered that Elias had allowed black magic to rule his heart and mind. He craved power and was willing to do anything to gain it. He sacrificed stolen cattle, goats, pigs, and chickens. But, when he suggested sacrificing his newborn niece, they took action to kill him. He was too obsessed to maintain clarity of mind."

"What happened to the rest of your family after they hung him?" Misty asked.

"They continued their journey through the Underground Railroad until their freedom was finally ordained and proclaimed by the government. But they didn't know Elias had survived."

"He never pursued them?" Frank asked.

"No."

"When we were on the isle with the tree," Eugene said. "You said that there are six tombstones there? Why six?"

"The only conclusion I've drawn is that he made five for his family members that hung and abandoned him. He considered them dead to him. The sixth gravestone was his own."

Hopkins' cell phone rang. It was the machine rental company. He gave directions to the spot where Frank had busted the rock on the side of Devil's Den.

"That's where we need to make an opening. Okay, thanks. We appreciate it." He disconnected the call.

"Good news?" Misty asked.

Hopkins smiled. "They delivered the backhoe and jackhammer and aren't charging any rental fees. They've also volunteered to cut out the opening for us. They want to help find Justin."

Tears formed in John's eyes. He wiped them away quickly. Frank clasped a hand on his shoulder.

"Since we know what the symbolism stands for," Hopkins said. "What do we do next?"

Marshall looked at John. "We need to find Ben. He should be able to provide answers to our questions about what we'll confront in the cave and why the cave sealed off after Justin advanced as far as he did."

John nodded. "We could drive out to his place. But, like I told Sheriff Hopkins, it doesn't look like he's been home in several years."

"How long do you think it will take them to make a new opening, Frank?" Marshall asked.

Frank shrugged. "An hour, maybe longer. They have to reinforce the opening to make certain it won't collapse."

"Then let's go," Marshall said. "We might find some evidence at Ben's house to aid us once we get inside Devils Den."

"Or he may have a map of another cave opening," Hopkins said.

"That would be our quickest route, if such exists."

CHAPTER 25

Justin and Belfry lay flat, propped on their elbows, in the putrid mud beneath thick-leafed shrubs as three dark robed men passed by. Hoods covered their heads, their faces hidden beneath shadow. Curved silver daggers hung from their belts. Bows were slung across their shoulders. The man in the center walked with his sword drawn. Their unison steps swept through the water with cold silence. Had Justin not seen them, he would have never known they were there. Their stealth made them deadly assassins.

Thunder rumbled.

Heavy raindrops pelleted the water and trees.

Belfry placed his index finger to his lips and the pointed to the right at a narrow path secluded between thick evergreens. The low-needled branches offered dense cover and, provided they maintained silence while concealing themselves, they'd be nearly invisible. The ground under the evergreens was firmer, allowing them to move faster, quieter.

The robed men disappeared down the swampy lane.

Belfry pushed himself from the mud and slung fistfuls of sludge into the ankle-deep water. Stooping down, he rinsed his hands and said, "Let's go."

As he walked ahead of Justin, he pulled his long hair back into a ponytail.

"Who were those men?" Justin asked.

Belfry parted evergreen branches as he walked. "Bounty hunters."

"How can you tell?"

"Their daggers are crafted by the Woodnog smith."

Birds fluttered from the thick foliage. A swarm of gnats moved around them like a tiny black cloud.

Justin stopped, waved the gnats from his face while he looked around. "They capture prisoners and return them?"

Belfry turned and glared with his one eye. "No," he said gruffly. "They return heads for gold."

"So," Justin said. "Woodnog banishes people out here only to send hunters to kill them?"

"It's how they train novice soldiers. Return with a head, you move up a rank. Five heads and you're enlisted in their militia."

Belfry began walking again. Justin stepped in behind him.

"Do you know where we are?"

Belfry shrugged. "The area is looking a bit more familiar. We have to stay off the main paths though. We can't afford to be seen by the hunters."

"But are we getting close to Woodnog?"

An arrow whistled past Justin's head and lodged into a tree ahead of them.

"Run!" Belfry said without looking back.

Justin ran, dodging the thrashing branches Belfry released while racing through the trees. The whisper of the next released arrow seemed amplified to Justin. Even with his back to their attackers, and the speed of the arrow, he knew where the arrow was as if watching its path in his mind. He pivoted to the left, the arrow zipped past his head, barely missing Belfry's ear.

"Blast the gods!" Belfry said as he forced his stubby legs to sprint faster.

They ran, fighting their way through stiff, slicing branches. Justin feared they'd never outrun all the arrows, but the layers of spiraling tree limbs shielded them by defecting the wooden shafts. Their pursuers didn't chase on foot because well-fired arrows travel remarkable distances, but that worked effectively in open fields, not in dense foliage. By the time they realized their error, Belfry and Justin were too far ahead to pursue.

As Belfry flailed through branch after branch with Justin ducking switching stings, the path dipped sharp onto a slippery slope, plummeting downward. They lost their footing and slid on dry twigs, leaves, and cones. Justin's descent was a blur. He couldn't differentiate what he passed on his way down.

They landed in shallow water.

Belfry gasped and pointed as he rose to his feet. "The Gates of Woodnog."

Justin stood and wiped water from his face.

"Come on," Belfry said, sloshing through the water.

The gates were crude and ruggedly hewn from enormous trees. From the corner watchtowers two horns sounded. Voices of skirmishing townspeople rose. Armed elves and humans flocked to the entrance.

"They don't look very friendly," Justin said.

Belfry remained silent and proceeded a bit slower to the gate.

The townspeople stared with a venomous gaze. Slowly the people parted enough for a horseman to slither through the crowd. He rode through the gate and down the cobblestone path to them. His heavy, gray hood hid his face.

"Belfry," the man said with an even tone. He drew his sword and stuck the tip against Belfry's throat. "You were warned never to come back except your head be in a bag."

Belfry nodded slightly. "Aye. But I come bearing a gift."

The man chuckled. "And what would that be? You're minus an eye since I last saw you. Are you going to cut off your own head for me?"

The townspeople laughed.

"No," Belfry whispered, pointing a stubby finger at Justin. "The Rana. I've brought him to you for the town's protection."

People in the crowd murmured, some with hope, at the sight of a Rana.

The man spat on the ground and turned to face the townspeople. "The Rana no longer exist! No one has seen one in ages."

"They do!" Belfry said, looking at the gathering crowd. He extended his hand and pointed toward Justin. "There. See?"

The man lowered his sword. "Come here," he said to Justin.

Justin walked and stood beside Belfry. The man studied him for a moment. "He's not a Rana. You've cast a spell over him."

"No."

"Don't lie to me. I sense the magic around him. Not from within, but flowing around him."

"I'm not lying. I swear."

"I'm impressed, Belfry. The quality of magic is more than I could accredit you. Who'd you hire to do the spell?"

"No one. He is what he is."

The man studied Justin carefully.

Belfry stuttered. "He's yours, just spare me. His powers could benefit the welfare of Woodnog."

Justin frowned at Belfry. "You're trying to trade me? You told me that you'd help me get home."

Belfry shrugged.

"Belfry, you should have kept running while you could," the man said, lowering his hood. "You only returned to find death. Unfortunately, the same fate comes to your companion as well. Bind them and take them to the town hall."

Justin's eyes widened when he saw the man's face. "Uncle Ben?"

CHAPTER 26

The houses along the winding road to Ben Whytten's home were abandoned. The overgrown lawns were weedy forests that needed more than a lawnmower to level. A bush-hog probably would suffer damage clearing away the thick growth.

Several houses needed fresh paint; some begged for shingles, and a couple older houses needed a match and fuel to end their misery. Bright yellow "No Trespassing" signs were posted on trees, doors, and at the end of driveways throughout the hollow.

"Doesn't look like anyone lives in any of these houses," Marshall said solemnly.

"Nope," John said. "When Ben bought all the owners' properties, he never rented them out. He left them to nature."

"Odd," Marshall said. "What a waste of houses."

Hopkins nodded. "It's odd that he ever obtained enough money to afford it."

"Are you implying he did something illegal to gain his wealth?" Marshall asked.

"I have no proof that he has. It's just mild speculation on my part. At least until I can question him."

"I've looked for him for years, Sheriff," Marshall said. "But not about property ownership or tax evasion."

"I know."

A pot-holed gravel road picked up where the paved road abruptly ended. Hopkins swerved, missing a deep hole, and quickly kicked in the four-wheel drive as the vehicle edged slightly off the road. The tires spun on loose gravel. The right rear tire left the road. The SUV tilted to the left, sliding, loosing grip.

Hopkins mashed the accelerator. The front wheels dug in and gained enough traction to pull the rear tire back onto the road.

"We're probably the first people to drive out here in months. I don't see any tire tracks and the road looks like a damn war zone," Marshall said, grabbing the handhold above his door as the SUV rocked back and forth. He glanced at the forty-foot drop Hopkins had saved them from falling over.

"I don't think he *wants* any visitors," Hopkins said.

Marshall grinned. "What was your first clue?"

"The road wasn't this bad last winter when Lib and I drove out here," John said.

Hopkins glanced into the rearview mirror. "We had a lot of spring rains that probably did most of this damage."

"But shouldn't the road department repair this?" Frank asked.

"Usually they do," Hopkins said. "But maybe they assume no one is living out here and are waiting until someone complains."

Marshall laughed. "That's probably the case."

The SUV drove around another sharp curve. The road straightened and ascended at a challenging forty-five degree slant. About a hundred yards further up the hillside was Ben's cabin. Hopkins put the gas pedal to the floor. The engine revved as the vehicle jerked forward and advanced up the road.

The house was flush with the mountainside. The driveway vanished into a garage built inside the mountain. Hopkins parked on the level drive and everyone got out.

Hopkins looked at Marshall. "My guess is that he isn't home."

Marshall nodded. "I agree."

"Then what exactly do you want to do?"

Marshall smiled. "We look for clues."

Eugene pushed his glasses against the bridge of his nose. Resting his hands on his hips, he studied the house and the garage opening. A pickup truck set outside the garage. Layers of dirt and grime covered the windshield. Wiping the driver window, he looked through. The keys were still in the ignition.

Eugene chuckled. "He's a trusting soul."

Marshall asked, "Why?"

"Keys are in the truck."

"Anyone who took it might not survive the deathtrap of driving it down the mountainside," Marshall replied.

Eugene chuckled and said, "I'll look around in the garage."

Misty followed Hopkins to the side door of the cabin. He knocked. Hard.

As he guessed, no one opened the door. He twisted the knob and it turned. He pushed the door inward.

"Door's unlocked," He called to Marshall and the others.

John frowned. "I *know* it was locked when we came in the winter."

"Maybe he's been back recently," Marshall said.

Hopkins took a step inside the door and Misty grabbed his arm. "Should you go inside without a warrant?" she asked.

"He's not a suspect. We're looking for any information to help us get Justin out of Devils Den. Besides, John is Ben's brother-in-law. I don't believe Ben would begrudge him for coming inside."

They stepped into the dim kitchen. Strange symbols were drawn on the floor, table, and the window. The musty air held the pungent odor of death. A thick layer of dust covered the furniture and counters. John flipped a light switch but no lights came on.

"Power's out," John said.

Hopkins covered his nose. "Be alert. We may have a body inside the house."

"I smell it, too," Marshall said, rummaging through a stack of mail on the table. "All postmarks are about two years old. I wonder why he's avoiding his home?"

Hopkins shrugged. "I don't know. He has no criminal record or never been in trouble with the law as far as I know. Not even a traffic ticket. Has he made anyone mad, John?"

John shook his head. "Not that I know of. I've never known him to make an enemy."

"He has always been a friendly individual," Hopkins said. He looked at a symbol drawn on the table. A melted ball of black candle wax set in its center. "Do you recognize this symbol? Is it like anything in your book?"

Marshall stared at it for a few seconds and shook his head. "No, it's nothing like the ones left on Ledbetter or at his murder scene. These . . . possess a different origin."

Frank separated himself from the group and entered the living room. He took a penlight from his back pocket and turned it on to look around. More dust, cobwebs, and a smell that indicated the house needed aired out. The light reflected off a silver object.

"What the?" he whispered.

Frank moved closer. A long sword was propped at the corner of a bookshelf. As he reached for the weapon, something gray and furry scuttled across the floor and disappeared under the sofa. It made a wicked chattering sound as it ran. The creature was larger than a rat and almost ball-shaped in the center with four stubby legs projecting out. Though strangely shaped, it moved faster than a cat.

From under the couch it hissed and spat. Frank grabbed the sword and ran toward the kitchen. The ball of fur rolled from the couch and sped for his leg. Trying to avoid the creature because he feared it was going to bite him, Frank lost his balance and tripped over his own feet. He crashed through the glass coffee table, wincing as the air was knocked from his lungs. He rolled over in the shattered glass to keep an eye on his attacker.

The little creature turned, flashed jagged teeth, and rushed at him, sinking its teeth into Frank's right boot. Snarling, it twisted and turned its head as if tearing meat from a bone, but the thick leather was more than it could sink its teeth through.

Marshall stepped through the door. "What happened?"

Frank pointed at the beast chewing on his boot. He kicked and dislodged the creature. It squealed, hit the wall, and dropped limp to the floor.

Marshall pulled his gun and aimed at the furry thing as he approached. He nudged its side with his shoe, but it didn't move. It was breathing. The impact against the wall had knocked it unconscious.

Misty hurried to see what it was. She frowned. "Is it a cat?"

Marshall shook his head. "I don't know what the hell it is."

Frank stepped closer, holding the sword in his left hand and steadying the penlight on the creature with the other. Blood saturated the back of his shirt where he had rolled in the glass.

"Looks like you're bleeding," Marshall said, brushing away loose glass fragments.

"Is it bad?"

Marshall inspected his back and shook his head. "No, looks more like abrasions than anything deep. Your shirt is quite thick."

"Yeah, I still have my caving shirt on. Gets cold inside sometimes."

"Lucky for you."

Misty knelt and reached toward the gray furry creature.

Marshall grabbed her hand. "No. We don't know what this is."

"But it's hurt," she whispered.

"It bites, too," Frank said, showing her the tip of his boot. Shreds of leather hung in tiny ribbons.

"Misty," Marshall said. "Find something to put the little thing in. A pet carrier or a wire cage. I'd hate to kill it since it's something no one's seen before."

She nodded and went back to the kitchen.

"What have you got there?" Marshall asked Frank. John and Hopkins joined them.

Frank handed the sword to Marshall.

"Well, I'll be," Marshall said. He wielded the sword and swung a quick, over the head and downward slash.

Hopkins frowned. "What is it?"

"A bastard sword. *Authentic*. This is *not* a reproduction."

"How can you tell?" Hopkins asked.

"The weight of the metal and the nicks in the blade. This sword has been in battles. Probably centuries old."

Frank said, "Looks like you know how to use it."

Marshall smiled. "Thanks. I've taken some swordsman training with some medieval renaissance groups. But, I've never seen a sword of this quality."

Hopkins looked at John. "Why would he have this? Does he collect old swords?"

John shrugged. "It's been years since I've sat down and talked with him. The one thing I know he loved collecting was insects, which is something that Justin loves, too. He has a massive collection that I was hoping Justin would get to see this summer, but I couldn't get in touch with Ben. Other than an insect collection, I don't know what other hobbies he has. I do know he loved teaching biology at the university."

Marshall said, "The IRS doesn't show any earned income by him in years. When's the last time he taught?"

"Your guess is as good as mine," John said.

"So, your saying there's no record of his employment for years?" Hopkins asked.

"That's correct."

"We passed, what, fifteen houses on the way up here?"

Marshall nodded. "At least."

"Combine the cost of those houses with their surrounding properties. That would be at a rough estimate, well over a million dollars," Hopkins said.

Frank shrugged. "Perhaps he played the lottery?"

"If he did and won," Marshall said. "The IRS would have shown records of his winnings, which they don't. If he had won and owed taxes, they'd be relentlessly looking for him."

"True," Hopkins said.

Marshall set the sword against the wall and pulled open a drawer at the base of a bookshelf. Two silver daggers were wrapped in silk cloths. Several drawstring bags rested to the side of the daggers. He opened one and poured a stack of gold coins into his hand.

"Frank, shine your light on these," Marshall said. Frank placed the narrow beam of light onto one coin. "Very old inscriptions."

Hopkins looked closer. "Definitely not a language I'm familiar with."

"No," Marshall said. "This isn't a language of our world."

Frank frowned. "You're implying he's gone to another world? First magic, now this?"

"Don't scoff," Marshall said. "You have to admit that the cave wall isn't something you've seen before."

"I know, but . . . ."

Marshall looked at Hopkins. "At least we know somewhat more about his wealth. These silver daggers are worth a good fortune. And each of these coins weigh about an ounce each."

Hopkins shook his head. "With the current price of gold."

"Exactly," Marshall replied.

Frank stared at the handful of coins with wide eyes. "If there's another world or realm with this kind of fortune, I want to find it."

Misty came back into the room with a small cat carrier. "I found this out on his patio," she said.

Hopkins crossed the room and took the cage. He unfastened the metal grid door and set the carrier on the floor beside the creature. Marshall used the sword hilt to gently scoot the breathing fur ball into the container. Hopkins closed the door and latched it.

Misty picked the carrier up and stared inside. "He's cute."

"It has teeth," Frank said. "Sharp teeth."

Misty smiled. "What is it?"

"Not an animal in any field guide I've read," Frank said.

"Then how did it get here?" Hopkins asked.

Marshall replied, "Remember you said something about magical portals when we were at the swamp?"

"Yes."

"You may be correct. This creature isn't from our world. Neither are these coins or weapons. He has no need to work at the university or anywhere else for that matter."

"Why would this creature be in Ben's home?" John asked.

"That's something only Ben would know," Hopkins replied. "Now that we have the animal locked up, we need to find the source causing this rotten stench."

Marshall left the living room and entered the adjoining room, which was the dining room. The smell grew stronger.

The bay windows across the room gave a panoramic view of the tree-tops below the cliff. A large mahogany table with claw feet was center of the room, surrounded by ten chairs. On the tabletop were a dozen open insect collection drawers. No butterflies or moths were pinned inside. All the drawers were empty except for the insect labels that had identified each specimen.

John shook his head. "This was his prized collection. I recognize the boxes, but all of his collection is gone."

A dark stain covered the carpet at the far end of the carpet. Frank shone the light on it.

"Blood," Hopkins said. "A lot of it."

~

ELIAS SLOWLY PULLED OPEN the screen door to minimize the sound of the stretching spring. Once he stepped past the threshold he eased the door shut.

Dishes clacked and water ran from the sink faucet. He balanced himself against the wall as he slipped to the door. Lib stood with her back to him as she washed plates and glasses, rinsed them, and then placed them into the drainer.

Elias took careful steps as he crept past the door and headed for the stairs. His vitality diminished with each movement he made, but he wanted to return to the room where Justin had slept the night before. If Elias found a place to hide and rest until the night fell, most of his strength would return. He had to reserve his energy.

Car doors slammed outside the screen door.

Elias hobbled faster toward the stairs, suddenly realizing how little time he had to get to the attic. He doubted he'd survive the climb.

"Mom?" Jack said.

"In the kitchen," she replied.

Elias gripped the stair railing and pulled himself onto the first step. It creaked. He hobbled to the next one, more carefully and without a sound. He took a deep breath and continued climbing. Five steps later, he reached the second floor. The twenty-plus steps that led to the attic were steeper and narrower. There was no way he could maneuver and expend that much precious energy.

He glanced down the hall. The door furthest on the left was open. He limped; dragging his right leg was he walked, leaning against the wall for support. He stopped at the doorframe and panted for air. After a few seconds, with the sickle in hand, he lay down on the floor beside the bed and crawled beneath the bedsprings.

Elias held the bone necklace in his hand and mouthed a healing chant over and over; careful not to utter the words aloud, for fear he'd be discovered. Warmth spread through his body as magic applied modest restoration to his decaying body and masked his putrid smell. The mantra wasn't enough to totally repair his body, but it applied stability to slow the deterioration and sustain him until night set in. Only the final sacrifice granted him an untarnished body, full of vigor and power.

His mind reached for his dark master, for his invigorating touch, but it was like an iron door blocked his access. He felt betrayed. Forsaken. The immortality granted him seemed further away than ever. Especially now. His master seemed to have retreated his blessings and power outside Elias' reach.

Closing his eyes, Elias craved undisturbed sleep and soon surrendered.

CHAPTER 27

$\mathcal{E}$ugene found a Coleman lantern in the garage and lit the wick. The garage went further into the mountainside than he estimated, but he didn't want to explore too far without a better light source or police backup. Although he had a strong stomach when he autopsied corpses, he wasn't exceptionally brave when it came to exploring dark places. After examining Ledbetter's mutilated body, he could assume nothing less than a soulless monster had been the killer. Encountering a ruthless murderer of that caliber wasn't on his agenda. *Ever.*

He had decided long ago to allow the police to do their investigations and apprehensions without him. He'd find the clues the dead bodies revealed and relate the information strictly to help their leads and pursuits, but that was all he could be expected to do.

The cold, stagnant air inside the garage chilled Eugene as he carried the lantern before him. Thick spider webs hung from the ceiling and in the corners and crevices of the carved out rock. Dried insect carcasses were spooled in webbed casings and tucked to the wall.

Square hay bales were stacked beside a small stable. An empty feed bucket and water trough were covered with dusty webs. The stable floor was clean. No piles of old manure littered the ground, which indicated a horse never spent long periods housed inside. But the outside terrain didn't have a place for a horse to graze.

Two old car frames set upon concrete blocks. Tools were strewn across worktables along the left wall. Empty paint cans and rags cluttered the floor. A table in the rear of the garage caught his attention. Stepping closer, he noticed a small furnace, a set of tongs, and several graphite crucibles.

"Interesting," he said.

Eugene set the lantern on the table next to a weight scale. Straightening his glasses, he picked up a rectangular mold and inspected it against the light. Traces of gold dust residue glimmered along the edges. Several draw-string sacks collected dust but held nothing inside.

"I see how you were able to buy all the property," Eugene said softly. "But where did you accumulate all the gold?"

"I'M NOT AN EXPERT," Marshall said. "But I'd estimate the bloodstain is a couple weeks old."

Hopkins nodded. "With that much blood loss, there should be a body nearby."

"I agree," Marshall said.

John followed a narrow trail of dried blood drops and opened a closet door. He covered his mouth and nose with his hand. "The body you're looking for is right here."

Hopkins and Marshall hurried to the closet as John stepped back. The released odor forced them cover their noses, too. A man lay scrunched in the corner with a gaping neck wound. Blood had seeped from his neck and soaked his shirt.

Hopkins turned to Frank and said, "Go tell Eugene we need him in here."

Frank nodded and left the room.

Marshall took a flashlight and inspected the dead man's throat.

"What do you think?" Hopkins asked.

"My guess is an animal bite," he replied.

Hopkins looked closer. "I think you're right. Probably that thing that attacked Frank earlier. Where's Misty?"

"In the living room," Marshall said.

"Misty!" Hopkins yelled, scrambling out of the closet.

"What?" she asked, peering into the dining room. She held the pet carrier.

"Put the carrier down," he said.

"Why? What's wrong?"

Hopkins pulled his gun. "Please, just do it. That creature is what killed the man in the closet."

Misty placed the cage on the floor. "Don't kill it."

He sighed. "I don't want to, but . . ."

"It looks harmless," she said. "It's awake now but doesn't seem aggressive."

"The man in the closet might beg to differ, if he was alive."

"You really think that something that small killed him?"

"I'll let Eugene make that decision after he compares the bite marks on the corpse to the shape of this thing's teeth."

The kitchen door opened. Eugene followed Frank to the dining room.

Eugene looked at the carrier and shook his head. "You found one of Ben's pets?"

Misty replied, "I don't know if it's his pet, but it's something very unusual."

"Don't name it," he said sternly.

"Why?" she asked.

"Once you do, it's harder to kill if we find it necessary."

She pouted her lips and knelt in front of the cage door. "Why would anyone want to kill you?" she said playfully.

Eugene rolled his eyes, straightened his glasses, and walked to the closet as he put on latex gloves. Taking Marshall's flashlight, he inspected the position of the body and moved closer to look at the neck wound.

"I believe he walked here on his own after he was attacked," Eugene said. "Other than the bite, there doesn't seem to be any foul play involved."

"So you don't think Ben was here?" Hopkins asked.

"I can't say that. I'm saying that he walked into the closet on his own freewill and probably died soon after."

"How long do you think he's been dead?" Marshall asked.

"Well, it appears the bottom of the door is flush to the floor, so little insect activity, but from the fluid markings beneath his body, he died in the position we see him. Possibly three weeks? I'll know more after I get him back to the lab. So, let's move him out of here."

Marshall helped Hopkins move the man from the closet. The horrific smell intensified when they lifted him off the putrid pool of body fluids.

Eugene said, "There seems to be some kind of trapdoor here in the closet. It was right beneath where his body lay."

"See if you can open it," Marshall said as they lay Deiko's body on the carpet beside the mahogany table.

"I'm afraid the door is locked," Eugene said.

"Any chance we can pick it?" Marshall asked.

"You could," Eugene replied. "If there was a keyhole. It's locked from beneath. No keyhole. Not even hinges."

Marshall stepped to the closet door and examined the trapdoor. "Odd."

"Very."

Frank looked at the dead man's face and said, "That's Dr. Deiko."

"You know him?" Hopkins asked.

"Not personally. He was a dean at one university in Lexington. He's been missing for a few weeks."

"He's not missing anymore," Hopkins said. "But why would he be here at Ben's home?"

John rubbed his eyes and sighed. "I don't know."

"Now," Eugene said, kneeling beside the body. "Let me look at those bite marks again."

Misty screamed.

Hopkins and Marshall rushed to the living room. She scooted away from the cage and rose to her feet.

"What happened?" Hopkins asked.

She pointed at the carrier. "It's trying to get out."

The little creature screeched and rammed its face into the door. Its yellow narrow teeth fastened around a metal grid wire. It tugged, snarled, twisted. Blood leaked from it gums as it pulled backwards.

While its teeth gripped the wire, Eugene came into the room and eyed the creature.

"I don't know what the hell it is," he said. "But that's Dr. Deiko's killer."

"You're certain?" Marshall asked.

"Those teeth. I have no doubt. That little beast killed him."

It twisted its head to the side. The metal wire bent. It pulled harder.

Misty ran across the room and stood behind Hopkins. "It's going to get out."

"Cover your ears," Hopkins said a few seconds before he fired.

The bullet tore through its midsection, knocking it off the wire door. Its little legs twitched and then it ceased moving.

Hopkins sighed and holstered his gun. "I really hated to do that."

"You had no choice," Eugene said. "Bring it to the table and let's examine it."

Marshall brought the carrier to the table and unlatched the door. He turned the cage upright and allowed the dead critter to roll out.

Misty wiped tears from her eyes. "Other than a nasty attitude, it was a very beautiful animal."

"But not from our world," Marshall said.

Hopkins frowned. "You really think it came through a portal?"

Marshall nodded. "You have a better suggestion?"

"No."

Misty looked at Frank and said, "There's no way I can cover this as a news story without being subjected to a mental evaluation."

"I was thinking the same," he replied.

"Or," Eugene said. "Ben brought it back from wherever it is he has disappeared. I found out how he was able to buy all the property along this ridge."

"How?" Hopkins asked.

"He has equipment in his garage with evidence that he has been smelting gold and producing one ounce bars," Eugene said. Without looking up, he used a pair of tweezers and a dissecting needle from Ben's table to pry open the creature's mouth to see the teeth.

Marshall smiled, reached into his jacket pocket, and brought out a handful of gold coins. "Gold, unique daggers, and a bastard sword. Ben spent years wandering through the cave's passages. So Devils Den has to be a portal to another world or dimension."

"And Justin is trapped inside," John said.

"Why would he bring a creature like this back?" Hopkins asked.

Marshall shrugged. "Perhaps to guard his home."

Eugene nodded. "It proved it could."

"Wait," Frank said. "We couldn't get past the wall that you believe magically appeared. Perhaps someone did it to protect us. What is going to happen once the workers bust through with the heavy equipment?"

"What do you mean?" Misty asked.

"What will we be allowing access to our world?" he asked.

John said, "We have to rescue Justin."

"In a sense," Marshall said. "Frank is right. The path was sealed for a reason and only after Justin stepped past. He's safe from Elias."

"But is he safe where he is?" John asked. "We have no way to contact him to find out. He could be in extreme danger."

"We don't know," Hopkins said. "But if we open the cave, there's no telling what will come out."

John's face flushed red. "That boy needs our help! We cannot leave him in there."

Hopkins took his cell phone and made a call.

Marshall said to John, "Before that new entrance to the cave is opened, we have to find Elias and destroy him."

"You go after Elias," John said. "I'll go find my grandson."

"No point arguing now," Hopkins said, disconnecting the call. "They've already busted a new cave opening. They're re-enforcing the opening, so it's safer for us to enter."

"Then we have to get back quickly," Marshall said. He gazed around the room and sighed. "There's so much more here to look through. Things that will probably help us. Especially if we can get that trapdoor open. There's no telling what kind of items he has stored down there."

Hopkins said, "I agree, but we can come back after we inspect the cave. Eugene, are you staying here with the body?"

Eugene nodded. "You go ahead. My assistant is bringing our Coroner SUV. I'll ride back with him."

Guards bound Belfry's hands behind his back. After he was secured, others came to take Justin into custody.

"No," The man on horseback said as he studied Justin. He frowned and waved them off. "Leave him with me. I have some questions."

The guards nodded and forcefully pushed Belfry through the gates. The angry townspeople jeered at him, throwing rotten food at his head.

When they were gone, the man said, "You called me Ben. Why?"

"You're my uncle."

A smile spread across the man's rugged face. He shook his head, and his graying shoulder length hair tossed side to side. "I don't know you."

Justin nodded. "Yes, you do. I'm John McKnight's grandson. Justin."

"My name is Roble, not Ben," He said, rubbing his beard.

"I've never met you, but I've seen your picture above their mantle. You're my grandmother's brother."

"What is your grandmother's name?"

"Lib," Justin replied.

Roble's eyes narrowed. "Are you a demon?"

"No."

"Then how do you know these things?"

"So it is true? You are Ben."

"If you are who you say," Roble said. "How did you take this form?"

"I don't know. I went inside Devils Den and couldn't find my way out. Sometime later, I became this."

"I would have imagined John to hold stricter rules about the cave. He forbade your father from entering. He should have done the same with you."

"No, he did. I was warned to never enter," Justin replied, looking at the ground.

Roble frowned. "Then why did you?"

He explained about the frog-jumping contest, the giant frog, and the reason he wanted to capture that frog so badly.

Concern furrowed Roble's brow. "John has lung cancer?"

Justin gave a solemn nod. Tears moistened his eyes. "That's why I want to go home."

"I can get you home," Roble said.

"Can you change me back to human?"

"Now that," Roble said. "You'll need to talk with someone who knows more about magic than I do."

"Who?"

Roble smiled. "My wife."

"When could I see her?"

"Soon. But one thing while you're here."

"What?"

"Call me Roble. That's how I'm known here. It's my name."

Justin nodded.

"You need a horse. My estate is a few miles outside town." Roble said as he took the reins and turned the horse around. Justin followed to the side of the horse.

Roble stopped at the gate and said to a boy about Justin's age, "Go to the stables and have them bring me a horse."

Roble handed the boy a gold coin. The boy's eyes widened.

"If you're really quick," he said, holding up two more coins. "You get these as a bonus."

The boy grinned, nodded, and ran down the cobblestoned street.

"As soon as he brings a horse, we head to my place," Roble said. "Perhaps my wife can reveal the source behind the magic that has ensnared you."

Justin looked at the mottle-skinned arms. "Are there other creatures like this?"

"Legend tells of three others that once existed. No one has seen them in a hundred years."

"Why are you living here?"

"I've lived here over twenty years."

"That's a long time. Why not go home?"

"It's a long story, but due to my successful efforts in different battles, Woodnog appointed me as one of their Guardians to protect the township. This *is* my home now."

Justin glanced back to the swamp where he and Belfry had traveled. "Protect it from what?"

"Evil grows beyond these swamps."

"I was taken prisoner by a dark wizard."

"In the cave?"

Justin nodded.

"The Dark Chancellor," Roble said with a grim smile. "But he's nothing compared to what we'll eventually face."

"What do you mean?"

"The Black Chasm is a scar upon this world. An evil sorcerer, Tyrann, rules over it. Each day, the chasm spreads a few inches further, and like a filthy plague, it contaminates and kills all it touches."

"How does Tyrann rule a land where everything is dead? Why would he?"

Roble replied, "He is undead. Any living creature trapped inside the chasm becomes undead beasts. Humans become Soulless Minions—mindless slaves that do Tyrann's evil bidding."

Justin thought of the face in the swampy water and the undead man that had come inside his room. He told Roble about the events, and as he finished, the boy returned with a saddled bay mare for Justin. The boy was breathing hard as Roble tossed the gold coins to him.

Justin climbed onto the mare.

"You saw this undead man?"

"Yes, in the backyard near Grandpa's barn." He explained the dead chickens and the blood pattern left on the ground.

"And when his face appeared in your drawing, he spoke to you?"

"Yes. He said that he was coming for me."

"We best hurry."

"Why?"

Roble nudged the horse's flank to get it moving. "Elias has returned."

"You know who he is?"

"His ties with the Dark Chancellor are known. I almost killed Elias twenty years ago."

"Why is he coming after me?"

"To kill you."

"Kill me?"

"To offer you as a blood sacrifice. He killed one of your father's friends twenty years ago."

"Maybe I'm safer staying here with you."

"You still need to return home. But first, we have to find a way to return you to human."

Justin smiled nervously. "I'd have a hard time blending in with my friends looking like this."

"That would be impossible." A shrewd smile crossed Roble's face. "It's necessary that I kill Elias before he finds a substitute sacrifice. If he succeeds, he gains immortality."

"How do you know this?"

"Torture a demon long enough, he spills his guts . . . literally. Of course, he answers questions during that time, too."

Justin responded with a puzzled expression.

"Don't worry over it. There are complexities that you don't need to understand. Once you're home, you won't have to think of this place again. You'll probably suffer nightmares over it, but nothing more than that."

Justin changed the subject. "What will happen to Belfry? Will he be released to the swamps again?"

Roble shrugged. "The council will decide his fate. He was a fool to return here."

"What did he do?"

"He cheated in a card game by using magic. He's lucky his opponent didn't slit his throat at the table."

"And for *that* he's being put to death?"

"Strict penalties apply to thieves."

Justin straightened on the saddle. "But, he's really not that bad a person."

"You hardly know him."

"He helped me escape the Dark Chancellor."

Roble cocked a brow. "Really? How?"

Justin explained the fight against the skeletons and how they escaped.

"You think that justifies his freedom?"

"Not freedom necessarily. But he shouldn't be killed. Give him some type of punishment that makes him repay the cheating he did."

Roble laughed. "You realize you're seeking to lessen the sentence of the dwarf that was willing to trade you as a slave?"

Justin shrugged.

"And you're okay with that?"

"Punish him, but don't kill him."

Roble rubbed his beard and nodded. "Very well. They'll keep him in stocks until I return. That should make him squirm for a while."

Roble's black horse steadily walked along the narrow mossy path between two green lanes of still water. The mare followed instinctively and without hesitation. As the path turned sharp to the left, approaching hoof beats alerted Roble to stop.

"Quiet," he said, raising his hand. His hand quickly rested on the hilt of his sword. He eased off when three elven riders came into view.

The elf in the center wore a green leather cloak stitched with silver thread. His vest and leggings matched the cloak. His long silver hair flowed down his back like smooth silk. His eyes shone like blue gems, and though older than his companions, age had not wrinkled his face. Confidence rained around him, not of arrogance, but elegance. His aura spoke regality.

His left hand held a tear-shaped shield the same shade of green as his clothes.

The two elfin companions wore tan colors. Bows were slung across their shoulders.

"Odlon!" Roble said as the silver-haired rider slowed and stopped beside him. They clasped forearms. "Any news concerning the Black Chasm?"

"Same as ever. It grows a bit each day. Our troops haven't encountered any Soulless Riders for days."

Roble took in the information and shrugged. "Doesn't mean Tyrann's power has weakened."

"No," Odlon replied. "He schemes. Activity has been building along the eastern border of the Black Chasm."

"An army?"

"Nothing big, but he's taunting us. I think he wants us to venture in."

"That's suicide."

"I know." Odlon peered around Roble and noticed Justin. "A Rana? Where did you find him?"

Roble laughed and introduced them. "This is my nephew, Justin. Justin, Odlon."

Odlon's piercing blue eyes narrowed beneath his frown. "I know you like to jest, but you're no more kin to him than I to this horse."

"He's from the Overlands."

"Ranas have never existed there."

"No. He's human and passed through the mystical caverns. He emerged as this."

"By the gods, how?"

Roble shook his head. "Your guess is as good as mine. To my knowledge nothing like this has ever happened before. Lesser things have occurred by men cursed into lower creatures. But not a Rana."

Odlon gave a slight nod toward Justin. "Good to meet you."

"You, too."

"Are you in a hurry to get back to Woodnog?" Roble asked.

"Why?"

"Accompany us to my estate, if it's not a problem."

"Expecting trouble along the way?" Odlon asked.

"Not really, but since a lot of people have seen Justin and most believe he's a real Rana, you never know what to expect."

"I'd love to ride with you, but with the activity building along the eastern flank of the chasm I need to gather reinforcements. Tyrann may send out scouts soon."

Roble nodded. "How many Soulless Riders did you see?"

"Too much rolling fog and ash to count. It may just be our eyes playing havoc, seeing what we fear *might* be there."

"Or Tyrann's placed a spell on the shifting shadows."

"That's always a possibility." Odlon stared at Justin for a moment and smiled. "Does he know?"

"Know what?" Roble asked.

"About his abilities? Or how much power he possesses?"

"I'm not certain he has any. He may only have the Rana's appearance."

"But if he does possess the power, Tyrann would never stand a chance."

Roble leaned forward and whispered. "Shawndirea can test him."

"Your wife can do that?"

"Better than anyone."

"It's best you get him to her quickly." Odlon stared into the thick tree canopy with an intense gaze. "Before Tyrann discovers this. His spies could lurk anywhere or in any creature."

"Very well. My two sons are in Woodnog. Take them to the Black Chasm to help stand watch."

Odlon studied Roble's face before he replied. "Are they ready to enter combat?"

"Of course they are. I trained them with swords and axes. You trained their archery skills."

Odlon smiled evenly. "I know how well they wield weapons. But what about mentally? Are they ready to shed blood without a second's thought? With the Soulless Ones, there's no time for hesitation. And the gods forbid whatever other creation that Tyrann will hurl our direction."

"Pawl and Bleys won't let you down. They've drooled over the chance to raise arms against Tyrann."

"I will insist on their coming then," Odlon said.

"As soon as Shawndirea deciphers the magic behind Justin's transformation, I will join you on the front lines."

Odlon extended his hand and shook with Roble. "Be well, my friend."

"Likewise."

CHAPTER 29

As Hopkins drove through John's pasture, the man driving the backhoe shook his head as they passed.

Marshall glanced at Hopkins. "He didn't look too happy."

"No," Hopkins replied. "I wonder if they had problems."

He parked the SUV near the cave. Two men stepped out of the opening with hammers. Several crossties were stacked outside. A crowd of volunteers stood around a fold out table grabbing snacks and canned drinks. The heat of the day had weighed harshly on them.

Deputy Shannons met Hopkins. "Sheriff, we've searched for hours, and we've had no luck at all. No clues that Justin wandered anywhere else than into the cave. What do you want us to do?"

Hopkins looked at the crowd of disappointed volunteers. "Folks, thanks for coming out and helping search for Justin. I'm afraid he's trapped inside the cave, so there's nothing more you can do. You're more than welcome to stick around while we search the cave. I know many of you are tired and hungry and have other obligations that need met, so going home is okay. Thank you all."

He looked at Shannons and said, "You can head home, too."

"Are you giving up?"

"Hell no. But you've worked a lot of hours the past two days. Go get some sleep. Come back later if you'd like."

Shannons nodded. "Okay."

Hopkins approached the torn wall. A man with "Earl" stitched on his badge said, "We did what we could, but there's rock in there that our tools cannot bust through."

Hopkins looked at Frank. "Are you certain you measured the proper distance?"

"Absolutely."

Frank walked past the two men and entered the opening. To the left of the hole was the rock slab exactly where he had estimated it to be. He walked straight ahead and said, "I'll be damned!"

"What's wrong?" Marshall asked.

"Another wall, just like that one," he said, pointing. "That's the first wall we came to inside the cave where Justin's footprint is cut in half."

"It was the damnedest thing," Earl said. "We cut through the rock. A cool breeze flowed out. We returned with a pallet of crossties and there stood that wall."

"It just appeared?" Frank asked.

"I swear. We had a clear opening, and then it disappeared. None of our tools can cut into it. It's too expensive to keep trying."

"I lost some of my tools, too," Frank said.

John stared at the wall and closed his eyes. He clenched his jaw and fists in frustration as he leaned back against a tree. "We're never going to get him out, are we?"

Hopkins sighed. "We're doing our best."

John pushed off the tree, turned, and walked away. His shoulders slumped, admitting his defeat. As he shook his head, fighting tears of desperation, he wobbled and nearly fell.

Another worker said to Hopkins, "With your permission I have some men bringing dynamite."

"Ask John," Hopkins said. "It's his property."

John turned around and nodded. "Do it! Blast that damn wall the hell out of here."

Earl said, "They should be here in a few minutes."

Marshall sighed, looking at the sun disappearing in the west. "We have an hour of daylight at best," he said.

"I know," Hopkins said. "What do you make of this?"

"The second wall?"

Hopkins nodded.

Marshall looked at the aged book in his hand. "Nothing in these pages would give us a clue as to why the cave doesn't allow us access. My guess is that someone or something doesn't want Justin to leave. Maybe it's for his protection, or maybe there's an ulterior reason."

"John is at wit's end. He's pale and tired, but I don't think he'll go home to rest," Hopkins said.

"Can you blame him?" Marshall said.

"No."

Frank shook his head as he joined them. "I've never seen anything like this. I never believed in magic, either. But something other than coincidence is at play here."

Marshall said, "I told you."

Misty approached Sheriff Hopkins and said, "I think I'll drive out to the Coroner's Office and wait for him to return with Deiko's body. Then I'll going to drive to Lexington to work on the news story of his death. Please call me at this number when you find Justin."

"I will," Hopkins said, taking her business card. "What will you report about this?"

She stared at him with nervous eyes. "I can only tell viewers that he's still missing. I'd ruin my career if I reported what's really going on."

Hopkins smiled. "I have to be careful how I write up my reports as well."

As Misty turned to leave, a hint of disappointment shone in her eyes.

Hopkins cleared his throat and said, "Will you come back to do a follow up on Justin's story tomorrow?"

"I plan to. Why?"

"Maybe I could buy you lunch then?"

She smiled. "Sure, I'd love that."

"Be careful," Hopkins said as she walked to her news car.

A truck turned off the dirt road into the pasture.

Earl said, "They're here. Sheriff, you might want to get people cleared out of this area."

"Certainly."

LIB POURED fresh coffee into mugs. Rita and Jack sat at the table.

"We need to head back to the cave," Rita said.

"I know," Jack said.

Lib looked at her son. "You're still bothered about Devils Den, aren't you?"

"You know," he said. "Until today, I really thought I had buried all that fear. I had pretty much locked it away. Then when we had the flat on the way here, and Justin helped me change the tire, we heard this savage cry in the woods. It wasn't an animal. Thinking about it now, I believe it came from the man that took Donnie. It wasn't until you called us about Justin disappearing that my fear returned. It crept back faster than I expected and overwhelmed me."

"If the cave makes you that uneasy, you don't have to go back up there," Lib said.

"No, Mom, I want to," Jack said. "I just feel useless once I get there."

Rita placed her hand on his. "I will go up and see how things are coming. Surely, they've cut a hole through so we can get inside. Justin is probably starving and scared."

"The sheriff thought my brother Ben could help, but I can't get in touch with him," Lib said.

"When's the last time you've seen Uncle Ben?" Jack asked.

"It's been a long time. A very long time."

A loud, thundering boom shook the ground.

"What was that?" Lib asked, standing.

"The sky's too clear for thunder," Rita said.

Jack stood. "It sounded like dynamite."

"We should go check it out," Lib said.

Rita grabbed the car keys as Jack and Lib followed her out the side door to the car.

JACK LET RITA DRIVE. Inside he quaked with nervous fear. He'd thought he had erased the memories, but now they seemed more vivid than ever. The fear on Donnie's face as the undead man wrapped an arm around his friend's neck and pulled him away. Donnie was too scared to scream or beg for help. The cold evil eyes of the undead man made him shiver. His deep solemn threat not to intervene or Jack was next seemed like words spoken seconds ago. He swallowed hard.

God, how he wished he had done something. Anything. Anything except run. But he did run, barely able to breathe as he watched over his shoulder, running, tripping, pulling himself back to his feet, running again, getting farther and farther away from the creature. From Donnie. His cowardice not only diminished the chance Donnie could be rescued, it shrank Jack's dignity and ate at him. He had failed to help Donnie, and Donnie was gone. Forever.

Jack's hands tightened into fists as they turned off the dirt road and entered the pasture. Anger burned inside him, slowly overcoming his fear. He might have failed Donnie, but there was no way in hell he'd do the same for Justin. One way or the other, he'd help find his son. He would not allow cowardice to conquer him a second time.

Rita parked behind Hopkins' SUV. Clouds of dust settled around the cave opening. As Jack stepped out of the car, Frank cursed and shook his head.

Frank said, "Like I thought, the dynamite didn't scratch that wall."

"So he's trapped?" Rita asked as she came closer.

Hopkins removed his cowboy hat. "I'm afraid for now, he is."

Jack walked through the chunks of rocky rubble and falling dust and pressed his hands against the cold wall. The dynamite didn't even heat the strange elements that structured the wall. Not one small fragment of the wall had chipped away.

Jack turned and Marshall stood behind him.

"What do we do now?" Jack asked.

"We need to destroy Elias before this night ends, before he has a chance to sacrifice another."

"My mother mentioned Ben and that you're looking for him?"

Marshall nodded. "We have been to his house. Found some interesting things and a dead body, but no clues that help us here. At least not yet."

"Whose body?"

"Frank identified him as a college dean that 's been missing for a while now."

Jack stared at the wall again. "So Elias is the one who took Donnie?"

"Yes."

"How do we find him?"

Marshall sighed. "He shouldn't be far. This is the area where it all started, and I imagine he doesn't have the strength to travel great distances."

"Should we try again to find Ben?" Jack asked.

Marshall looked at his watch. "No. Sun will be setting soon. Nightfall is the best time to find Elias."

"Why?"

"Cooler temperature. Darkness enables him to prowl without being seen, too."

"I want to help, ever how I can," Jack said.

"Can you shoot a gun?" Marshall asked.

Jack nodded.

"Good. I don't have to tell you how dangerous he is. He killed the pastor and an armed deputy, so you have to remain alert."

"I know."

Rita grabbed Jack's hand and squeezed. "Do we need to wait here?"

"There's nothing coming or going through these walls," Marshall said. "We'll be wasting time if we continue. It's best we return to the farmhouse and wait. Since he wants Justin, he may attempt to find him there."

"But what about Justin?" Rita asked. Her eyes narrowed.

"We have to find another route into this cave system," Marshall said. "I have a hunch we'll find that at Ben's house."

"Why?" Jack asked.

"Your father told us that Ben spent a lot of time in the cave. He has probably mapped out the tunnels, and my guess is that since he owns the entire ridge along Boykin Hollow, there must be an entrance to the tunnels on that property as well."

"But you don't know?" Rita asked.

"Nothing is certain," Marshall said. "But rest assured, I won't stop looking. I won't give up."

Jack extended his hand and Marshall shook it. "Thank you, sir," Jack said.

"Let's get back to the farmhouse and set up a perimeter. We have to find Elias tonight."

~

ELIAS' eyes opened when the house shook from the dynamite blast. The kitchen door opened and slammed. The Lexus drove away.

He peered out from beneath the bed. The house was getting darker. Sunset wasn't long. He crawled closer to the wall and lay in a fetal position. His strength was growing. Left undisturbed a few hours more, and he'd have enough energy to stalk the night. He possessed a few more magical tactics that he hoped he didn't need to use until necessary. They were a last resort because the power drain was possibly more than his body could sustain.

CHAPTER 30

Roble and Justin rode their horses around a narrow path. Between two massive trees Roble stopped his horse. Deep green moss covered decaying logs and rocks all along the forest floor. Thick thorny vines with purple flowers hung from the trees. A scent sweeter than jasmine filled the air. Hundreds of brilliantly colored butterflies, unlike any Justin had seen, fluttered and drifted from flower to flower. The masses of butterflies were like spectacular curtains hanging from the trees and reminded him of the Monarch butterfly migration in Mexico he had watched on the Discovery Channel.

More butterflies puddled in wide circles near the gentle, flowing stream. Other than the gentle flow of trickling water and the pattering whisper of delicate butterfly wings, the forest spoke with no other sounds.

"I wish I had my butterfly net," Justin said softly as a lavender-colored butterfly drifted past him.

Roble turned with narrow, angry eyes, and shook his head. "That hobby isn't something you dare bring up in this realm. Understood?"

Justin shrugged. "I guess? But why?"

"You'll learn soon enough."

"How far to your house?"

"We're here."

Justin looked around. "You live in the forest?"

Roble dismounted and said, "Come with me."

The two towering trees held widths as wide as Giant Sequoias. Roble took the reins of his horse and walked to the trunk of the right tree. He spoke words that Justin didn't understand. A slight click sounded. Seconds later part of the tree opened, revealing a wide door. Two men stepped out and took the horses, went back inside, and the door sealed shut behind them.

Roble turned to the other tree and spoke similar words. A smaller door opened. He motioned Justin to follow. Once he entered, the tree door sealed shut.

They descended a hundred steps down a spiral staircase, which seemed to take forever in Justin's mind. At the bottom of the stairs they entered a large room. Shelves carved into the walls were lined with leather bound books. Old books. Lit candles burned softly on tables, in sconces, and from hanging holders.

"How long have you been married?" Justin asked.

Roble smiled. "Over twenty years."

"What's your wife's name?"

"Shawndirea."

"And you never told Grandma or Grandpa?"

"No."

"Why not?"

"I have my reasons. It's a long story. One we don't have time to discuss right now."

"Do you have kids?"

Roble nodded. "Three. Two sons and a daughter. You'll meet Erin soon. She's about your age. My sons are Guardians of Woodnog and will soon leave with Odlon to patrol the Black Chasm."

"Roble? Are you home?"

"Yes, dear," he replied. "Come meet our guest."

"We have company?" Shawndirea asked from the adjoining room. "Who?"

"It's a surprise."

Shawndirea graced the room. Her face held radiance that glowed as bright as a moon pool. She stepped with pure elegance and finesse. When her eyes met Justin's, he gasped. Justin never suspected his uncle's wife to be a faery. He always imagined fairies to be miniscule creatures, but she stood near the height of his uncle.

Her wings were magnificent, covered with what he thought to be jewels. The brilliant iridescence illuminated even in the dim candlelight. As she moved further into the room, dozens of butterflies flittered around her and some returned to their perch on her wings.

She studied Justin with keen interest. "A Rana? Where did you find him? None have been seen in almost a century."

"Shawndirea, meet my nephew, Justin. He's from the Overlands."

She looked from Justin to Roble and back to Justin again. Her eyes narrowed as she stepped closer. "Your nephew?"

"Yes. He passed through Devils Den and came out in this form."

Shawndirea pursed her lips and walked around Justin. "Odd. I perceive *his* magic, but not the magic of whoever cast this upon him."

"So he has powers?"

"Weak ones presently, but in time, they will grow stronger."

When she stepped around him and stared into his eyes, Justin said, "I just want to go home. I don't want to be like this."

Roble walked to the long table. "Let's sit."

After everyone was seated, Roble said, "So he has the magic of Rana in him."

She nodded.

"How?"

"I don't know. I've never known any sorcerer or sorceress to cast such a powerful spell on a human and for what purpose except to manipulate an unscrupulous scheme? I need to consult with my mother about this."

Roble rolled his eyes and shook his head. "Must she be involved?"

"She'd know better than I would," Shawndirea said, cocking one brow. "Besides, with the Black Chasm growing, we don't know what purpose someone has to make your nephew a Rana. It may be another ploy of Tyrann to gain more power."

"Perhaps, but she's not the only person that could decipher the source or reason."

"She's the best authority not tainted by an obsessive need for magic. I know you're not fond of her."

"*She's* not fond of me," Roble replied.

With a narrow smile, she said, "She's not happy about my choice. That's all."

"We've been together more than twenty years and she still cannot accept you marrying me."

"She's more disappointed that I renounced my position to rule by marrying a human. I was next in line for the throne. She's bitter that my cousin, Dirk, will replace her."

"Politics."

Shawndirea smiled, shook her head, and stared at Justin. "Tell me, what happened while you were inside the cave?"

Justin explained how the tunnel he had followed abruptly changed and when he tried to exit the way he had entered, nothing remained the same.

Shawndirea glanced at Roble. "Did you ever experience anything like that when you explored those tunnels?"

"No. Someone has cast a spell on those caverns."

"The Dark Chancellor?" Justin asked.

Shawndirea said, "How do you know about him?"

"He took me prisoner," he replied and explained how he eventually escaped. "Do you think he made the tunnels change?"

"Doubtful. If he had, it's unlikely you'd have escaped the way you did or that easily."

Looking at his webbed fingers, Justin asked, "How can I change back to human?"

"That's something I will have to ask my mother."

Roble said, "We don't have a lot of time."

"No, we don't," Justin said. "My grandfather has cancer. He told me that he has six months to live. I want to go home."

"Let me speak with my mother. It won't take long. The magic cast over you may only last while you're here. If you return to the Overlands, it is very possible you'll become human again."

Roble smiled. "And if that's the case, I can have you home quickly."

Justin's eyes widened. "I don't want a confrontation with that wizard again."

"There are other routes to the surface," Roble said.

"But what if I'm stuck like this?"

"Don't lose hope," Shawndirea said. "*Never* lose hope."

Shawndirea stood and a swarm of butterflies circled around her.

"How long will you be gone?" Roble asked.

"No more than a couple hours," she replied. "Have Erin show Justin around our home. She'll enjoy the company and meeting her cousin."

"Erin!" Roble yelled.

Shawndirea extended her arms and summoned power from the earth. Green light shimmered beneath her feet, slowly building, growing, until the radiance flashed around her, forcing Justin and Roble to shield their eyes. When the light vanished, so had she.

Justin lowered his hands from his face. Across the room stood a young lady that left no doubt that she was Shawndirea's daughter. Her facial features were almost identical but younger. The most radical difference was her lack of wings. She had slight arcs, delicate projections, but not the fullness like her mother. Erin's wings appeared wilted, damaged.

Roble introduced her to Justin.

She responded with a shy nod and smile.

"What is he?" she asked, looking at her father.

"He is human, just temporarily altered into this Rana form," Roble replied.

"Why?"

"Your mother left to see if she could find out. Show Justin around."

"Okay," she said.

"Justin," Roble said. "Are you hungry?"

"Starved."

"While you and Erin get acquainted I'll find you something to eat."

Erin smiled as her father left the room.

"This is my favorite room," she said. Her voice was cute, slightly elevated. "It's where all the books are."

"I like to read a lot, too."

Several small butterflies glided around before finally seeking rest on Erin's shoulders.

"Those are the most unusual butterflies I've ever seen," Justin said. "There were hundreds around your mother earlier."

"Of course," she replied. "My mother's the Butterfly Queen."

Justin frowned. "Not sure what you mean."

"Butterflies, when their wings are old and worn, seek her out. She gives them new wings so they can live longer. She's their protector."

"We have butterflies where I'm from, too. We have some pretty ones, but nothing like the ones I've seen here."

"I know. My father told me. He also told me that people where you're from like to kill them by cramming needles through their chests and viewing them in glass boxes. That's so savage."

Justin took a quick breath and looked away.

"I mean," she continued with anger rising in her voice. "How could someone be so cruel to one of the most beautiful creatures in the world?"

"I don't know."

Erin gave him a stern look. Though smaller than he, her temper made her seem so much bigger. She frowned, pointed her finger, and asked, "Would you do something that horrible?"

"No," Justin said nervously, shaking his head. In his mind, he thought and swore to himself, "*Not anymore. Never again.*"

"Good," Erin said. "Because if you would, you might as well do the same to me. Butterflies and fairies are somewhat related. And I'm part faery, so . . ."

"Really?"

"Yes," she said, pointing back toward her wing nubs with her thumb. "Don't you see my wings?"

"Of course," Justin replied. "But I always imagined fairies to be so much smaller. Well, about the size of a butterfly."

"Normally, we are," she said. "And we probably would be except my mother fell in love with my father. Of course, she was tiny, and to marry him, she had to sacrifice some of her faery qualities. Size was one, and there are other things but my parents won't discuss the details. Said that I *have to be older.* Typical of parents, I suppose. But whatever else she gave up, my grandmother is still ticked about it."

"Why are your wings . . . ."

"So small?" she asked with narrow eyes.

Justin nodded.

"Mother's not certain. She thinks maybe they'll eventually grow to equal hers, or because I'm part human, they may just stay this size. Neither of my brothers have wings. They never complain about it because I believe they *like* blending in with humans. Not me. I want wings just like my mother's."

"What do you like to do besides read?" he asked.

"Oh!" her eyes widened. "I have a horse! Want to see him?"

"Sure."

"Let me tell my father first."

Erin hurried to the other room with several butterflies flying after her. Justin released a long sigh. He was thankful he was at her home and not his for their first meeting. He didn't want to imagine what wrath would explode from this feisty young faery once she discovered his insect collection and his lie.

Until he met Erin, he had never felt guilty about collecting butterflies and moths. Now, he understood Roble's warning not to mention butterfly collecting. And once he returned home, his days of collecting butterflies and moths were over. Just from the few minutes of conversation with his cousin, he would never view a butterfly as a coveted prize for his collection. He'd see it for what it was. A blessed creation.

CHAPTER 31

Dusk settled around the McKnights' farmhouse. Whippoorwills called from the shrubs, answered by a desperate owl in the far distance. Katydids, crickets, and cicadas added to the chorus with the chirping background of bullfrogs and toads.

Since there wasn't any way to get through the walls of Devils Den, Frank packed up his gear and headed home after eating dinner with the McKnights. Sheriff Hopkins promised to return in a couple hours after he checked in at his office and met with the deputies that had volunteered for night duty. He also hoped to get in touch with former Sheriff Douglas.

After dinner was over, Marshall sat in a rocking chair on the front porch while John glided back and forth on the porch swing. A Browning 12 gauge shotgun lay across his lap.

Marshall had changed out of his suit into a pair of John's overalls, which were tight around his shoulders and crotch, but not overly uncomfortable. However, the pant legs were well above his calves. He cleaned his fingernails with a pocketknife while rocking.

Looking across the front lawn, Marshall said in his deep voice, "It's been a long time since I've done this. Just sit out and listen to the night. Hell, I was probably a boy the last time I sat and enjoyed the sounds of nature."

John forced a smile, trying to hide his inner heartache. "I've lived here all my life, but it wasn't until I turned my business over to Jack and retired that

I truly enjoyed life. And now, with Justin gone, I'll never have inner peace again before I die from this cancer."

Marshall spun the rocker and faced John. "Mr. McKnight, I'm a man of my word. I never make idle promises. We're going to find your grandson. It might not be as quickly as you or I want, but we're going to find him. But, Elias needs to be eliminated first. That way, we know Justin will be safe."

John nodded. "I know that's what you said, but I can't stop worrying about him."

"I understand your heartache. Any good parent or grandparent would feel the same way. If those magical walls are there because someone is trying to protect Justin, they may disappear after Elias is killed."

"And if they don't?"

"We'll find a way. I want to go back to Ben's home and see what other information we can find. The fact that he's been making gold bars and has weapons with unfamiliar markings is a good indication he has found access to some other place *not* on our maps."

Lib pushed open the screen door. "Marshall?"

He turned and said, "Yes, ma'am?"

"I wanted to show you your room before it gets much later."

Marshall stood and smiled. "Okay, but I'll probably be up most the night."

She gave a feeble smile. "I wish I could, but I'm exhausted. I have to sleep some, though I'm certain it won't be restful."

"Yes, all of you need to get some rest. Don't worry, Sheriff Hopkins is returning with a couple of deputies. We'll watch the house while you sleep. This is probably the last night Elias will seek a sacrifice."

He stepped to the door and held it while she went back inside. He followed her through the living room and up the stairs. She grabbed a pillow from a closet and an extra sheet. Handing them to Marshall, she turned and walked to the last room on the left.

Heavy footsteps down the hall aroused Elias. His eyes opened quickly. As he had hoped, his energy had increased.

He slid away from the wall and peered out to watch the open door. The footsteps thudded closer. The old woman wore slippers that scratched the floor as she walked. Someone else was behind her. She paused at the door and flipped on the light switch.

The instant light made him squint. Tears leaked from his eyes. Pressing his hands against the box springs, he waited. She stepped aside and a large man entered the room. His hands were full. Rushing an unexpected attack, Elias believed he could kill the man before he had time to defend himself.

~

MARSHALL ENTERED the room with the sheet and pillow in his hands. As he headed to the bed, something scratched the bottom of the bed.

He tossed the sheet and pillow at the bed, reached for his gun, and said, "Move, Lib! He's in here!"

Lib ran out the door.

Marshall pulled his gun and clicked off the safety. Elias shoved the mattress and box strings upward. Before Marshall squeezed off a round, the mattress struck his right arm and shoulder. The impact knocked the gun from his grasp and it slid across the room and under an oak dresser. Marshall fell backwards, catching himself against the wall.

Elias gnashed his teeth and growled. He rushed Marshall.

Marshall grabbed Elias' forearms and spun him around. Elias bared his teeth, opened wide and tried to bite Marshall's neck. The stench of Elias' breath choked Marshall, making him gag. Marshall shoved him away, releasing his arms. Elias toppled back, his feet slipping on the hardwood floor. He was in the hallway before he mastered his balance and ran.

Marshall dropped to the floor and reached under the dresser to retrieve his gun. By the time he grabbed it and ran to the door, Elias was at the stairs. Lib was nowhere in sight. He aimed and fired.

The bullet ripped through Elias' shoulder. He roared in pain and staggered down the steps. Marshall ran. As he rounded the top of the stairwell, Elias was hobbling through the living room. Marshall aimed, but didn't fire. Lib screamed in the living room.

Jack grabbed Lib's hand and pulled her behind him. He held a 9 mm but was hesitant to fire.

"Move!" Marshall yelled. "Jack, get out of the way!"

Jack and Lib moved from the living room into the hallway where Rita stood.

Elias was no longer in view.

Marshall ran downstairs with his gun held against his side. He turned, positioned the gun with both hands, aimed, and fired. The bullet struck Elias. The slug appeared to have crippled his left leg.

The screen door slammed shut. Elias limped across the porch. Marshall tore through the living room and flung open the door, ready to fire again.

A loud shotgun blast reverberated on the porch. The pellets struck Elias in the back and propelled him over the porch rail. The undead man screeched in pain, then mumbled words in a language Marshall didn't recognize. John stood beside Marshall with his shotgun raised to fire a second shot.

Marshall aimed as Elias' dropped to the front lawn. He squeezed the trigger, but Elias's body rained down like a dense dust cloud.

"What the hell?" Marshall said. "He disintegrated."

John lowered the shotgun. "I see that. Is he dead?"

"I don't know."

Marshall stepped off the porch with his gun pointed at the ground. He eased near the spot where Elias had vanished. No bone or ash. Nothing.

"Dammit!" Marshall said. "We had him! But there's no trace of him."

Marshall turned on a flashlight and held it against the side of his gun as he scanned the ground. John nervously glanced around the yard.

"He shouldn't be far away," Marshall said.

He and John backtracked to the porch while searching through the darkness for Elias. The faint porch light didn't project far enough to aid them, but Marshall didn't want to leave the view of the others. He was there, not only to kill Elias, but also to protect the McKnights. Stuck in the thick hedge was an object that he had overlooked while running after Elias.

Elias' left foot.

Other than the foot, there wasn't any other sign of Elias. No sounds that gave away his position.

Lib stood on the porch with Jack and Rita. Her face was pale and her hands shook.

"It's okay," Marshall said. "He's gone. At least for now."

Lib nodded abruptly. She looked like she was agreeing, but her head shook so badly, she was seconds from passing out.

"John," Marshall said. "Help Lib get to a chair."

John took Lib's hand and led her to the rocker.

Brittle chunks of mossy clay crunched under Marshall's feet.

"Looks like I'll have to sweep the porch again," Lib said.

"This has been here before?" Marshall asked.

"Yes."

"This was left by Elias," he said.

Her eyes widened. "You're sure?"

"Had to be, if you have already swept the porch."

"This dirt and moss was also in Justin's room."

"When?"

"The same morning Justin disappeared."

Marshall frowned. "Which room is his?"

John pointed up and said, "In the attic."

"Mind if I check it out?"

"Not at all."

Headlights brightened the porch as Hopkins pulled his SUV down the drive. A deputy followed behind in a squad car.

Hopkins approached the porch. "What's everyone doing out on the porch?"

"He was here," Marshall said.

"Elias?"

"Yes."

"Did you kill him?" Hopkins asked.

Marshall shook his head. "No, but he left something behind. Follow me."

Hopkins glanced back at his deputy and motioned him to come along.

Marshall pointed at the decaying foot. "I must have clipped his ankle with one shot as he was running away. The rest of his body vanished."

"Vanished?"

"He exploded into a cloud of rotten dust would be a better way to describe it. But his foot was dismembered before that happened."

Hopkins said, "Deputy Shannons, get some gloves and take this to Eugene for evaluation."

John looked at the foot and said, "We should have a box if you need one."

Hopkins smiled. "That would be good." He glanced at Marshall and asked. "So Elias is gone?"

"For now, it appears so. But I have the suspicion he's lurking nearby. Lib informed me of something we need to investigate in Justin's room."

"What?"

"Apparently, Elias has been in Justin's room."

"How does she know?"

"The mud on the porch was also in his room."

Hopkins replied, "She showed me the path of muddy tracks on the porch. The same was at the scene of Ledbetter's murder. We sent samples from both places to a lab for comparison, but I wasn't aware any was in his room."

"Since Elias was up there, we need to check it out. Just in case."

"I agree."

"Sheriff, would you happen to have a UV light in your vehicle?"

"Yes. Why?" Hopkins lowered his voice and asked, "You want to check for blood?"

"The timeline is too narrow not to."

"Let me get it."

CHAPTER 32

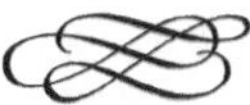

Shawndirea's spell not only transported her outside the Faery Queen's throne room, it shrank her to faery size. Two guards bowed slightly before turning and opening the doors.

Shawndirea glided through the throne chamber. Her mother stood on an open balcony overlooking the green forest floor below. The overhead canopy blocked the harsh sunlight. In her hand she held a square crystal mirror. Her gaze into the opaque mirror was so intense she never noticed her daughter step beside her.

"Troubling news, Mother?" Shawndirea asked.

The words jarred her mother as if awakening her from a trance. She smiled weakly. Her eyes were dull, worried.

"Shawndirea," she said with a tired voice. She hugged her daughter, pulled back, and smiled. "Good to see you."

"The mirror. Is there trouble?

"Nothing that concerns you, dear," her mother replied as she passed her hand over the crystal to break the visual connection.

"Whatever it is has you concerned. That makes it my business, too."

"You renounced your right to the throne for a human, and yet you consider my problems yours?"

"Mother, I didn't come to argue."

"I'm surprised you come here at all."

Shawndirea rolled her eyes and turned away. "Must you hold a grudge after all this time?"

"Our Kingdom needs you."

"I've never left."

"You gave away your claim to the throne for a human."

"Does that make me any less your daughter?"

Istrell gazed into Shawndirea's eyes. She placed the mirror on a table and sighed. "No."

"Dirk isn't a bad choice for the throne."

Istrell shook her head. "He *isn't* you."

"He will always have my council, if he chooses to call on me."

"He won't. He's too stubborn and pompous to ask for help of any sort."

"You exaggerate."

"Do I?" she said sharply. "Things are changing within our world. Dirk is not the cousin you grew up with. He's changed, and not for the better."

"It's been a long while since I've seen him."

"You're not missing anything."

"He's become that bad?"

"I'm old, Shawndirea. I force myself to live to prevent him from taking the throne. If you were still heir, I'd have released my spirit a few years ago."

Shawndirea picked up the mirror. It remained cold to her touch. She focused on the flat black crystal. Nothing happened.

"Your magic fades," her mother said.

"Nonsense."

"Your human husband weakens your connection to the earth."

"Roble is a wonderful man and a loving father."

"He's human. He cannot undo all the damage his kind has inflicted upon the earth, no matter how good he is."

Looking at the mirror until the black crystal shimmered, Shawndirea said, "What did *you* see in the mirror?"

"Evil is growing."

"The Black Chasm?"

Queen Istrell nodded. "Yes. You see it, too?"

Shawndirea stared at the mirror. Images of dark shifting fog swirled, but she was unable to see through the veil. "Yes."

"The more territory Tyrann claims, the more his power increases."

"Woodnog is preparing their forces to counterattack."

The queen smiled bleakly. "It won't be enough."

"Perhaps Hoffnung will ally with us?"

"No," Istrell said. "They have to fortify their position. The Black Chasm grows outward from all sides. No other cities or towns can spare additional troops."

"It will take a united front to stop Tyrann," Shawndirea said.

"It will take far more than that. Now, I know you didn't come to discuss feeble war tactics or accepting your destiny as the next queen. Why are you here?"

"Roble's nephew came through Devils Den. He wants to return home."

Istrell shrugged. "What prevents him?"

"The cave path altered after he travelled inside. His way back was sealed."

"So? Roble knows other ways to the Overlands. I know you do, too."

"But that's not the only problem. His nephew was transformed into a Rana."

Istrell's eyebrows rose. "You've seen him?"

"Of course."

"Can you sense his magical abilities?"

"He has a magical aura surrounding him. But, I have no knowledge of what it's like to be in the presence of a real Rana since I've never encountered one."

"Are you sensing the magic of the caster instead?" Istrell asked.

"No. That eludes me."

Istrell took the mirror from her daughter. "This may be what we need."

"Are you implying he attempt to defeat Tyrann? He's only a child in a Rana's body."

"But harness his power . . . ."

"Mother, he's still a boy and not mentally keyed to endure such a battle."

"What other reason would there be for him to be transformed?"

"What insane person would cast such a powerful spell on someone so young?"

Istrell frowned and pointed a withered finger. "Careful, dear."

"You?" Shawndirea asked with wide eyes.

Istrell looked away.

"How could you?"

"Tyrann has to be defeated."

Shawndirea shook her head. Butterflies flitted into the air and spiraled around her. "Mother, you've overstepped your bounds, placing a spell like this over a child."

"I had no other choice. He is still innocent at heart. Grant those powers to an adult and their lust for authority and wealth tarnishes their soul. Their greed corrupts them."

"This is a hypocritical move on your part. As much disdain as you hold toward humans, you chose him because you believe humans are expendable?"

"No."

"Justin wants to go home. That's the desire of his heart, which contradicts your aspiration for him. His grandfather has cancer and a few months left to live. That inner conflict makes him weak and unfit to train."

Tears filled Istrell's eyes. She turned and walked to the balcony. "Then let him leave."

"Will he return to normal or do you need to remove the spell?"

"The spell only works while he is in the Underworld."

"We will find a way to stop Tyrann."

"His kingdom grows more each day. Everything we hold sacred is endangered. I fear we're running out of time."

Shawndirea placed a gentle hand on her mother's shoulder. "If Roble and his men could have killed Tyrann when the chasm was first created, this chaos would not exist."

"Roble is bold. I'll give him that."

"He's the only one that survived."

"I know." Istrell smiled at Shawndirea. "Did he ever tell you how he escaped death?"

Shawndirea shook her head. "No. He won't talk about what happened. He holds too much guilt for their deaths."

"I watched the battle in this looking glass," she said, holding it out. "No blood was shed once they got past the guards at the bone gates."

Shawndirea frowned. "How did they die?"

"The black air that looms around Tyrann's fortress is toxic. Worse than anything humans have produced in the Overlands. Roble and his twelve men had found a breach in one of the fortress walls. A black gaseous cloud drifted from the grayish moat, settled around them, and choked them to death."

"I thought they were attacked by demons."

"No. Tyrann never even called on them."

"And Roble? How did he escape?"

"He never told you?" she asked.

"No, Mother. How?"

"A crystal portal. He probably had less than a minute to live before the toxic air killed him. I projected a portal, grabbed his arm, and helped pull him through."

"He didn't recognize you?" Shawndirea asked.

"Dear, he was barely conscious enough to crawl through the portal."

"And you've never revealed to him that it was you who saved him?"

Istrell shook her head. "No. And don't you tell him, either."

"Why not? Why keep this animosity between you?"

"It will always be there."

"It doesn't have to be."

"Of course it does."

"Why?" Shawndirea asked. "He doesn't think ill of you. He stays distant because of how you've always treated him. If you told him about this, you could remove the wall between you."

"I cannot. Doing so means I condone your marriage."

"Then why did you save him?"

Istrell lowered her gaze. "Because he makes you happy."

"That can't be the only reason."

"It's all I'll confess to."

Shawndirea laughed, shaking her head. "You're impossible."

"They know I'm old. Some believe I'm too old to reign and it's time to pass the throne to Dirk. Maybe so, but they'll never rumor I'm soft on humans."

"Mother, it's highly unlikely anyone would have you removed from the throne."

Istrell sadly shook her head. "You're getting out of tune with the earth, my dear."

"No, my powers are still strong."

"I never implied they aren't. But, listen to what the earth is saying. The Black Chasm is spreading its poison. Some of the Sidhe have drawn tainted magic from the earth without realizing it, and they are no longer allies. Tyrann is drawing them together to wage war against us. That's why I placed the spell on Roble's nephew. Although I was unaware he was the one to be enchanted by the spell."

"How could you not know he was enchanted?"

"I hung the spell to fall upon the first innocent venture to pass through the cave. Race and age didn't matter."

Shawndirea embraced her mother. "I must tell Roble that Justin can return home. I wish there was a way this could help our cause against Tyrann, but Justin isn't the proper one to lead this battle."

"Perhaps you're right."

"There has to be a way to stop him," Shawndirea said.

"There is no other way."

CHAPTER 33

Elias wasn't certain where the spell had transported him. Darkness surrounded him. He was weaker than ever. Jagged throbbing aches centered in his back, shortening his breath. The pellets had embedded in his flesh with some burrowing deep enough to damage lung tissue.

Pain shot through his left leg like burning fire. He grabbed his left calf and discovered his foot was gone.

Filled with dismay, he closed his eyes. Even if he managed to sacrifice Justin, he didn't want to gain immortality with only one foot. He had to retrieve the appendage and magically reattach it, provided he could. He had never suffered injuries during the past six sacrificial periods. Until now, he had never failed, but he feared that was his imminent outcome.

Elias focused his attention on Devils Den and reached with his mind to find the Dark Chancellor. No connection stirred. A cold veil blocked him. He pushed with his mind again, harder, but still came up empty. The chancellor was avoiding him.

Losing hope that his master would aid him in his despair, he searched the area around the farmhouse to find his foot. At the front of the house where the shotgun blast had ripped chunks of flesh from his back, two men stood at the hedges, pointing at his foot. A few seconds later, another man put it in a box and headed to a vehicle. Elias followed with his mind's eye until the man got inside the car. When the engine started, Elias focused his spirit through the window and kept his attention on the cardboard box.

Elias' spirit rode with the officer to the Coroner's Office. Once there, he crept alongside the deputy to see where the box was being taken. A man wearing glasses eagerly accepted the box and the deputy quickly left.

The man studied his foot while Elias drifted around the room, making interesting discoveries of his own. Seconds later, he was back inside his body.

He rubbed the bone necklace between his thumb and index finger, chanting a spell over and over. His time was over, unless his magic obeyed his commands.

～

HOPKINS SCANNED the UV light across Justin's desk, chair, and bed without finding any trace of blood.

Marshall pointed at the large muddy thumbprint that had dried on the butterfly spreading board. "He was here."

"There's dried mud on the chair, too. But if Elias was here, why didn't he kill Justin then?"

"Not sure. My guess would be that he was waiting for a more opportune time outside the house or the moon wasn't in its proper phase yet."

Marshall stepped to the window and peered out. Along the edge of the window seal was a partial handprint. He lifted up the window and shone his light on the trellis. The rose vines were bent and broken in places. Some of the dying leaves were wilted.

"He came up the trellis," Marshall said, lowering the window.

"He did a lot of traveling for someone that has a deteriorating body."

Marshall gave a slight nod. "Yes, but he's staying close to the farmhouse now. That's the biggest sign that he's desperately searching for Justin."

"And the cave has made it impossible for us to find him."

"Exactly. Someone wants Justin protected."

"Who? Ben?"

"Could be. There are a number of unknown possibilities."

Hopkins rubbed his chin and said, "A great number of unknown dangers, too. With the strange animal Ben had in his house, I'd hate to run across an unruly creature that's any larger."

"I find it fascinating."

"Why?"

"Another world, full of creatures and people we've never seen."

Hopkins shook his head. "I am quite satisfied with what I know,

Marshall. Never been fond of exploring outside my home county. I have everything I need and want here. I certainly don't want dangerous animals and undead people burrowing their way up into my comfort zone. If Justin didn't need rescued, I'd never do one thing to reopen Devils Den."

"I don't think we'll have to."

"God, I hope not. What's your plan?"

"We watch the farmhouse tonight in case Elias returns. Once daylight comes, we go back to Ben's house. I believe we'll find some clues that will enable us to get to the place Justin is. I also want to see if we can open that trapdoor."

"I don't want to imagine what might be on the other side of that door."

"If we can open it, I volunteer to go down first."

Hopkins smiled. "No argument from me."

"Were you able to contact Sheriff Douglas?"

Hopkins looked troubled. "Not directly. I did talk with his daughter."

"Does she know where he is?"

"Yes. That's part of the problem."

"What?"

"He's in a nursing home and suffers from severe dementia."

"Damn," Marshall said. "So he probably doesn't remember anything from all those years ago."

"That's how I took it."

Marshall frowned and nodded before he said, "I'm going to walk around the farmhouse one more time before we secure the house and wait it out."

"Okay," Hopkins said, glancing at his watch. "I'll have Lib make us a pot of coffee. It will be a long night."

EUGENE RECEIVED the box from the deputy. He didn't act a bit surprised when he found Elias' foot inside. He was more intrigued than anything else.

The gray skin was splotched with little abscesses, scabs, and moldy patches. He removed a peeling flake of skin with a pair of tweezers and placed it on a glass slide. After placing the slide on the microscope tray and adjusting the ocular, he studied the tissue at the highest magnification. Weaved within the skin cells were long green filaments that he didn't recognize immediately. He backed away from the microscope and frowned.

Eugene grabbed the data analysis sheet for the dirt samples from his desk. The clayish material was composed of decayed plant matter. The moss was identified as sphagnum. With a quick Internet search he obtained a microscopic photo of sphagnum, which was a match for the green filaments in Elias' cell slide.

"Interesting," he said, returning to the microscope.

He looked at the slide again. The cells were still attempting to divide. The green strands were attached to the human cells in various places and appeared to be pumping sustenance through tiny fingerlike projections.

"Symbiotic relationship? That's damn impossible."

Looking again, he had no choice but to accept it as fact. Cells that should have been dead for decades were still undergoing mitosis. It had to be the science behind the magic that was making Elias able to live for well over a century.

Eugene flipped open a lab notebook and scribbled down his observation. Midway down the page, he stopped writing. Metal clanged behind him. A tray of dissecting instruments clattered on the floor. He turned to see Ledbetter's corpse traipsing toward him. The laceration pattern Elias had carved on the man was outlined by faint green growth. The same moss filaments attached to the skin cells in the microscope slide.

Ledbetter staggered forward, his dead eyes dark and unblinking.

"Dear God!" Eugene exclaimed, running toward the doorway.

One of the refrigerated drawers thudded. A second later the door where he had placed Meeks' body popped open. Meeks pushed against the sides of the unit and slid the tray he laid upon came out the storage door.

Ledbetter changed direction, walking for the door.

Eugene paused at the door and looked back. Meeks picked up Elias' foot. Ledbetter was coming after Eugene but at such a slow speed, the coroner could walk and escape. Although he had never believed in magic or given Voodoo much validity, something from the dark, mystical realms was at work.

Not owning a gun, Eugene did the only thing he knew. He ran for his car, hopped in, and drove away. He guessed Hopkins was still at the McKnight farm, which was only a few miles away, so that's where he'd go. He knew a lot about death, but he didn't know how to kill something after it came back to life. Perhaps the sheriff or Marshall knew a way to destroy these undead people.

～

FRANK STOPPED his truck alongside the narrow back roads. He stared at the starry sky and shook his head. Under his breath, he berated himself for excusing himself and fleeing from what he had promised he'd see to the end. He turned his truck around and headed back. He might not be able to help them get through the wall, but he could help protect the McKnights.

~

CLIFFORD LAY IN BED, trying to sleep. James was on the bunk above him, and Zeke was in a single bed across the bedroom beneath a window.

"Wonder what really happened to Justin?" Clifford said.

"A monster ate him," Zeke replied.

James leaned over the edge his bunk. Looking down at Clifford, he said, "Don't worry about it. You're safe here."

"But," Clifford said softly. "What if it gets us?"

"Don't be a baby," Zeke said. "It's not going to come out here."

"How do you know?" Clifford asked.

"Cause it lives in the cave," Zeke said. "That's why it took ol' city boy."

"We don't live that far from the cave."

"Just go to sleep, you big baby," Zeke said, throwing a pillow at him.

"I'm not a baby, Zeke!"

"Go to sleep, Cliff," James whispered. "Things will be better tomorrow."

Clifford sobbed.

"See?" Zeke said. "You're crying. Just like a baby."

"Leave him alone, Zeke," James said.

"Or what? You know I'll put a whipping on you, James. I've done it before."

James said, "Yeah, just wait until Mom and Dad get home. He'll use the belt on you again."

"You best not say a word if you know what's good for you."

James lay down and stared at the ceiling.

Clifford cried quietly.

Something scratched the window screen. Zeke sat up and swung his feet off the side of his bed.

"You hear that?" Clifford whispered.

"Yeah," Zeke replied.

A shadow moved across the window.

Clifford pointed and screamed. "It's outside! Don't let it get us, Zeke!"

Zeke ran across the room and into the hall. He pulled the door closed

209

behind him, holding the doorknob tight. Clifford grabbed the doorknob and tried to turn it. Couldn't.

"Zeke!" Clifford wailed with a tear-choked voice. "Open the door and let us out!"

Glass shattered.

"Zeke!"

Zeke held the door closed. His eyes were shut tight. His body trembled and for a few moments, he heard nothing due to the fear consuming him. When sounds became audible again, his two brothers cried with muffled screams as they were forced out the window.

Zeke convulsed with heavy tears and sobs. He held the door so tight his hands hurt. Finally, he let go and slowly pulled open the door to look inside their bedroom. Nothing moved or breathed. He flipped on the bedroom light.

Clifford and James were gone.

~

ERIN SMILED when she introduced Lily to Justin. Lily was a spectacular horse. Her coat was the color of a snow leopard and extremely soft. Her eyes were glass bluish-white She whinnied gently when Justin petted the side of her head.

"She's beautiful. Do you ride her much?" he asked.

Erin held an apple in her hand for Lily and said, "Some, but only if my father accompanies me."

"You think he'd let us now?"

She shook her head. "No. It's dark outside."

Justin looked around the stable. "We're underground. How can you tell?"

"Being a faery, the earth lets me know."

"So you can't ride after dark?"

Erin shook her head. "The forests are dangerous enough in the daytime. Much worse after dark."

"I hope your mother has good news when she returns."

"You don't like it here?"

"No, it's not that. I think the area is beautiful. But my grandfather is sick, and I really like being human more than what I am right now."

She laughed. "Do you feel different?"

"Not really. Not until I see my reflection at least. My eyes are too big."

"Have you done magic?"

Justin smiled. "Some."

"That's new for you?"

"Yes."

"How does it feel?"

"It's hard to explain, but it feels good. I felt this warmth rush through my body."

"I know. I love that."

"So you do magic, too?"

"Since I was able to walk."

"I couldn't imagine doing that all my life."

"It's second nature for us."

"What are you able to do?"

Erin looked away. "I'm not permitted to say."

"Oh."

She led Lily to the stable. "We should get back in case my mother shows up. Especially if you want to return to your home sooner."

∾

EUGENE CALLED Hopkins on his cell phone.

"Sheriff, we have a situation."

"What's wrong?"

"Pastor Ledbetter and Deputy Meeks are still alive."

"What?"

"They're like Elias."

"Zombie-like?"

"You could say that."

"Where are you?" Hopkins asked.

"I'm driving to the McKnight farm. You are still there?"

"Yes."

"Good. I should arrive in a few minutes."

"Did you have a chance to examine the foot?"

"I did a tissue slide. What I discovered is a bit unusual, to say the least."

"The whole situation here is disturbing"

Eugene slowed his vehicle as he rounded a sharp curve. "There may be more than magic involved with Elias' ability to live all these years."

"How's that?"

"His human cells have somehow developed a symbiotic relationship with the sphagnum moss. The moss feeds the human cells."

211

"How is that possible?"

"Technically, it shouldn't be possible at all."

"So magic is also involved."

Eugene chuckled. "I'm not a fan of magic, nor do I intend to become a believer. However, with all the events we've seen the past couple days, I have to accept there are things outside science that even I cannot dismiss. How are things on your end?"

"Marshall has patrolled the outside of the farmhouse. We're all inside locking doors and windows."

"So no more signs of Elias?"

"Not yet."

"Keep an eye out for when I arrive. I don't want to be stranded outside."

"We'll be watching. Blow the horn when you pull in just in case."

"Okay."

Hopkins said, "Elias lost his foot, but he also suffered a shotgun blast to his back. Marshall believes he sustained sizeable damage, which may prevent him from emerging again tonight."

"That may be," Eugene replied. "But, Deputy Meeks took Elias' foot."

"I wonder why?"

"Ask Marshall. He seems to know a lot more about the situation than we do."

"I will."

"Ahh, I see the McKnight mailbox. I'm turning in the driveway now."

"Come to the side door."

Eugene parked behind the Lexus. Hopkins swung open the door and stepped down to the drive. He held his gun at his side while watching the drive and side buildings. Eugene hurried around his vehicle and ran into the house.

Hopkins latched the screen door. He peered out a few more seconds before shutting the inside door and locking it.

"There's coffee in the kitchen," Lib said to Eugene.

"Thanks, ma'am. I think I'll pour a small cup."

Hopkins followed him into the kitchen. Marshall sat at the table, carefully flipping through Elias' journal.

"Tell Marshall what you told me," Hopkins said.

"About the foot?"

Hopkins nodded.

"Deputy Meeks took Elias' foot."

Marshall looked up from the book. His eyebrows rose. "Meeks has resurrected?"

Eugene shrugged. "Yes, and so has Pastor Ledbetter."

"Damn. How long ago did this happen?"

Eugene looked at his watch. "No more than twenty minutes ago."

Marshall glanced at Hopkins. "We have to find Meeks and get back that foot."

"Why?"

"Elias may not be able to gain immortality without it."

"So he had Meeks take the foot?"

"That's a fair assessment," Marshall said. "They are under his control."

Eugene seated himself at the table. "Neither of them walked very fast."

"Hopkins and I should head back to your office," Marshall said.

"You don't think Elias will try to attack the McKnights?" Hopkins asked.

"Why would he chance anything without his foot? Besides, we find Meeks, we'll find Elias."

"How?"

"Meeks is under Elias' command. He'll take the foot to Elias and that's how we're going to find him."

Eugene sipped his coffee and said, "What about Pastor Ledbetter?"

"I'm not sure."

Hopkins' cell rang. "Hello? What?"

He quickly disconnected the call.

Marshall read the concern on Hopkins' face. "What's wrong?"

"Zeke just called the dispatcher. Both of his younger brothers were taken by what he described to be a living corpse."

Marshall stood, closed the book, and quickly checked the clip in his gun. "We have to hurry. If he gets back his foot, he'll sacrifice those boys instead of Justin. We have to find Meeks and those boys."

"How do we kill them?" Eugene asked.

"We'll figure out something," Marshall said. "Our best bet is killing Elias. The other two are controlled by his magic. Kill Elias and they should drop where they stand."

CHAPTER 34

Shawndirea returned home.

"So what did you find out?" Roble asked.

"Where are the children?" she asked.

"Erin took Justin to the stable to see Lily. Why?"

"They don't need to hear what I have to tell you."

"Bad news?"

"Not necessarily. That's not to say you won't be upset by it."

Roble replied with an even smile, "Try me."

"Justin can return home anytime. When he does, he will be human."

"How did she determine that?"

Shawndirea shook her head. "Specifics aren't necessary."

"*How* does she *know?*"

She closed her eyes and released a long sigh. "She is responsible for his transformation."

"What?" he asked with anger in his voice.

"She didn't intentionally cast the spell on Justin."

"You saw him. How can that not be intentional?"

"The spell was cast months ago. Justin simply stepped into where she hung it."

"What reason did she give?" he asked.

"She wants to stop Tyrann before his power and territory increases any further. She believes a Rana can stop him."

"Justin is too young to face Tyrann."

Shawndirea nodded. "I told her that."

"Why did she cast such a spell to begin with?"

"Some of the Sidhe have been affected by Tyrann's magic. So not only are the humans, dwarves, and elves being corrupted, the faeries are, too."

"I wasn't aware."

"She's keeping it as quiet as she can, but her concern is valid. She'd never have placed such an incantation if she didn't deem it necessary."

Roble sighed. "Your mother would have more support if she'd join counsel with Woodnog."

"I know, but her pride is too much for that."

"Sadly, her pride is what will destroy her Kingdom."

"I fear that she doesn't have much longer to live. The toll of the Black Chasm has worn her down. The stress has aged her tremendously."

"After I take Justin home, I am to meet Odlon at the edge of chasm. Our sons will be there."

Worry creased Shawndirea's face. "They volunteered?"

"They've begged to go for months now."

"Their eagerness can be dangerous."

"Odlon will keep an eye on them. He certainly won't send them into the chasm. This is just patrol. Not an attack."

"Our sons are men," she said, wiping away a tear. "I have to accept that."

"They'll be an asset in preserving what we know and love."

"We all have to fight for what we believe in."

Justin and Erin walked into the room.

"Good news, Justin," Roble said. "You can go home."

"When?" he asked.

"We'll leave in a couple hours. I have to get some things together first."

Justin smiled. Erin looked disappointed.

FRANK SLAMMED the brakes hard enough for the truck to skid sideways. Smoke billowed from the rear tires, and the smell of burnt rubber drifted on the air. At the edge of the road the headlights brightened the walking dead man as he carried two boys through the ditch. The boys' muffled screams barely rose above the truck's engine.

The light allowed Frank to see the carved symbols across the moving corpse's midsection.

"Ledbetter?" Frank said. "How?"

Ledbetter had each arm wrapped around a boy. He clamped a hand over each of their mouths. Even though the boys struggled to get loose, they didn't have enough strength to break free of the corpse's grip.

Frank flipped the headlights to bright, striking Ledbetter in the eyes, but the brightness didn't make him flinch. Ledbetter continued walking closer to the truck, dragging the boys along with him.

Frank recognized the two boys from Harper's Grocery earlier in the day when Hopkins had admonished them.

He assumed Elias was somehow responsible for Ledbetter's strange resurrection, but Marshall would know more about that than he did.

Had Frank not known about Elias or the undead phenomenon that defied science and logic, he would have thought these boys were being dragged home by a drunken, half-naked parent. He'd have stopped to rescue them anyway, but for different reasons.

He put the truck in park, grabbed his backpack, and searched for his gun. Once he found the 9mm, he clicked off the safety and loaded a round into the chamber. Stepping out of the truck, he aimed and then hesitated. The last thing he wanted to do was accidentally shoot one of the boys.

The older boy, James, shook his head violently and freed his mouth from the Ledbetter's hand.

"Kill him!" James shouted.

Frank's hands shook. He tried to steady his aim, but he couldn't. He had always shot paper targets. Never at a human. Undead or not, this man was still human.

"Shoot him!"

The dead man's eyes were glazed over, covered with a white film. If he could see at all, there was nothing that indicated he did. Frank had no choice. He'd have to make a headshot. Nothing lower or he risked hitting one of the brothers.

"He's not alive," Frank whispered to himself. "He's not alive."

He steadied his aim and fired. His shot was wide to the left. The sound of the gun blast brought no surprise to Ledbetter's corpse. He continued his slow march.

Staring down the site, he fired a second time. The bullet struck the man in the center of the forehead. The impact slung the man's head back and a large hole exploded through the base of his skull.

James yanked himself free and reached for Clifford. He pulled Clifford away as Ledbetter's body slumped and dropped into the ditch.

"You boys okay?" Frank asked.

They nodded.

"Get in the truck. I'll take you to Sheriff Hopkins."

They never hesitated. They ran out of the ditch and rushed through the open driver-side door.

Frank's hands quaked. It took a couple minutes for him to click on the safety. After he slid the gun behind his belt, he climbed into the truck. His heartbeat thudded hard against his chest. Clenching the steering wheel tight, he took a couple of deep breaths.

"Are you sure you're okay?" he asked.

"Yes," James said.

"How about your oldest brother? Is he okay?"

Clifford sobbed heavily as he said, "He's the reason that man got us."

"What?"

James nodded. "When the man came through our window, Zeke ran out of the room and held the door so we couldn't get away."

Frank frowned, put the truck in gear, and drove down the road. "You're okay now."

Hopkins' SUV sped around Frank's truck with the lights flashing. Frank pressed the horn and flashed his lights off and on. The taillights of the SUV brightened as Hopkins stopped.

Frank parked behind the SUV and got out.

Hopkins rolled down the window. "Frank, I thought you were headed home."

Embarrassed, he nodded. "I was, but I decided to come back. I have to see this out, too."

"Good," Hopkins said, smiling. "We're headed to the Butler house. Two of the boys were abducted by Ledbetter's corpse."

"I know. They're in my truck."

Hopkins's eyes widened. "Really?"

"I rescued them from Ledbetter. His body is in a ditch a quarter mile back."

Marshall leaned across the seat. "Where did you shoot him?"

"In the head. I had no choice."

Hopkins glanced at Marshall. "Is that enough to prevent Ledbetter from getting back up?"

"I believe a headshot should be sufficient."

"What do you want me to do?" Frank asked.

"Take the boys home. I'll radio a deputy and them him you're on your way. Their parents returned home a short time ago."

"Then what? You want me to go to the McKnights' farm?"

Hopkins nodded. "That would be good. Eugene is there. We're going to the Coroner's Office, and then we'll head back to the farm, too."

"Okay."

Marshall said, "Nice shooting."

Frank smiled. "Thanks."

ELIAS CLASPED his hands over his chest when the bullet ripped through Ledbetter's head. He gasped for air. Choking, he sat up in the darkness and clutched his throat. The pain slowly subsided, but for those few moments, it was as painful as losing his left foot. In his case, a magical arm had been severed because he had leashed his power into Ledbetter. When that link was instantly broken the backlash smacked to his inner core, weakening his power.

He searched with his mind for Meeks. The deputy still possessed Elias' foot, but regaining the appendage wasn't enough. Without the proper sacrifice his long journey to claim immortality was soon to be over, and he no longer had enough time to find another substitute. Unless Justin returned to the farmhouse, Elias was dead.

MARSHALL AND HOPKINS drove to Eugene's office. The office door was still open.

"He will be difficult to track in the darkness," Hopkins said.

"I understand that, but it's our best option right now."

"There was no sign of him along the highway."

"I know. That means he cut through pastures and perhaps some forest."

Hopkins stepped out of the SUV. "Then why come here?"

Marshall looked at his watch. "To figure out which direction Meeks' corpse is heading. Once we discover that, we narrow down where we need to look."

"One problem we have is that Meeks' corpse is in a lot better shape than Elias."

"Yes, but the dew is heavy tonight." Marshall clicked on a flashlight and combed alongside the driveway in the thick grass. "How far away is the Butler house from here?"

"Half mile? Certainly not more than that."

"Which direction?"

"West. Why?"

"Because I found footprints headed East."

Hopkins ran to Marshall and looked at the ground.

"Nice work."

Marshall smiled and shrugged. "How far do you estimate the McKnights' farm to be from here?"

"About six miles."

"Cross-country?"

"The way these roads wind around, probably a mile."

"That direction?"

Hopkins nodded. "Yes."

"Then I suggest we hurry and find him. We can take the SUV across the pasture. The gate is over there."

Marshall walked to the gate and opened it while Hopkins got the SUV. He stopped at the gate and Marshall climbed inside.

"So Meeks will walk all the way?"

"If Elias had the capability to teleport the foot, he'd have no need to use Meeks to bring it to him. Besides, I'd guess a foot is a lot easier to magically teleport than reviving a body and transporting it. He has progressively gotten weaker."

Hopkins drove across the pasture, down a steep hillside, and across a narrow stream. On the other side, Marshall pointed at the edge of the field. Meeks was stuck in a barb-wired fence. He continued pushing against the wire, walking in place while the sharp, rusted barbs cut deeper into his flesh.

Marshall shook his head and stepped out of the vehicle. He pulled his gun.

Hopkins looked at Meeks. "Wait. Don't shoot him."

"Why?" Marshall asked, lowering the gun.

"If we kill him here, we'll never find Elias."

Meeks feet walked in place. He held the foot in both hands as he moved. His body pushed against the barbed strands. Holes dug deeper the more he moved. Hopkins shook his head, fighting tears. He knew it wasn't Meeks, but he didn't want to see any further damage done. Based on Marshall's theory, a headshot was the only way to end Meeks' body tampering.

Hopkins reached and grabbed the foot. He pulled but Meeks had a firm grasp. Hopkins yanked harder.

Meeks turned his head and faced Hopkins. Where caring eyes once were, red demon eyes glowed. Meeks opened his mouth but no words came. Instead, he gnashed his teeth and a gurgling sound came from his throat.

Hopkins jerked the foot free of Meeks' grasp.

"We have the foot!" Hopkins said.

Meeks turned and pulled away from the fence. The jagged barbs sliced through leg muscle fibers with a sickening, mushy sound. He reached for Hopkins' throat with both hands. Hopkins stepped back, lost his balance, and rolled through the wet grass. He lost the foot when he tumbled and rolled.

Marshall fired. The round missed Meeks' head and struck his shoulder. He swayed side-to-side and staggered down the hill toward Hopkins.

Hopkins unsnapped his gun holster and pulled his weapon. He felt sorry for his deputy and regretted that to put his friend to rest there wasn't anything else they could do except put a bullet in his brain.

Meeks stooped forward, reached for Elias' foot, and each movement he made seemed mechanically and unnatural. Marshall aimed.

"No!" Hopkins said. "Let me do it!"

Marshall lowered his gun. "You sure?"

"Yes," he said, nodding. "It has to be me."

Hopkins kicked the foot out of Meeks' reach. Meeks growled and ground teeth. His reddish eyes glowed and his brow narrowed.

"You see me, Elias?" Hopkins asked, clicking off the safety and aiming his gun.

Meeks stood still. The mention of Elias' name was recognized through Meeks' facial expression. Ever how Elias controlled Meeks and from whatever distance, he was able to see and hear the things around the deputy's vicinity.

"I know you can hear me, Elias," Hopkins said. "And know this, we're going to find and kill you for what you've done."

Without any warning, Meeks rushed and lunged at Hopkins, wrapping his arms around the sheriff 's waist. The gun was knocked out of his hand and into a deep, sandy sinkhole. The unexpected attack put Hopkins at a disadvantage. Meeks locked his arms and rolled, pulling Hopkins down the steep hill where it was darker.

Marshall hurried through the grass, aimed, but he didn't have a clear shot.

"Hopkins! Are you okay?"

Meeks rolled again and slug Hopkins beneath his body. He wrapped his hands tight around the sheriff's throat and squeezed.

"Sheriff Hopkins! Answer me."

Hopkins felt the pressure around his throat increase. He couldn't breathe. His eyes bulged and for a moment, he was certain he'd lose consciousness.

Although Meeks was dead, his strength was more than Hopkins had credited the undead deputy to have. Hopkins thrust the palm of his hand against Meeks' sternum, failing to realize that Meeks suffered no pain. He didn't even grunt in reply to the blow.

The lack of air pained Hopkins. Colorful dots blurred his vision. He placed his hands above his face and in between Meeks' wrists. With all his strength, Hopkins thrust his hands apart and dislodged Meeks' hold. Meeks dropped atop of Hopkins, forcing Hopkins to push Meeks up and roll from beneath his former deputy.

Hopkins leaned over on all fours, gasping and coughing for air.

"Sheriff? Are you okay?"

"Barely," Hopkins replied with a raspy voice.

Meeks growled and pushed himself to his feet. His red eyes were haunting.

Hopkins took another deep breath and prepared to run when his hand found the gun in the sandy pit. He grabbed the 9mm and sat down.

Marshall stepped to the edge of the pit and shone the flashlight on Meeks.

Hopkins aimed at his deputy's forehead, closed his eyes, and squeezed the trigger. He did a mental count to ten and opened his eyes. Meeks lay facedown in the grass. The red eyes dwindled like a dying coal and returned to normal.

Marshall stepped closer and offered his hand. "You okay?"

"I will be." He grabbed Marshall's hand and climbed out of the pit. Marshall picked up Hopkins' bent hat and handed it to him. Hopkins placed his hand inside it and popped out the bent places the best he could.

Marshall said, "Just accept the fact that it wasn't really your deputy."

"I know it wasn't," Hopkins replied. "But it's still difficult to deal with."

Marshall found the foot and picked it.

"Do we head back to the McKnight farm or to Ben's house?" Hopkins asked, massaging his throat.

"We should probably check in with the McKnights. We can check out

Ben's place when daylight comes. But, before we do that, let's find some gasoline and destroy this foot."

"Will that make a difference?"

Marshall placed his huge hand on Hopkins' shoulder. "If you were to live forever, would you want only one foot?"

"No, not really."

"I imagine Elias feels the same way. We destroy this and it will cut his enthusiasm a bit. Those who wish for immortality are usually consumed with vanity and perfection.

ELIAS WAILED when the bullet shattered the deputy's skull and imploded the brain. The fiery pain stabbed blindingly, undulating through his body. He gasped and writhed where he lay. Grabbing the sides of his head, he shrieked a high-pitched cry. When the blindness and pain subsided, he felt the floor around him. His hands grabbed handfuls of dog food pellets. He knew where he was.

John McKnight's shed.

CHAPTER 35

*E*rin hugged Justin.

"Will you ever come visit again?" she asked.

Justin shrugged. "I hope so."

"Justin, it's time to go," Roble said. To Shawndirea, he said, "I'll be back as soon as I can."

"Hurry," she replied. "I don't want our sons out there without your guidance."

He kissed her. "It won't take long."

Roble walked up the long spiral stairway. Justin followed. Instead of stopping at the door where they had entered earlier, Roble continued upward.

"Where are we headed?" Justin asked.

"To the very top."

"What's there?"

"You'll see."

Ten minutes of climbing stairs ended with a steel door overhead. Roble said a few words and the door rose. A rotten stench drifted through the trapdoor.

"Something smells dead," Justin said, coughing.

"Come on," Roble said, pulling himself upward. He extended a hand for Justin and helped him into the closet. Looking around in the darkness, he said, "Someone's been here recently."

"Where are we?"

"My house."

"I need to call Grandpa."

Roble laughed. "No phone and no electricity."

"Really? Why not?"

"I've not been here in months. Until you showed up, I never intended to come back."

"I like it where you live, but I don't think I'd want to stay there."

"I have ties there that you do not."

Roble grabbed a candle from a drawer and lit it with a match. "Careful," he said, looking around. "I have a pet."

"You left a pet here for months? How did it get food and water?"

"It has a pet door. It eats insects and vegetation." He handed Justin several more candles and the box of matches. "Light those."

"Okay."

Roble said the pet's name over and over in a language Justin didn't understand.

"Odd," Roble said. "He generally responds quickly."

Roble carried the candle to the dining room table. He set it down when he noticed the pet carrier. A line of blood dried on the inside bottom and wall of the carrier. His jaw clenched tight.

"Dammit," he said. "Someone killed him. And it looks like they took him."

Justin brought another candle to the table and inspected the cage, too.

"I knew someone had been here," Roble said.

Justin noticed the empty insect cases on the tabletop. "You collected butterflies and moths?"

"Did."

"Shawndirea's the reason you stopped?"

"It's a long story how that happened, but yeah, collecting them and being married to her would be a direct conflict of interest. I'd advise if you ever plan to venture back to the Underworld that you find new hobbies yourself."

Justin nodded. "Erin sorta changed my mind about it."

"You never told her that you . . . "

"No."

Roble sighed. "That's good. It's best you never do. She's one fiery little girl."

Justin smiled. "I got that impression."

Roble clasped Justin's shoulder. "You've a lot to learn about girls and women."

He took his candle and walked to the living room. In the faint light, he saw fingerprints on the dusty shelves.

"When will we go to my grandparents?"

"Come daybreak."

"Why not now?"

"Elias is why. Since it is night and a full moon, it's best we keep you here where it is safer."

Roble opened a drawer and rummaged through the contents. "Ahh, there it is."

"What?"

"I want you to have this," he said, holding out a large silver coin. "Actually, it's something you need to give John."

"Why? What is it?"

"A healing medallion."

Justin held the coin to the light. On the front side was a blue Pegasus with wings spread wide.

"Place it under his mattress or pillow. Shawndirea blessed it long ago. The medallion will cure his cancer as long as you hold no doubt in your heart."

"Should I tell him?"

"You could, but it's probably best you don't."

"Why?"

"Because he may doubt. Choose a couch."

Justin lay on the couch and stared at the flickering shadows on the ceiling. He wanted to go home more than anything, but thinking back on the drawing, the haunted cave, and Elias' threat, he knew Roble was right. He needed to wait until morning. He knew he'd be hugging his parents and grandparents more in a few moments than he probably had all his life.

After Marshall and Hopkins set Elias' foot ablaze on Eugene's driveway, they drove back to the McKnight farm. John opened the side door and let them inside. He held the shotgun tight.

"Still nothing?" Marshall asked.

"Just the loud cry of a bobcat earlier."

"You sure that's what you heard?" Hopkins asked.

John nodded. "We have a lot of them in this area."

Jack and Rita sat at the kitchen table. A 9mm lay on the table in front of Jack.

Hopkins and Marshall filled mugs with more coffee.

"You folks can go to bed and get some sleep," Marshall said. "We can handle things from here."

"You sure?" Jack asked.

Marshall nodded.

"Hon?" Jack said to Rita. He offered his hand and she took it. They went into the hallway and headed for their room.

John handed his shotgun to Hopkins. "Lib went to bed some time ago. I guess I should try to sleep, too."

"You should," Hopkins replied. "You'll feel better in the morning."

"Eugene's asleep on the couch," John said quietly. "And Frank passed out in the recliner. He got the Butler boys home safely."

"That's good," Marshall said. "I don't believe Elias will make an appearance right away. He's missing a foot and since we destroyed it, he has no way to get it back now."

John gave a feeble smile. "Goodnight, folks."

"Goodnight," they replied.

Once John's door closed, Marshall said, "I'd hate to know the worry and fear they're suffering over Justin."

"I know. It's a heartache no one should suffer." Hopkins removed his crumbled cowboy hat, set it on the table, and then ran a hand through his hair.

"I've seen a lot of it. I've worked a lot of missing children cases over the years. There aren't any words that ease the pain, especially if you never find the child."

Hopkins shook his head slowly and then sipped his coffee.

Marshall pointed and said, "You're going to have some bruises in the morning."

"I'll survive. Do you really believe Justin is alive?"

Marshall nodded. "Absolutely. Elias wouldn't have attempted to kidnap those two boys if Justin was dead. If Elias doesn't make a move by morning, I believe he'll be dead this time tomorrow."

"That's the best news I've heard all day."

~

RITA SAT at the edge of the bed, waiting for Jack to finish brushing his teeth. When he finally came to bed, she embraced him. He leaned down and kissed her.

"All we've worked for to make a better life for our family feels so empty," Jack said, shaking his head. "Without Justin to share it with."

"I believe Marshall will find him," she replied, pulling back the bedspread.

"I hope so."

"For some strange reason," Rita said. "I believe he's alive. I sense he's close."

Jack climbed into bed beside her, pulled the blanket over them, and wrapped his arm around her waist. "When he comes home, things are going to be a *lot* different."

"How?"

"We're selling the business."

She faced him with a broad smile. "Really?"

Jack nodded. "It's time to settle in closer to home. My parents won't be around forever, and Justin loves it here."

"What will we do for careers?" Rita asked.

"We won't be hurting for money for a long while. McAbee has made a huge offer."

"What if he's changed his mind?"

Jack chuckled. "With the greedy gleam that flickered in his eyes the day we met, he hasn't changed his mind."

Rita kissed him, and then she reached over and turned out the bedside lamp.

CHAPTER 36

The sun barely touched the horizon when Roble drove Justin to the McKnight farm.

"A lot of people have been looking for you," Roble said. "See all the vehicles?"

"Yep. I don't recognize a lot of them."

Turning into the driveway, Roble said, "I hate to rush off, but you know the problems we're facing in the Underworld."

"The Black Chasm?"

"Yes. So I really need to get back. Whatever you do, keep the things you've seen and heard a secret."

Justin nodded. "I will."

"And don't forget about the medallion."

"I won't."

Justin smiled at the old farmhouse that was little less than a lost friend. Before the pickup was fully stopped, he had taken off the seatbelt and opened the door. He ran to the side door and knocked.

Roble put the truck in reverse and stopped a second later when he saw the 9mm in Sheriff Hopkins' hand.

"Morning, Ben," Hopkins said with a gentle smile. "Don't rush off until I've asked you a few questions."

"Hi, Sheriff. I really need to be going."

"It won't take long. I'm surprised you got here without Special Agent Marshall Jackson stopping you."

"Who?"

"He's headed to your house to look around. We were hoping to find you to see if you could help us find Justin. But it looks like you got him home safely."

"What kind of questions do you need to ask?"

"First, hand me your truck keys and get out."

"Am I under arrest?"

"Not at the moment. We have some questions for you. That's all."

Roble handed the keys through the window and then stepped out of the truck.

Hopkins put the keys in his pocket and said, "Turn around against the truck."

"What's going on?" He turned around and faced the truck, placing his hands on the door.

Hopkins patted him down. "Hands behind your back."

"Why?"

"Ben, I need to take you back to your home. You need to talk to Marshall."

"I don't have a problem with that, but why are you wanting to cuff me?"

"We found a body in your house yesterday."

Roble turned his head and faced Hopkins with a furrowed brow. "What? Who?"

"Dr. Deiko, a dean at one of the state colleges."

"I don't know him. As far as I know, I've never met him."

Hopkins handcuffed Roble and led him to the SUV. He opened the rear door and let him get inside.

"We'll sort it all out in a while."

LIB OPENED THE SIDE DOOR. Seeing Justin she squealed with laughter. Justin wrapped his arms around her. Seconds later, John, Jack, and Rita embraced him tightly.

"Oh, my boy!" John said, hugging Justin fiercely. "You okay?"

"I'm fine."

Rita wiped tears from her eyes. She hugged and kissed his cheeks. "We've worried ourselves sick over you."

"I've missed you. I tried to get back out of the cave but I couldn't find my way back out."

John shook his head. "Why did you go inside the cave? You know not to."

"I know," Justin replied, looking down. "But I was trying to catch the biggest bullfrog ever. It hopped into the cave, and I went after it."

John hugged his grandson tighter. "You're home safe. That's all that matters now."

Lib frowned. "How'd you get home?"

"Uncle Ben brought me home."

"Ben?" Lib said. She hurried to the door and looked out. Her brother was cuffed and getting into the back of the SUV. She turned to John and asked, "Why is Sheriff Hopkins arresting him?"

"What?" Justin asked.

John walked down the steps and into the driveway, but Hopkins' SUV roared in reverse down the drive, onto the dirt road, and sped away.

"I'll be," John said.

"Why would he arrest him?" Justin asked.

"I don't know."

"Perhaps," Eugene said. "He's taking him to answer some questions. And since it's morning, I need to get back to my office and do more work on those autopsies."

Frank extended his hand to Justin and said, "So glad that you've made it home. You've a lot of catching up to do, and in a few days, I'll be back to visit. I'd like to know what you experienced on the other side of the portal."

Justin gasped. "What?"

"Marshall believes a magical barrier blocked your way back out after you went inside Devils Den," Frank said. "Again, glad you're safe."

"Thanks," Justin replied.

Eugene nodded at Justin. "As am I, young man. I'll want to hear your adventure, too, but at a time when work doesn't demand so much from me."

Eugene and Frank walked to their vehicles.

Lib smiled at Justin. "What would you like for breakfast this morning? Anything at all. What will it be?"

"Biscuits, gravy, sausage, bacon, and hash browns," Justin said, smiling.

Lib winked at Rita. "We'll get right on it!"

Jack cleared his throat. "Before you get started with that, Rita and I have some news. We've decided to sell the business and move back here."

"Oh, that's wonderful!" Lib said, hugging them.

"Really, Dad?" Justin asked.

"Yep."

"That's great, son," John said, embracing Jack. "Let's allow the women to get started on breakfast, and we'll go feed the livestock."

When they stepped onto the driveway, Charlie chuffed and wagged his tail. Justin knelt and petted the dog.

"Come on, boy," John said to Charlie. "Let's get you fed."

Eugene pulled his SUV up the drive. Getting out, he said, "I believe I've forgotten my medical bag in your house. Sorry for the intrusion."

"It's no trouble at all." John smiled. "Go on in and get it."

ERIN STARED up the long spiral staircase where her father and Justin had ascended a few hours before. Timidly she looked around. Not seeing her mother, she slipped up the winding stairs. Once she reached the top, she placed her hand against the cold, metal door. It was partway up. Cautiously, she pushed it and peered into the dark closet. The stench was enough to make her hesitate, but only for a few moments.

She shoved the door all the way over and climbed through the door. Stepping outside the closet, she studied the odd house with great curiosity. It was nothing like their home below. Her bare feet slid across the thick carpet, which was a new sensation for her.

Outside, the sound of a roaring engine silenced. She took a quick breath and stood still. A door opened and heavy footsteps entered the house. She squatted and crawled beneath the dining room table. A very large man stepped into the living room.

HOPKINS LOOKED at Roble in the mirror. "So, Ben, where have you been?"

"Call me Roble."

"Roble? Why?"

"That's the name I prefer."

Hopkins nodded. "Okay. Where have you been for the last few years?"

"Traveling."

Hopkins chuckled. "Lib and John insist that they've not been able to contact you in a long time."

"That's true. I'm seldom in this region anymore."

"Marshall's been trying to find you for the last six years. He says that you've practically fallen off the radar."

"What reason does he have to find me?"

"Elias, for one," Hopkins replied. "It seems you interfered in killing him twenty years ago."

"Consider it a mutual interference. I almost had Elias dead at the same time Marshall attempted to shoot him. The gunshot distracted me and allowed Elias to break free."

"And I'd like to know how you managed to acquire all the property along Boykin's Hollow when the IRS doesn't report any income for you in over six years."

"You might say that I work out of state."

Hopkins shook his head. "We found your smelting equipment in the garage. You've been making gold bars and selling them?"

"Is that a crime?"

"Not as long as you report you income. And you're certain you don't know Dr. Deiko?"

Roble shook his head. "I've never met him."

"Why would he be dead in your dining room closet?"

Roble shrugged. "I have no idea. If he were alive, he'd be charged with trespassing. He's dead from stupidity. You just don't wander around inside someone's house without an invitation, which apparently is something you and Marshall have done?"

"We went inside your house, hoping to find maps of Devils Den because John said that you knew that cave better than anyone else."

"I do, but the only map I have is inside my head. Did you have a warrant to search my house?"

Hopkins shook his head. "No. John came with us."

"I'm supposing John didn't have a warrant, either."

"No."

"I'll also go as far as to accuse one of you for killing my pet."

"We didn't have a choice. It's what killed Deiko. And it was trying to attack us."

"Of course it was. That's what it is supposed to do. Just like a dog will protect its home and family, my pet did the same."

"What the hell was it?" Hopkins asked.

"A Moorbat."

"It tore a chunk out of Deiko's throat. I hated shooting it."

"You?"

"I'm sorry."

"I've told you all you need to know, Sheriff. I didn't know Deiko and his death was his own fault."

"I believe you. Marshall probably has a lot of questions though. Much different than mine."

~

JOHN WALKED to the shed and said, "I don't know what happened to all my chickens. All of them were decapitated."

Justin wanted to tell his grandfather what had happened, but he promised Roble that he wouldn't.

John pulled open the door.

Elias growled and dove at John. Jack froze.

John stumbled backwards, but Elias grabbed his shirt with both hands.

Elias gnashed his teeth, trying to bite John's throat. Justin shoved Elias and knocked him off his grandfather. John fell to the ground, and Jack hurried to help his father to his feet.

Elias faced Justin, immediately recognizing the boy. A smile creased his wrinkled face. He hobbled toward Justin, but the boy pushed Elias back into the shed. Elias growled like a mad animal. Charlie ran with his tail between his legs.

"Run, Justin!" Jack said, as he and John ran across the driveway.

Elias braced himself against an inner support post, trying to maintain balance on one foot. Justin grabbed the garden sprayer from right inside the door. He swung the two-gallon sprayer hard, striking Elias in the face. The impact slung Elias off the shed floor and against the wall but cracked the plastic sprayer along the base. Liquid seeped from the split container.

Justin smiled. He still had his strength.

Elias snarled and pushed off the wall. Justin struck him again and again. Elias seethed and fought to stand. Justin swung the sprayer again, but Elias ducked. Although Justin missed, a stream of the liquid splashed across Elias' chest. Elias howled in pain. The liquid ate his decaying flesh like acid.

Justin twisted off the lid and doused the entire contents onto Elias' face and chest. His undead body shook. Flesh melted off Elias. His face sank and bone crumbled. His exposed brain shrank and shrank until the liquid had consumed it. Nothing except goo remained where his head had been.

Elias ceased moving.

Justin stepped back to the door.

John and Jack stood behind him.

Eugene carried his medical bag out the door, saw them at the shed door, and joined them.

"What's going on?" he asked, peering into the shed..

Jack pulled Justin to him and hugged him. "He just killed Elias."

"What was in the container, Grandpa?" Justin asked.

"Herbicide."

Eugene shook his head with a chuckle. "Why didn't I think of that?"

"What do you mean?" Jack asked.

"I studied skin cells from Elias' foot. His skin tissue had a symbiotic relationship with sphagnum strands. That explains why the herbicide ate away his skull and brain. I'm certain Marshall and Hopkins will be pleased."

"I know I am," Jack said.

Eugene smiled. "I'll have my assistant come gather the remains and take them back to my lab. I'll also notify Hopkins and Marshall. Young man, you're a hero. Although this whole *undead* thing isn't something we should not make public."

Justin nodded. There were a lot of events he couldn't tell his family. No matter how badly he wished to, they had to remain secret.

~

MARSHALL STOOD at the dining room door with his flashlight in hand. The bastard sword Frank had found lay on the table.

Movement stirred beneath the table. With the light he knelt and peered under the table. The little winged girl closed her eyes tight and held her breath.

"Easy," Marshall said. "I won't hurt you."

Erin's eyes opened. She entertained a small smile.

"Where did you come from?" he asked.

Erin crawled from beneath the table and stood. She pointed at the open closet door. Her wings were underdeveloped. She had somehow come through the trapdoor, and he was eager to discover what was below that door. If a faery, what other wonders awaited?

Marshall took a step into the room, and Erin backed toward the corner.

"It's okay. I promise."

A door slammed outside. Marshall turned and walked back to the kitchen. Hopkins stood at the back door of his SUV.

~

HOPKINS OPENED the door to let Roble out. Roble swung his legs out the door and after he stood, he handed the handcuffs to Hopkins.

"How'd you do that?"

Roble smiled and walked to the front door.

The transmitter on Hopkins vest beeped. He tapped his earpiece. "What is it?"

"Eugene wanted me to pass word that Elias has been killed."

"Really?"

"Yes. He said that he'd contact you with more specifics later."

"Copy that."

Marshall met them in the kitchen.

"Ben?"

"Roble," he corrected.

Marshall frowned.

"Let's just say I've assumed a new identity," Roble said with a grin.

"Very well," Marshall replied. "Tell me about the little faery in the dining room."

"What?" Roble asked.

Hopkins followed Roble and Marshall to the dining room.

"Erin?" Roble said. "How did you get in here?"

"The door was open," she replied.

"You know her?" Hopkins asked.

"She's my daughter."

"You have a wife?" Marshall asked.

"In the realm of Aetheaon in the Underworld, I am. She's a faery."

"I thought faeries were tinier creatures," Marshall asked.

"It's a long story. I need to take my daughter back home immediately."

"We'll let you, but after Elias is dead," Marshall said.

"I was just informed," Hopkins said. "That Elias is dead. Eugene will get us more information soon."

Marshall frowned. "And what about Justin?"

"I brought him home," Roble said.

"Through the trapdoor?"

"Yes. So can we leave?"

Marshall smiled. "That depends."

"On what?"

Marshall took the bastard sword in hand. "You have another one of these?"

Roble laughed. "You want it? It's yours."

"But do you have another?"

Roble sighed. "I have lots of swords."

"Retrieve your best."

"For what purpose?"

"I'll make a wager with you. If you get past me, I'll let you leave."

Roble smiled. "Don't be foolish."

"But, if I can hold you to a draw, I get to go with you."

"You want to go to the Underworld?"

Marshall nodded with a broad grin.

"Now is not an appropriate time."

"Why not?"

"A war is coming."

"So test me. I'll fight by your side."

"In all fairness, sir, I'd think you'd rather retire here than enter combat against such dark forces."

"We all die sometime. And what better place than a land I've yet to see."

"Dying isn't the problem. It's not dying and being controlled by the evil sorcerer, Tyrann. You could end up like Elias or much, much worse."

Roble walked across the room. Marshall brought the sword up and held it with both hands. He gave a simple nod and smile.

"You really don't want to do this," Roble said.

"It's the only way you're getting to the trapdoor."

"Erin," Roble said. "Go with Sheriff Hopkins into the living room."

Hopkins motioned for her to follow. Roble pulled open a drawer beneath the dining room table. He took out a claymore.

"Ahh," Marshall said. "I never suspected a drawer there."

"Seems I need to hide everything in this house. Pet killers, dead trespassers, and a crazy old man with a sword fetish. What's next?"

Roble approached quickly with an overhead attack and slashed downward. Marshall parried, swung upward, and sliced off a lock of Roble's hair.

Stepping back, Roble smiled. "You're not bad."

Roble came again, striking hard, fast, and deflected Marshall's parry. As Roble turned, he swung his elbow into Marshall's gut. Marshall groaned and shoved back. His strength sent Roble off the floor. He caught the table at the waist and rolled over to the other side. Landing on his feet, he parried

Marshall's attack and riposted. Marshall defected the counterattack and kicked. He missed Roble's knee by an inch.

The clashing metal lasted another five minutes before Roble bowed and said, "Hell, old man, if you wish to go that badly, I'm not going to stop you."

"I can hold my own," Marshall said.

"You're good. I'll admit that. But I wasn't going for blood. Were you?"

"No."

Roble laughed. "Good. Because had you said, 'yes,' I'd have to leave you here."

Marshall panted and wiped sweat from his eyes. "Let me make a quick phone call to my secretary and I'll be ready."

"You really going to go?" Hopkins asked.

Marshall smiled. "Of course."

When his secretary answered, Marshall informed her that Justin had been found and that he was retiring. He'd return in a few days to complete his paperwork and gather his belongings. After he disconnected the call, he shook hands with Hopkins.

"It's been a pleasure working with you, Sheriff," he said.

"Same."

"When I return, I'll pay you a visit."

"Good."

Hopkins' cell phone rang. "Misty? Yes, Justin came home today. Sure, be glad to see you when you come to do the news report."

Erin went down the stairwell, followed by Marshall, and then Roble descended and sealed the door with an incantation.

AFTER BREAKFAST, Justin snuck into his grandfather's bedroom and slid the silver medallion between the mattresses on his grandfather's side of the bed.

Odlon sat on his horse, watching the edge of the Black Chasm. Shifting fog swirled and drifted. Too thick to see through or to discern the shifting shadows, Odlon and his troops had no choice but to wait it out.

Pawl, Roble's oldest son, was thick chested with big arms. His long blonde hair was braided down his back. His face sported a short, blonde beard. A heavy bow hung across his shoulders and a crossbow rested on his saddle.

Bleys was two years younger with jet-black hair. His face was smooth and his eyes dark as coal. A sword hung on his belt.

The shadowy chasm moved and swirled. Two dark riders darted from the fog and headed for the evergreen forest.

Pawl raised his crossbow and fired. The arrow lodged in the second rider's back. He dropped forward in the saddle.

Bleys kicked the sides of his horse and rode after them.

"Hold!" Odlon commanded.

Bleys kept riding.

"Hold your position!"

Bleys kicked his horse's flanks harder. His horse galloped into the trees after the two dark riders.

Odlon's piercing eyes darted at Pawl. "Is your brother deaf?"

"He just wants to prove himself."

"He'll prove foolishness is an early grave."

WITH SWORD DRAWN and his horse swiftly catching the two horsemen, Bleys eagerly awaited his first attack. The slumped rider with the arrow protruding from his back was easy to catch. Coming to the rider's left side, he swung the blade and removed the man's head.

Without noticing the second rider had turned and waited with his own sword drawn. Bleys turned his horse sharply to the right. The enemy's sword nicked his left arm. The pain was instant. He turned his horse around two small trees and prepared to attack again.

The dark horseman laughed and waited for Bleys.

Bleys kicked the horse's side. It reared and shot forward. As he neared and readied his sword, the rider lowered his sword and leaned his head back, offering his throat for an easy target. A target that Bleys couldn't resist.

SHAWNDIREA'S MOTHER appeared in the study. She was so weak; she could barely hold her head up.

"Why are you here, Mother?"

She held out the crystal mirror. "You must look."

"What is it?"

"Bleys. He's in trouble."

Shawndirea took the mirror. She focused intently on the crystal until the surface shimmered. Bleys came into view. He rode his horse through the thick evergreens with his sword held up for an attack.

The horse sped swiftly through the trees. A second later, he brought down the sword and removed the dark rider's head. The man's body crumbled to ash.

Bleys dismounted. With the tip of his sword he brushed through the ashes. Gold glittered. He reached down and picked up the ring. He held it up for a few moments and studied it against the faint light before putting it on his finger. The ring tightened and form fit itself to him. His dark eyes filled with blackness.

Bleys climbed on his horse.

Shawndirea focused on the crystal, tears flooding her eyes. Her mother looked, too. Bleys' face came into view. Horns like a demon protruded on his forehead. Without thought or hesitation, he encouraged the horse to ride faster. Instead of joining Odlon and the others, he rode into the Black Chasm. The dark fog swallowed him, obscuring their view in the mirror.

The Faery Queen placed her hands on the mirror with Shawndirea. Both focused their energy until they swept through the fog and Bleys became clearer. His face tightened. Anger claimed his features.

The Soulless Minions that stood guard around Tyrann's castle bowed as he rode through the gates. He dismounted outside the chamber hall. The tall doors creaked open.

Bleys marched to the throne. Demons and undead minions stood at allegiance.

Bleys stopped at Tyrann's throne. He knelt before the dark sorcerer and kissed his signet ring. Standing around the throne were several members of the Sidhe. Tyrann smiled and the mirror turned black.

Shawndirea looked at her mother.

"Was that?" Shawndirea asked.

"Dirk," she replied, nodding. "I'm afraid so."

Shawndirea shook her head in disbelief.

"Now, do you see, Shawndirea? You have to bring Justin back. He's the only one who can rescue your son." The Faery Queen had never looked so frail. So defeated.

Shawndirea focused on the mirror, but it was cold to her touch. She shook her head and wiped away tears. Even if it were true, she didn't know how Justin could preform such a miracle.

AUTHOR'S NOTE

Thank you for purchasing this novel. If you enjoyed this book, please check out my website and join my mailing list at www.leonarddhilleyii.com to receive a free digital copy of Forrest Wollinsky: Vampire Hunter.

If you could also take a moment, please leave a review, it is greatly appreciated!

Blessings to you and yours.

ABOUT THE AUTHOR

Leonard D. Hilley II grew up a quiet, shy kid with an inquisitive mind. Learning to read at an early age, he fell in love with books. He read every book he could get his hands on and stacks of dark comics about ghosts, monsters, and creepy things that stalk the night.

Like a lot of boys, he caught beetles, wooly bears, butterflies, and had an ant farm. When he was ten, his interests in science increased even more after seeing a professor's insect collection. Soon he set out on his quest to build his own collection. He also learned to rear butterflies and moths to obtain perfect specimens. He learned botany, gardening, and set his goal to become an entomologist.

At eleven, he saw Star Wars. His imagination soared. Soon after, he discovered Roger Zelazny's Chronicles of Amber. Six months later, he had written the first draft of a novel. A novel he later discarded, but the characters stuck with him. Years later, these characters came to life in Shawndirea, which Hilley intended to be a novella for Devils Den. The characters, however, refused to be ignored and took the opportunity to unveil Aetheaon in their first epic fantasy. Lady Squire: Dawn's Ascension was quick to follow.

Shawndirea was Hilley's farewell to butterfly collecting, and those who have read the novel understand why. He has taken Ray Bradbury's advice to heart: "Follow the characters." He does. He follows, listens, and take notes—often never knowing where they're going to take him, but he's never been disappointed in the results.

Hilley earned a B.S. in Biology and an MFA in Creative Writing to combine his love of science and writing.

Sci-fi Titles: Predators of Darkness: Aftermath, Beyond the Darkness, The Game of Pawns, Death's Valley, The Deimos Virus.

Epic Fantasy: Shawndirea (Aetheaon Chronicles: Book One), Lady Squire (Aetheaon Chronicles: Book Two), Frosthammer (Aetheaon Chronicles: Book Three), Shadowfae (Aetheaon Chronicles: Book Four), and Devils Den.

UF/PR: Succubus: Shadows of the Beast (Nocturnal Trinity Series: Book One), Raven (Nocturnal Trinity Series: Book Two), A Touch of the Familiar (Nocturnal Trinity Series: Book Three).

YA UF/Paranormal: Forrest Wollinsky Vampire Hunter; Forrest Wollinsky: Blood Mists of London; Forrest Wollinsky: Predestined Crossroads.